BOHEMIA HEAT

by

Lucy Lakestone

VELVET PETAL PRESS

Florida

Published by Velvet Petal Press, Florida

Learn more about the author at LucyLakestone.com

Jacket design, shell and beach photography
by Sky Diary Productions;
additional photo by George Mayer

Paperback ISBN: 978-1-943134-07-6
Kindle ISBN: 978-1-943134-08-3
ePub ISBN: 978-1-943134-09-0

First edition

PART 1

I have learned the hard way that I would much rather judge a man by what he looks like with his clothes *on*.

I don't say that just because I'm a costume designer. I say that because my wits have a way of leaving me once the clothes are *off*.

I've made mistakes. I won't deny it. Some of them were divine. One was cataclysmic. But now I pick and *choose* my mistakes. This sentiment presumes, of course, that all men are mistakes, which, of course, they are.

I had to remind myself about the clothes, especially at times like these, when my friends were gathered around the bonfire. The more formal attire of earlier in the day had given way to shorts and bathing suits. Who knew how much less the more untamed of us would wear once it got truly dark?

This beautiful twilight on Bohemia Beach followed a party that followed a wedding, so most of the more staid guests had gone home. That left the rest of us, who'd received the invitation within the invitation to Gary's mom's house.

His mom had gotten married — in the dress I designed — and was already off on her honeymoon. Gary had disappeared somewhere with my friend Ez, but the rest of us were enjoying the last private party outside this gorgeous old beach house before the whole thing was turned over to the Bohemia School of Art and Design.

The roaring flames cast an orange glow on happy, laughing faces as folks sat around on low beach chairs, coolers and towels. A fire was hardly necessary on a late-spring Florida night, but its heat caressed my skin as the air cooled just enough to make the blaze pleasant.

The surf band was long gone, but a couple of people plucked at guitars. A few had drums, too, but Damien, who wore black swim trunks and a black T-shirt that didn't quite conceal his tattoos, had exiled them a hundred yards down the beach. They still made a low, pulsing tribal racket, but somehow it meshed with the ocean and the breeze, the fire and guitars.

"I don't want to hear some goddamn hippie drum circle tonight," Damien said as he flopped down on a towel next to my low chair, smelling slightly of gin. His black hair was spiky, and his one earring caught the light. "I can't hear myself think."

"So you *think,* do you?" I teased, sipping my plastic cup of champagne.

"How do you think I make such fabulous art?" he exclaimed, a little too loudly. His sister, Calista, the blonde to his brunette, shot him a glower from where she was leaning against her boyfriend. Her camera still dangled from her neck after shooting all afternoon.

"Any meetings of the Bon Vivant Theatrical Society in the offing?" I asked him. Though Damien was an artist, not an actor, he and I were both in a small group of friends who occasionally were asked (for a small fee) to appear at local parties to, well, make them more interesting. We were good at making parties more interesting. And I could always use a few extra dollars.

"Next Friday, I think," Damien said. "And what are you wearing tonight, Miss Penelope? It looks kind of like the dress you had on earlier, but it isn't."

"Exactly," I said, happy someone had noticed. I'd made the hot-pink pencil dress I'd worn to the wedding. "The skirt and part of the bodice come off to reveal these cute little shorts and the halter bikini top," I explained. The retro outfit's secret weapon was the matching tie-back heels; I almost always wore heels, so everyone thought I was taller than I was.

"If only I went in for that sort of thing," Damien responded, acting bored. "But it does fit your whole pinup vibe. And matches the pink streaks in your Marilyn Monroe hair."

"You may not notice women or fashion, but you can't help but notice color."

"Sometimes I notice fashion," he said. His eyes strayed to the stranger among us, the actor who'd moved from Broadway to Bohemia for a mysterious summer project at the Chamberlain Theater, my sometime employer.

Jace Edison was his name. Those of us in theater had known it for a while, and now everyone else did, too. He was a hot young property on Broadway — by young, I meant somewhere around my age, twenty-five-ish. I'd actually seen him perform once, in *Acid Candy,* the wild hit musical about a psychedelic pop band and the breakdown of the '60s revolution, during a whirlwind visit to New York a couple of years ago. His performance had been breathtaking; rumor had it he might be in the pending film, too.

In New York, he'd been in a handful of highly successful shows, had been nominated for two Tonys and had made a splash in a featured role in a dark TV crime drama, fanning the flames of his budding fame. He'd just starred in an indie film whose ecstatic buzz indicated he could make the hop from Broadway to Hollywood whenever he wanted. And then he'd dropped out of sight for six months before showing up in Bohemia Beach.

Jace had recited a sonnet at the wedding. Now he reclined in one of the beach chairs, his legs stretched out and propped up on a cooler. He looked thoughtfully into the fire, his brown eyes nearly black but sparking with the light. They were framed by a brush of devilish eyebrows, almost sinister in repose. He had thick, short, wavy, dark brown hair with meticulously trimmed sideburns that accented a long, angular face, the kind that begged to appear in advertisements for *haute couture.* Dark hair dusted his chin and upper lip. He wore snugly fitting jeans and a clinging, long-sleeved black T-shirt. His only nod to the warmth was his bare feet. They begged my eyes to follow the line of his body, up the long road of his legs, to the hint of muscles under the thin shirt as he clasped his hands behind his head and stared into the flames. My eyes were drawn to the chunky silver watch flashing on his wrist, then to the hollows under his cheekbones and the strong jaw that narrowed sharply to a square chin, softened only slightly by sensual, full lips.

"It's hard not to notice him." My words of appreciation were masked by the noise around us. "Too bad he doesn't play in my sandbox."

"I wouldn't be so sure," Damien said.

"That's his reputation. Everyone knows it. He doesn't date women."

"Maybe he doesn't date anybody. I still look at *People* and *Us* at my mom's house. I've never seen him linked with anyone."

"Maybe that's why the young girls love him so much," I murmured. "He's sexually harmless."

Just then, Jace Edison's gaze flicked to mine from across the fire. He couldn't have heard what I said over the crackling, the waves and the music. But there was nothing harmless about his volcanic gaze. I caught my breath at the sheer intensity of his expression.

"Holy eyes of Mars," I whispered to myself as Jace shifted his stare back to the fire, unfocused again.

Damien laughed wickedly next to me. "Well, if he's gay, my gaydar is broken."

"How does your gaydar do on asexuality?"

"Not so hot. It's focused on incoming missiles, if you know what I mean."

I rolled my eyes and drained my cup. "Then you're useless. Go get me more champagne," I said, handing it to him.

"As you wish, mademoiselle." He staggered to his feet and bowed, then made his way to the cluster of coolers and tables that held snacks and drinks higher up the beach.

The wedding arch, stage and piano had been cleared away, as had the catering tents and truck, by an army of worker ants after the official reception was over. Left behind was this delicious bonfire and my friends, these artists and actors and writers and musicians who'd become my family. And Jace.

At a smattering of applause, I reluctantly pulled my eyes

away from him and looked up at the reappearance of Gary and Ez, now in casual clothes. Gary shrugged, unable to keep a grin off his face, and Ez gave the guys who were clapping the finger, to a round of laughter. Despite her gesture, Ez and Gary were holding hands. Finally. Love must have found a way. I was happy for them, of course. I just wasn't a believer myself.

Where the hell was Damien with my drink? I peered into the circle of deepening darkness beyond the campfire and couldn't see him. I plucked off my heels and left them by the chair, giving in to the shifting sand, and picked my way to where the coolers were illuminated by tiki torches. That's when I saw Damien chatting up another actor I knew, a regular at the Chamberlain. Flirting had trumped drink duty.

I found another cup and filled it from a bottle of champagne nestled in a tub of ice.

"Is that for me?" came a voice from behind me.

I knew that voice. Half of America knew that voice.

I turned slowly to face Jace Edison. He wasn't smiling, but something playful glinted in his eyes in the flickering light of the torches.

"Is that for me?" he asked again.

"That's the wrong question," I said in my best theatrical lilt, hanging on to the plastic cup, regarding him evenly.

"What's the right question?"

"If you want something, you have to ask for it." I took a sip out of the cup, fluttering my eyelashes at him over the rim.

He took a step closer, just a step away from me, and I ordered my body to freeze. I was no fangirl. Besides, I might have to work with him, this freaking celebrity man-hunk. Despite my resolve to stay cool, the heat rolling off him engulfed me until all my nerve endings fired. I found myself wishing for my heels so I could get a little closer to his height and look him, almost, in the eye.

And the lips.

"May I?" Jace asked, his voice lower, more intimate.

He still hadn't asked for champagne. Just what was he asking for?

"You may not," I answered in the same suggestive tone. "But I'll pour you a glass of champagne if you want one."

His face broke into a broad grin that was almost as dazzling as the serious, sexy persona.

"That will do," he said. "For now."

Good lord, he's flirting with me! Probably just part of that keep-away game he plays with everyone.

I silently filled a cup for him and handed it over. His fingers brushed mine as he took the cup, and a shiver rippled across my skin. His eyes widened slightly.

"You're cold," he said. "Here." He set his cup on a cooler and pulled his shirt right over his head.

I don't believe I shut my mouth at all in the few seconds it took him to drape it around my shoulders and tie it in a loose knot in front.

"It looks good on you. You're Penelope, aren't you? Penelope Locke? Will you be at the meeting Monday?"

It took me another five seconds to get my mouth shut, formulate an answer and open it again to speak. The man was built like an Olympic swimmer. The firelight shone softly over every shift in his muscles as he leaned over to pick up his cup and took a sip.

Oh, lord, his skin . . . his dark, flat nipples . . . the valley that led right down past his belly button and into his jeans . . .

I tried to lock my wandering eyes on his. "I — I wasn't sure it was mandatory."

"Consider it mandatory. You're the costume designer, aren't you? And you do know why I'm here?"

"Not exactly." I had no fucking idea. The executive director and the artistic director had been whispering about Jace for weeks, but they'd never let me in on the details.

"You're needed," Jace said. "Monday at 10. You're designing costumes for the next play. My play. I hope they're at least as fetching as your outfit tonight."

He lifted an eyebrow, smiled and headed back to the fire, where he took a seat next to the guitar players and started to sing along. I walked to the edge of the circle of undulating light, transfixed. There he was, the Babe of Broadway, singing Green Day's "Good Riddance (Time of Your Life)" like it was no big thing. Ez and Gary joined in, along with a few other drunk, brave souls. Jace's serious mien was gone. Now he relaxed and drank champagne, shirtless.

Did I mention he didn't have his shirt on?

No. Yes. *I* had his shirt on, and the soft cotton smelled like him, a masculine scent that evoked forests and stars. I hugged it closer and watched him in wonder, my carefully cultivated persona lying in pieces on the sand, leaving nothin' but a dumb country hick who'd done lost her damn mind again.

THE CHAMBERLAIN THEATER had come a long way in just a few years. A capital campaign had renovated a quaint old movie theater — and a store that once adjoined it — turning it into a state-of-the-art complex with two performance spaces and ample backstage facilities. Located in downtown Bohemia, just across the lagoon from Bohemia Beach, it was part community theater, part professional, with mostly volunteer actors. But it was on the brink of becoming a big deal, with all the rules and expense and opportunity that came with it.

"And the thing is, Penelope, you might be out of a job," Anne Friar, the artistic director, said casually in my office Monday morning. I sat at my desk, which was crammed into the space with a drafting table, a couch, a sewing machine, a full-length mirror, an extra chair and a rolling rack of costumes. A poster from our production of *Alice in Wonderland,* featuring a photo Cali had taken of actors in my costumes, was framed on the wall above me.

"I — what?" I asked, stunned at the change of topic. Anne had just been telling me about the latest greyhound she and her husband had adopted.

She adjusted her nerdy, red-rimmed glasses and smoothed her silver braids and colorful tie-dyed dress.

"Now that the board has some money, it's looking to make some prestige hires. I'd be concerned myself, except that I know Boris loves me," she said of the executive director. "Now, don't worry," she added as she registered my increasing horror. "You're very talented, and we all know that. I'm just saying you really need to hit a home run this summer to justify your being here. It's not like you came from New York."

New York. *Ha.* I came from central Florida, with an internship at a summer theater program in North Carolina. But I'd earned my theater degree, and I knew I had the chops.

"So you're saying my job depends on this Jace Edison show?"

Anne smiled dreamily at the mention of Jace Edison. "Isn't he a doll? Yes, you're going to have to make all his dreams come true." She winked at me.

"Very funny. We all know I'm no help in *that* department," I said, thinking of his rep. "But I swear I can make brilliant costumes. Can you tell me what show we're doing?" I wanted to start planning as soon as possible.

"He prefers to announce it himself — oh, look," she said, glancing at her watch. "Five minutes. Meet us on the main stage."

"See you there!" I said with false enthusiasm as she sauntered off. *Fuck.* They didn't pay me enough to feel this much stress. But I liked this job, even if it wasn't really full time, and I didn't want to lose it. It was hard to find employment in the arts. And as much as I enjoyed creating the occasional wedding dress or special frock on the side, theater was in my blood.

I stood and moved to the mirror to make sure I was presentable. I'd opted for white capris, a sleeveless white blouse with big black polka-dots and a short, sheer black scarf today; it was an outfit that looked especially good when I rode my Vespa over here from my funky apartment on the lagoon. Too bad I couldn't bring my scooter to the meeting. It was a great accessory.

I quickly brushed my hair, still a bit flat from the helmet. It fluffed into a cloud of yellow, with those streaks of cotton-candy pink I loved. I touched up my red lipstick and regarded my perfect makeup. I worked so hard to look this effortless, I sometimes found myself ridiculous, but looking good was one of my few areas of expertise.

I looked myself in the eye, my pale green eyes, and thought about the way Jace Edison had reduced me to my component parts with a few words and a hot look at the bonfire. I'd stayed for a while at the party, listening to him and the others sing, engaging in the usual shallow banter that kept my friends entertained. Then I'd left his shirt on my chair and slipped away.

There was a reason I avoided risks in the relationship department. There was a reason I dabbled in online dating and selectively chose my brief affairs — mostly because I knew they would be brief. My heart was no longer open for smash-and-grabs.

A powerful attraction to a man I'd just met, a man who couldn't have the slightest interest in me, a man I'd be working closely with — that kind of attraction was only going to fuck with my mind.

This was business. Or rather, it was art. Theater had been my home when my own home became unbearable, and it was still the thing that held me together, that fired my imagination, that got me up in the morning and kept me up late at night. No man was going to ruin that for me.

I grabbed my tablet computer and stylus and hastened down the hall and downstairs, clattering in my perky black heels.

The Alistair Chamberlain Theater, the main performing space, held a versatile thrust stage. It wasn't raised. Instead, a large section of the floor was surrounded on three sides by ascending rows of seats. The back half of the stage was still framed by the old-fashioned proscenium arch from the movie theater, which had been built in the 1920s, but the renovation allowed the set designers to create a variety of imaginary worlds in the heart of an immersive audience experience.

Jace Edison stood front and center in that space, chatting with Anne and Boris, who stood next to him. The house lights illuminated a dozen of my colleagues sitting in the first couple of rows. They weren't what drew my eye. A few spotlights highlighted Jace's head like a halo and ignited amber sparks in his dark brown eyes. They also limned that long, lean, muscled figure, which today was clad in jeans and a short-sleeved black T-shirt. I was struck with a strong desire to make a costume for him. Underwear optional.

I shook myself back to reality and politely sat in the third row. I had it to myself. As Anne and Boris sat, Jace glanced at me and smiled briefly, then crossed his arms and swept his gaze across the room.

"I'm Jace Edison," he said. "You may have heard of me." His small audience laughed, and for a moment, Jace looked taken aback. Then it seemed to occur to him that he had, indeed, made a joke, and he chuckled, too.

What a curious fellow.

"I'm here this morning to tell you what we're going to do on our summer vacation," he said. "My friends" — he paused for dramatic effect — "we are going to improve upon Shakespeare."

There were a couple of chuckles and more than one wry exclamation. I settled for a "hmph" at his arrogance and waited for him to proceed.

"OK, I'll grant you, it's hard to improve upon Shakespeare. But we're going to do something that I think Will would've enjoyed. We're going to play with Shakespeare — specifically, *A Midsummer Night's Dream.*"

Just another old Midsummer *revamp?* It was a classic comedy, of course. The authority figure in the play, the duke, wants Hermia to wed Demetrius, who wants her. But she wants Lysander, and Helena wants Demetrius. The would-be lovers are subject to the whims of the fairy king and queen, Oberon and Titania, as they flee to the forest to make their matches. Eventually order reigns over chaos, with the extra fun of silly rustics doing a play within a play. They were all good fodder for costumes, but *this* was why he'd come to Bohemia?

"I can see that Penelope has her doubts," Jace said, and I bit my lip as my colleagues laughed. "Just to be clear, we are not staging *A Midsummer Night's Dream*. We are staging my contemporary play that spins *Midsummer* into the near future. We're exploring the idea of nature versus technology in a world where nature, and natural emotions, are under threat."

OK. More interesting. I granted him a small smile as he glanced at me to check my reaction.

"Dirk Paladin here will be our director." He waved at the short, balding man with large red sideburns, a red beard and mustache and an outrageously colorful print shirt — not my favorite guy to work with, given his occasional temper tantrum, but he *was* considered somewhat of a Shakespeare specialist. "We're having auditions Thursday night. Millie here is going to hand out scripts so you can get familiar with it, and Wednesday, we're going to meet and talk concepts. I know it's a lot to get done in a short period of time, but we're going to open on June 19 and run through the end of July. It's going to be tight, but I hope it will be fun. Any questions?"

"What's the play called?" asked Karen, the set designer, a thin whip of a woman with silver-streaked black hair who was as clever with a drawing as she was with a hammer.

"*Midsummer at Midnight,*" Jace said.

"That sounds ominous." *Whoops.* I hadn't meant to say that out loud.

Jace's mouth quirked. "It is somewhat ominous, but I promise, it will be funny, too."

"Oh, I didn't mean — um," I tried to recover myself. "Do you have a vision for what it will look like?"

"Sort of steampunk meets *Metropolis* meets Silicon Valley," Jace said, and my imagination started spinning. I sketched on my tablet as he continued: "Think gears, art deco, fun with LED lighting and, of course, the trees."

"The trees?" Karen asked.

"I should explain. In this play, in this future, the forest that the fairies inhabit in Shakespeare's version has been surrounded by the city. It's now a lush park in the middle of a crowded urban landscape, and there's a debate among the fairies — especially the king and queen — about their future. Oberon likes the idea of becoming as technical as the foolish mortals. Titania wants to hang on to the magic of nature, and she's stolen a clockwork baby from an inventor in hopes of turning it into a living thing."

"Creepy," I said.

Jace chuckled. "But so it is in the original — remember, Titania has taken a child from one of her followers? And in this version, she and Oberon hide in plain sight, running a coffee kiosk at the heart of the park. The potions they distribute are in the form of coffee."

"Now that's fun," Anne said, and there were murmurs of approval.

"The young women are right out of 'Sex and the City' culture," he continued. "Demetrius is an investment banker; the duke is Mr. Duke, a business bigwig. Lysander is a popular actor. The fairy Puck is sort of like a bicycle messenger — but I think if we can put him on a unicycle, that would be great."

"Casting challenge No. 1," Dirk said, to laughter.

"As for the rustics who put on the play within the play,"

Jace said, "they're spaced-out virtual reality game designers. You'll have to read it to really get it."

He was so animated, so into it. It sounded crazy to me, but I liked crazy, and I was already getting ideas for costumes.

"We've discussed thematic imagery," Dirk interjected, "and we want you think along two lines: clocks and the moon."

"Yes," Jace agreed. "The gears of time grinding on as chaos reins, with the implied threat of the doomsday clock, and the natural order represented by the moon, which will be full in the final scene as order is restored and the couples marry off."

"That's the opposite of Shakespeare," Dirk added.

"Correct," Jace said. "In the original, the full moon represents the full strength of Diana, the virgin goddess, and the couples are moving away from that chaste virginity to wed. But in my vision, they have already moved far from it, as we do in modern life. With a waxing moon, they are moving back to the purity of nature. In my play, that purity is also sensual."

I worked to wrap my mind around his concept while trying to ignore the way he said *sensual.*

"What role are you going to play?" I asked, imagining him as the magnificent Oberon, or perhaps the dreamy Lysander.

"I'm not."

Stunned silence swept the room. Jace Edison would be huge box office. How could he *not* be in the show?

"That's not why I'm here," he said. "I'll be here throughout the rehearsals, of course. I'm honored that you all agreed to be my host and workshop my play, but I'm not getting on stage."

I wanted to ask "why not?" Judging from the murmurs

that percolated around me, I wasn't the only one. But he was so adamant, I didn't see a way to inquire without sounding like I was harassing him.

"OK, everyone," Jace was saying. "Go read. We'll meet Wednesday at noon — the director, the designers and relevant personnel — and we'll talk production design. Think fast. Come to me or Dirk with questions. I wrote my number on your scripts. Call me if you need me."

I accepted a script from Millie, an energetic brunette I knew from around town and one of her other jobs, at The Double Diamond Diner. She'd taken the Chamberlain's admin position.

As my colleagues filtered out of the theater, I exited my row and looked up to see Jace staring at me.

Damn. That *stare*.

I tried to keep my poise as I took the two stairs down to meet him, but my blood heated with every step.

I crossed my arms. "You look like you have something to say."

"You don't like my concept?" he asked.

"I haven't read it yet, but no, I mean, yeah, I think it sounds — cool. Intriguing. It definitely has costume potential. Of course — " I hesitated.

"What?" he asked, his voice lower, his eyes searching mine. Someone cut the stage lights, so only the center house lights illuminated the large space. The dimmer lights softened the severe shadows the spotlights had wrought in his handsome face, and this star, this ego-driven force, abruptly seemed vulnerable. Struggling to find the right thing to say, I pursed my lips and blew a puff of air to get a stray hair out of my eyes. He reached over and slowly tucked it behind my ear, his fingers warm, brushing my ear, my neck.

What is he doing to me? My body lit up like a pinball machine, and I could barely remember my own name, let alone what I'd been thinking, as he held my gaze.

"It sure would have been fun to design a costume for you," I managed to say.

He gave me a half-smile that almost killed me. "A fitting would have been exquisite torture."

Did he mean that the way it sounded? Is he flirting, or can't he stand the idea?

"So why aren't you performing in the play?" I asked to change the subject.

His expression darkened. "I'm here as a playwright."

"Is that your true ambition? I noticed you haven't been in anything for a while."

"No. I mean — " A strange look came over his face. "I have to go. I'll see you Wednesday."

Jace spun and walked out, stage left, leaving me alone in the dim theater, my thermometer on boil, wondering what I'd done to piss off the Babe of Broadway.

I SPENT the next two days practically memorizing *Midsummer at Midnight* and sketching until my eyes blurred. The play was quirky. Sometimes it made me laugh out loud. Parts of it were poetic, and Jace had even quoted some of Shakespeare's most beloved lines. It also had a surprising romantic heart.

Though the couples fell in love in Shakespeare's comedy, I'd never felt moved by their relationships. Amused, yes, but never drawn in. Here, their relationships got more lines and more heart. There was a speech Demetrius gave to the awkward Helena in Jace's version that softened the hard

Demetrius and built up Helena with such aching tenderness, it gave me goosebumps.

Yet I could see where much would depend on the actors. Jace didn't have it all down on the page. A natural talent like him could simply walk into one of these roles and make it soar; I didn't know if he had any idea what he'd be dealing with when it came to our community players. Some of them were very, very talented, and we got a pro now and then, but this was no wacky British sex farce. This was complex stuff, and it would be a challenge even for experienced professionals.

My job, as the costume designer, was not simply to make stunning outfits that supported the theme of the play. It was to create the shell of each character, a chrysalis each could step into and emerge from, one with the role.

I had lunch Tuesday with Karen to talk about her ideas for set design, and we came up with colors and themes that we thought would work: silver and black for the city folk, gold and green for the fairies, and lush greens and blues for the forested park where much of the story would take place. She thought the coffee kiosk should be a small trailer, silver like a vintage Airstream, which I loved. I toyed with a swank '50s style for the young men and women, with funky futuristic twists in collars and accent colors. Of course, it didn't hurt that my own closet was filled with retro fashion; I understood and loved the lines of it, the hopeful geometry.

Karen liked the idea of making the design mid-century-futuristic. It wasn't quite *Metropolis* or steampunk, but it had art-deco influences, and I thought the designs would transfer well to Jace's fictional near-future. We would have to sell Dirk and Jace on it, though. The couple of times I saw Jace around the theater, he barely gave me a nod before ducking into an office, or he turned around and booked down the hallway as if he'd forgotten something. His performance was insincere, I thought. I knew when actors were acting, and his clear avoidance of me was irritating. Had I made him angry? Did he just not like me?

Of course, he couldn't be interested in me romantically, given both his reputation and his brusque departure from Monday's meeting. All well and good. But I still couldn't help a stray fantasy or two that involved him in a tuxedo, or out of one.

Wednesday, designers and directors met at noon in the theater's only meeting room, a tight, windowless affair with a long table and a large-screen monitor on one long wall. On the opposite wall was a massive black-and-white collage showing a faceless theater audience that, frankly, kind of freaked me out.

At least there were sandwiches catered by Picasso's. I grabbed one of the delicious crab cakes on a roll, one of my few options as a fishatarian. As I settled in with a lemonade, my tablet computer and a sheaf of larger sketches, the others packed the room — a bevy of technical and design staff, including set designer Karen, lighting designer Alan, sound designer Bill, artistic director Anne, executive director Boris, play director Dirk, laptop-carrying Millie and, last, Jace.

Jace nodded at Dirk, who cleared his throat, stroked his red beard and talked a little about what he saw as the themes of the play, echoing Jace's previous thoughts on technology versus nature, order versus disorder and the pressures of time.

"Karen, what are your thoughts?" he asked the scenic designer.

She explained what she and I had discussed in terms of

the overall look. "I see a clock in a streamlined deco style, projected onto a large convex circle at the top center of the proscenium that transitions to a full moon by the end of the show."

"My costumes would complement the kind of '50s deco she's talking about," I said, "rather than the '20s of *Metropolis*. This is a style we can update and spin ahead with details and fabrics."

"How would you give us that clockwork feeling, the idea that the mechanical world is constricting nature?" Jace asked.

"The city folk will wear a lot of blacks, grays and silver at the beginning, along with severe jewelry." I showed him a sketch of the Duke and Hippolyta; her bracelets looked almost like manacles, while he had a large, militaristic watch on his wrist. As I presented the drawings, I realized how much the watch resembled the one Jace wore. "As the young lovers ramble and the forest insinuates itself into their affairs, their costumes become less severe. Bits of flowers and leaves become part of their attire, some left by fairies, some added by themselves. A sleeve is rolled up, revealing crimson or yellow. A jacket is flipped open, revealing a bright silk lining. Later they become more sensual, too, more open, revealing hints of lingerie underneath for the girls, a bit of chest for the boys." There were titters around the table at this idea.

"Clever and sexy," Jace said.

"There seemed to be a subtext in your interpretation," I said, "especially with your reversal of Shakespeare's moon phases. Nature's primal power is also erotic."

"I like that," he said with a warmth I hadn't yet heard from him. He granted me a small, beautiful smile, and I had to tear my gaze away from it before I could continue. I shuffled to the next drawing.

"And then there are the game developers." I showed him a sketch of Nick Bottom and a couple of the others wearing sleek light-up glasses with just one lens. "Sort of virtual reality meets Google Glass."

Dirk nodded and glanced at Jace, then back to our sketches. "I think that could work. Jace?"

"I was picturing something more steampunk, but I like this better. It makes more sense. It's hard to be art deco *and* steampunk. The virtual reality headsets are great. And Karen, I love what you're doing with the park and the coffee kiosk. Penelope?"

I looked up from the drawings and started drowning in those eyes again. "Yes?"

"What about the ass?"

"Excuse me?" I briefly imagined his ass and what a shame it was to keep it hidden under those jeans.

Shit. I snapped out of my reverie as low giggles told me I'd been silent a moment too long.

"Oh, Nick Bottom, you mean? When he's turned into a donkey?" I ignored the buzz around me and the smile quirking at one corner of Jace's mouth. "Since he's kind of a modern ass, I thought he might wear a baseball cap on backward with big ears sticking out of it and an extra-large false nose, attached to a pair of the virtual-reality glasses — since he thinks he might be stuck in the game they've created. Unless you'd like something more literal. I'm still conceptualizing it."

I flipped to my drawing, and there was a good laugh all around at the goofy Nick Bottom I'd created.

"Perhaps some buck teeth as well? Just because we can?" Jace said with a grin.

"Whatever makeup wants to deal with is fine with me." I

smiled, partly from relief that my designs had not been rejected out of hand.

"We'll talk more about the details and the fabrics," Dirk said.

"And what looks good under my lighting, especially if we can incorporate some LED magic into the fairy costumes," Alan added.

"Of course," I said.

We discussed more details and the brutal schedule, including the auditions planned for Thursday. Even though I wasn't needed at those, I usually went. It was good for me to hear actors speak the words as I worked out the details of the costumes.

And, not that it mattered at *all,* Jace would be there. If I couldn't have him, at least I could watch him. And it might be fun to push his buttons and see just how far he would take his manipulative little game of flirt and run.

MOST OF THE usual suspects turned out for auditions, along with a lot of people I didn't know. To be specific, there were a lot of young women who mainly seemed to be there to meet Jace Edison. He was stunning in jeans and a thin black sweater that only our arctic air conditioning made tolerable. The giddiest of the girls quailed as he read lines with them under Dirk's direction.

They weren't all awful. One woman, a striking actor named Holland Ivey from Orlando with long, dark hair and an almost scary, volatile intensity, made an impression on everyone. Jace barely smiled at her raw sexuality, but Dirk was obviously impressed. While Jace appeared to be unmoved by men or women, Dirk was known to voraciously sample both.

Holland's brazenness irritated the hell out of me, but after she left, Jace and Dirk spoke animatedly about how good she'd been.

"She'll crackle as Titania," Dirk said.

Sitting in the darkness in the middle of the theater, I said nothing, just took notes on her shape and coloring in case I might need it later. And wondered again, looking at Jace, what it must be like to be the asexual male god everyone wanted.

While a few of our local actors seemed a bit intimidated by Jace's height, assurance and resonant voice, to their credit, most of them held their own, and some were even great.

When my friend Wendy Lilac finished her audition and the director called for a break, she dropped into the seat next to mine and sighed. Other actors who'd already read or were waiting their turn milled about, laughing, chatting, hugging one another. We were a huggy crowd.

"So what's he like?" Wendy asked.

"Not you, too," I scoffed.

"Oh, he doesn't like you, either?" She laughed.

"I don't think he likes anyone," I said as we watched Jace and Dirk on stage comparing notes.

Wendy ran a hand through her cloud of ebony curls and pursed her pink lips. "Too bad. I thought at least one of us might have a story to tell after this summer."

"Yes, a tale to keep us warm at night during all the frigid Florida winters as we grow old and remember that summer we didn't sleep with Jace Edison."

Wendy and I giggled. Jace looked up briefly, caught my eye and scowled, then turned back to Dirk.

"What the hell did you do to him?" Wendy asked, surprise in her voice.

"Apparently my very existence offends him, though the man throws off so many pheromones when I'm around, my temperature goes up about fifty degrees."

"Seemed like a cold fish to me," Wendy said.

"He's a puzzle. I was hoping he'd at least be fun."

"Forget it," she said. "We'll have some fun tomorrow. The Bon Vivant Theatrical Society is on."

"Whose party is it this time? And please tell me they're not going to play limbo like at the last one."

"Oh, that was a harmless diversion," Wendy said.

"Not in four-inch heels."

"At least we got to do more than mingle and chat and do our parlor tricks."

"Don't forget flirting with donors," I said.

"Not this time. Apparently this is some new, rich couple in town. They want fresh, funky faces to give the impression that they're fun and exciting, or something. They heard we were *bohemians*."

"Ha. Our highly exaggerated reputation precedes us. This isn't some kinky thing, is it?"

"Not to my knowledge. You know the deal. If things get weird, we walk."

The parties pretty much never got weird — at least the ones we were hired to attend. Actual parties held by my friends? There was always a dollop of weird.

For the Bon Vivant gigs, usually half a dozen of us showed up. Some played instruments (Wendy had a ukulele), one did card tricks and minor magic, and others, like Damien, sported big personalities. I did a little fortune-telling. It always entertained people, and sometimes it spooked them

— and me, too, because I really didn't think I had a talent for it until I got something dead-on right. I called it my women's intuition.

"They want us to wear masks," Wendy was saying.

My skin prickled. "Masks? It's not Halloween."

"It's a black-and-white party. They want everyone to wear black, white or some combination thereof, and they want masks. They don't have to be elaborate."

"You forget who you're talking to," I said.

"I know exactly who I'm talking to."

I laughed. "Come by the costume shop tomorrow afternoon, and we'll come up with something ridiculous."

Wendy grinned. "I love you, Pen."

"You too, Wen. By the way, you were great up there."

She rolled her eyes and stood. "Except I'm competing with fifty girls who escaped from the Barbie factory."

"Bah. No competition at all," I assured her, and she smiled and walked away. She had a point. She couldn't look any more different from most of the women auditioning, with her glowing dark skin and slender figure. But the difference was all to the better. She had a presence and a talent they didn't.

The second half of the auditions offered a healthy mix of decent actors and reminded me of why I'd gotten into theater in the first place: the heady escape of becoming someone else. The time went swiftly, and with it came a perceptible relief among those in the room that we might actually have good options for our cast.

I stuffed my tablet in my cute little pink backpack, slipped it on and straightened up my dress (casual, for me: a pink flamingo print on a mint background with thin straps). As the crowds headed for the main employee exit, I slipped backstage so I could make my way through the workshop and prop rooms, taking a shortcut to the back parking lot and my beloved Vespa.

The scenic pieces in the vast room we'd nicknamed The Attic were a jumble. They created an obstacle course in the dim glow cast by the ghost light, the caged bulb on a post in a corner. I dodged Cinderella's magical coach, subtly sparkling, then moved past a detached house porch and around a faux fire escape attached to a glassless window. My mind was elsewhere when I bumped into a figure who popped out from behind the giant's foot from *Into the Woods*.

I let out a startled cry and recovered myself.

Forests. Stars. Heat.

"Jace. Excuse me," I said, trying to sidestep him.

"Wait." He grabbed my wrist. His touch was light, but to me it felt like a steel handcuff.

I debated yanking my arm away and somehow didn't. His hand felt warm, smooth. I could almost feel his pulse in the delicate touch of his fingers.

"I'm sorry I bumped into you," I said. "What are you doing back here?"

Regret and relief warred within me as he released my wrist. Then he took a step closer. "Just wanted a moment in the dark to think about our options while the readings are still fresh in my mind."

A laugh escaped me. "In the dark? Amongst the junk?"

"Away from everyone."

"Oh, you're one of *those* actors," I said, deliberately provoking him.

Jace's eyes narrowed. The shadows of his face looked dangerous in the feeble ghost light.

"What do you mean?" he asked.

"The introvert who can express himself only on stage."

"I've expressed myself in the play."

I didn't say anything. Something like doubt flashed across his face and was gone.

"Why aren't you on stage? You have the looks for it," Jace said after a moment. The compliment seemed cold, but his eyes flickered with the spark of — something.

"I started on stage in school, but then I discovered costume design, the perfect marriage of my love of history and my love of dress-up."

He crossed his arms and did a slow scan of my outfit, much more than casual. Now he provoked *me*. Trails of fire followed wherever his gaze touched my body until he caught my eyes again. "Dress up a lot, did you?"

I shot him a sardonic smile, determined he wouldn't get the better of me. "I *do* dress up a lot, but as a kid, it was mostly paper dolls. The best-dressed paper dolls in Osceola County."

He answered my smile with a tight one of his own. "I'm sure. What did you think of the auditions?"

"I think you'll have plenty of good people to choose from. And if you want to add an army of pretty groupies to the script, you'll have lots of candidates."

Jace chuckled, and he seemed to relax a fraction. "That kind of attention gets embarrassing sometimes."

"Not convenient?"

"What do you mean?"

"I mean you'll never want for company."

"That's not the kind of company I want." He'd snapped back into that soldier-tense posture, as if he were bracing for attack, and his eyes burned into mine. Fucking with me.

Time to push some buttons.

"There were some good-looking men tonight, too," I said casually. "One or two I wouldn't push out of bed."

He looked troubled, and his voice dropped lower. "I didn't notice."

"Not your type?"

"Nobody's my type." Now Jace sounded almost angry. But in his agitation, he'd moved even closer to me. My nostrils flared, breathing in his scent. *Get out of here, Pen,* I told myself. And then, *Shut up, Pen.*

"What are you doing here?" he demanded.

I blinked. "Uh, going to auditions? Going home?"

"No, I mean, what are you doing *talking to me?*" His voice was dark, almost anxious. His eyes were stormy, those plush lips parted.

I echoed his tone. "I thought *you* were talking to *me.*"

"You know what I mean."

"Jace, I'm beginning to think you're just a little bit crazy. In a perfectly charming way, of course."

I took a deep breath and pushed past him. He grabbed my arm, spun me and yanked me to him. My breathing quickened as he lowered his face close to mine, hovering, arresting me with his dark eyes. *God.* Was he going to kiss me or bite me?

I decided either would be fine. I was tired of waiting for him to make up his mind. I reached up with my free hand, grabbed his hair and pulled his head down, slanting my lips across his.

He made a sound of surprise and froze — and then he caught fire. He pushed me back against the stupid giant foot and took charge of the kiss, reaching up to cradle my face in both hands. He opened his mouth over mine, consuming me with those decadent lips. He slipped in his tongue, sliding it against mine, tasting me in a heated erotic dance that instantly melted my composure. I could feel his arousal pressing against me through my thin dress. He moved his hands to my back, where they slid under the now damn annoying little backpack, and then he pressed one warm hand behind my neck, kneading the muscles there, holding me in place, fucking my mouth with his tongue. Dizziness washed over me. This was no sweet first kiss. It was tinged with anger, desperation. Jace Edison was a starving man, and I was the sleek animal he'd slain, pumping red-hot blood, even as I feasted on his hunger. He shifted again, gripping my ass and pulling me harder against him. I felt him through his jeans as he strained to get to my aching, needy core. I hung on to his neck, drowning in his kiss, and whimpered.

And he released me with a gasp, panting, staring at me with haunted, almost feral eyes as he took a step back.

"I can't do this," he whispered.

"What?"

"Go!" Jace shouted.

He rushed past me and the big foot, leaving me wet, wanting, anguished and furious.

AFTER A NIGHT OF FEVERISH DREAMS, I was, for once, glad to climb out of bed in the morning — my empty bed — the bed where I'd entertained frustrating fantasies about rolling in the sheets with Jace Edison. And a few fantasies about slapping him in the face.

The window air-conditioner struggled to cool the room, and the living room and adjacent kitchen were even warmer, despite another window unit there. This apartment, half of the lowest floor in a creaky Victorian in old Bohemia, had appealed to me with its vintage details and view of the lagoon, which most of us called the river. I'd first rented it one winter a few years ago, when heat wasn't an issue. Every spring and summer, I was reminded of my impulsive decision as I began to perspire almost as soon as I stepped out of the shower each morning.

Still, I cranked my old Vornado fan, made myself up and donned one of my dozens of 1950s-style dresses so I could get to work at the theater, Jace Edison or not.

I brewed my daily dose of caffeine in my tiny coffeemaker and looked past my living space, out the big window to the glittering water. The shiny, curved backs of dolphins occasionally broke the surface as they searched for breakfast. The view was framed by cabbage palms and oaks that swished in the morning breeze. In the summer, that breeze would push the baby clouds over the ocean inland, where they would grow into towering pillars of vapor that might, if we were lucky, drift back east and cool us off with a delicious thunderstorm.

Growing up as I did on a minor lake in a mobile home with even less A/C, I always welcomed Florida's afternoon dose of summer rain. Unfortunately, at the start of May in Bohemia, we had the heat but not the storms. The sweltering tension was almost unbearable as we waited for the rainy season to start.

Despite the warmth, I loved this apartment. It had funky charm, a small bonus room that housed my sewing machine and much of my wardrobe, and it didn't have my mother in it. I was still paying student loans, but I was out of that Skunk Lake hellhole and had a life of my own making.

The last thing I needed was an affair with a volatile co-worker, no matter how hot he was.

Then why couldn't I get him out of my mind? I was haunted by Jace's fervor, by the anguished need in his kiss. This was the man who didn't sleep with women? And what about his rough dismissal last night? He'd let go of me as if I'd burned him. I couldn't forget that wild look in his eyes. It had scared me a little — scared me and intrigued me. No one had ever reacted to me with such intensity.

And maybe part of me liked playing with fire.

I slipped out to the back patio and one of its comfy chairs, sipped my lightly sugared coffee, munched a biscotti and scanned my phone for updates. There was buzz on social media among my theater friends about the auditions and how soon the cast list would be posted. And I had to work on my sketches and plans, pull fabric swatches and get Dirk to OK my concepts. I probably wouldn't create and print any fabrics for this show, though I'd done that in the past; there was already plenty to do. I loved putting on a new show, but the next six weeks would be like trying to dance in roller skates on a runaway train.

I left my cup in the sink, grabbed my backpack, donned my helmet and walked around the side of the house to my mint-green Vespa. It was parked next to the vintage VW bug I drove only when I had to, or when it decided to start. Sometimes I needed a car. But right now, I got a thrill revving up the scooter and accelerating onto the road toward downtown and the Chamberlain Theater, where a dream world of the imagination and one bizarre thespian awaited my attention.

I SPENT the morning refining my designs in my office, then talked Cali into meeting me for a quick lunch between photo sessions. We discussed the merits of dating famous people (her boyfriend was a fairly well-known big-wave surfer). For her, the merits were obvious. He was gorgeous, smart and a photographer as well, and he pushed her to be her best. In my case, I hadn't even really progressed to a date, just a lust-filled kiss followed by lunacy. But it was fun to talk about anyway.

Then it was on to the sunlit costume shop, with its big windows, racks of clothes of every description, pod of four sewing machines, washing machines, work tables, dummies, wigs and accessories. I was in a closet, going through boxes of masks, when Wendy found me. Her face was shiny, and she seemed a bit breathless.

"Are you that excited about the party?" I asked after giving her a hug.

"You didn't hear? They've posted the cast list. I got Helena!"

"That's fantastic!" I hugged her again. "I knew they'd cast you. I'm going to make you so beautiful. I mean, even more beautiful!"

"Ha, ha," Wendy said, but her eyes shone with happiness. "I noticed Jace Edison wasn't on the list."

"He says he's not performing in the show." I shrugged at Wendy's baffled look. "So who's your Demetrius?"

"Oh, hell, it's Paul."

"Paul Terrimore? Is he still a drunk?"

"That's not funny."

"I know it isn't," I said. The last time Paul was cast, it was for a farce that called for him to hide behind the drapes and eavesdrop on a conversation. He'd fallen asleep during the scene and slid to the floor with a crash. He'd turned it into a comic bit, but it had shaken all of the actors on stage. "I guess Dirk thinks he can handle it."

"He's really good," Wendy said, "when he's not falling down. And he's handsome, which makes him irresistible to directors."

"People with good looks tend to have an advantage."

"You would know," joked Wendy, whose large, brown eyes lent themselves to the comic expressions at which she excelled. Her nose was a bit overlong, her smile too wide. She would never be labeled a beauty, but her energy made her attractive, and she was luminous on stage.

"Thanks," I acknowledged her backhanded compliment, "but I don't think my looks are doing me any favors this week."

"What's that supposed to mean?" She opened another box and joined me in the hunt for masks to match our black-and-white outfits for the party.

"I don't think I should say at this time," I said wryly.

Wendy shot me a look. "This doesn't have anything to do with our playwright-in-residence, does it?" I said nothing, and those expressive eyes widened. "What happened? Are you going out?"

"Nothing happened. Or, at least, it amounted to nothing. Just a passing moment of insanity, I think. Don't say anything to anyone. This production doesn't need any more distractions."

Wendy shook her head with a mischievous smile. "Don't worry. How can I gossip without details? Have you seen him today?"

"No. But he may be avoiding me."

"What did you *do?*"

"Now why would you think *I* did something?" I asked innocently, and she laughed again.

Five hours later, Wendy and Damien came by my place to pick me up in her SUV, a much more comfortable car than what I drove. Wendy had a day job as a software engineer, doing contract work, so she could afford a nice car. She had the air blasting and the stereo cranked to the max with a high-energy dance tune.

"Someone's ready to party," I said.

"Gotta get pumped up," Wendy said.

"I'm relying on gin and tonics to get in the mood," said Damien, clad in a slim, ruthlessly black suit. He sipped from a covered plastic cup. He already wore a simple black mask; his longish black hair was fluffed and spiky, and he wore black eyeliner.

Wendy rocked a short black dress that clung to her narrow curves. Between the seats was her ukulele and the black mask we'd found for her. Oversized and shaped like a butterfly, it sparkled with teal and clear rhinestones. Two fluffy teal feathers formed the butterfly's antennae.

"You look amazing," she said as I climbed into the back seat.

I loved wearing black, but tonight I'd gone with the opposite look — a white dress with a strapless corset bodice that plumped my breasts into creamy curves above the line of the fabric. Its white satin skirt was overlaid with a diaphanous, sparkling organza. A black ribbon demarked the waistline, and a black crinoline puffed the skirt out so that it felt like a lightly swinging bell around my hips. The entirety of the white dress was dotted sparingly with tiny black gems to catch the light. I wore a choker of black rhinestones with matching earrings, and my lipstick was cherry red.

"I don't look too virginal, do I?" I asked.

They both laughed out loud.

"Hardly," Damien said.

I pouted. "You don't have to make the idea sound so ridiculous. Though I suppose it is." We all laughed then.

"It does look a little like a wedding dress," Wendy said as she navigated toward the causeway that would take us to the beach, "only totally different."

"It was someone's wedding dress once upon a time," I said. "I found it in a thrift shop. I shortened it, expanded the skirt and added the overskirt. Today, I sewed on the gems. I think it looks great with the mask."

The black and white mask, which I carried for now, would cover the upper half of my face. Sparkling flourishes and lacy details were accented by a red sequin at the outside corner of each eye. White rooster feathers and bobbing ostrich plumes formed a loose fan that sprouted from the center and would add several inches to my height, which was already enhanced by my tall black heels. White ribbons fluttered from the sides. Adding to my sense of mystery, I'd worn a straight, shoulder-length white wig over my blond and pink hair.

"So do we know any more about this party?" I asked.

"Suzy was the one who arranged it," Damien said. "She's meeting us there with the others. From what she told me, this is a young couple who just bought a mansion on the beach after making a fortune, and they want to break it in with a very special party. They've invited a lot of the well-known people around here, or at least the ones who are younger than our usual clientele. Hipsters, I guess."

"How'd they make their fortune?" I asked.

"Suzy will tell you it was with an Internet company,"

Damien said, "but I can tell you after a little research that they made their fortune in Internet porn. They ran a popular video site and just sold it."

"No shit," Wendy said. "Remember, if it gets weird, we walk."

"It's Bohemia Beach," Damien scoffed. "And they're basically software geeks like you. How weird can it get?"

Wendy smacked his arm as she drove the car over the causeway bridge, and I grinned at his "Ow!" This was going to be fun.

WHENEVER I SAW a house as grand as this pile of stucco on Bohemia Beach, I was reminded that I was and probably always would be a have-not. Still, what I did have was a chance to express my creativity with oddball friends like these, so that was something. Right?

The two-story, contemporary house was white, with sparse, light-gray trim, multiple balconies, and a forbidding metallic double door that looked as if the Wizard of Oz might be hiding behind it. Instead, it was opened by a young woman in a black-and-white harlequin dress, checkerboard tights and exotic makeup — a hired model, I came to realize — to reveal the cacophony of a party.

There was nothing particularly odd about the crowd on the surface, except for the costumes, some of which were beyond extravagant. As a striking black-and-white fashion duet, Wendy and I drew stares, though I had no idea who was staring at us behind their disguises. Damien was a diabolical vision in black, and he looked like trouble, which guaranteed he'd draw admirers.

Suzy and the others from the Bon Vivant Theatrical Society were already there and introduced us to our hosts, a mild-mannered young couple in matching black-and-white outfits who looked as if they'd walked out of a 19th-century ballroom. It wasn't the scandalous stuff I'd been led to expect by Damien. They were polite but treated us like the employees we were. We had a brief chat, then scattered to engage the guests and keep them entertained.

I had a strange feeling about this party, even as I chatted and told a few whimsical fortunes with the crystal ball I'd packed in the wee purse that hung from my wrist. There was something unnerving about not being able to see anyone's faces. Not all of the faces were completely masked, but I wasn't sure if there were people I knew here or not. It was a younger crowd than I was used to seeing at Bohemia Beach's elite parties, but as I made the rounds, I learned that some of the guests were from out of town. I suspected that at least a few were involved in our hosts' purported profession. Some of the costumes were scandalously revealing, making my mounding cleavage seem tame by comparison.

It had been a long time since I'd felt like a stranger at a Bohemia party. Despite the insistent bass and slinky beat of the electronic lounge tunes pervading the house, with its white furnishings and bland art, I had trouble getting into the groove.

And I felt as if someone was watching me.

I stood by the refreshments table and scanned the room, a glass of wicked rum punch in my hand, trying to figure it out. Wendy sidled up to me.

"Having fun?" she asked, drawing a ladleful of the punch.

"It's OK. I just feel off tonight. Or confused." I sipped the strong punch and made a moue.

"It was OK when I was out on the deck playing the ukulele, but I have to agree, there's something a bit odd about this crowd."

"If Tom Cruise shows up, I'm definitely leaving," I said.

She laughed. "No one's naked. That's probably a good thing."

"Maybe almost naked," I said, using my eyes to indicate a particularly voluptuous blonde with a taut, sculpted face under her lacy black mask and a dress that left little to the imagination.

"Maybe Damien was right," Wendy said. "Still, no one's bothered me. If anything weird is going on, it's not in the living room."

We both glanced up at the ceiling, then exchanged a look. There had been quite a bit of traffic heading for the second floor in ones and twos and the occasional three.

I shook my head. "I also — oh, it's nothing."

"What?" Wendy asked.

"I keep thinking I'm being watched."

"That's because you are. See the guy in the silver suit?"

"Where?" I asked keenly, following her nod. The man in question seemed to sense my glance and slipped outside. I got a glimpse of a handsomely tailored, shiny, dark gray suit hugging a tall, lean body, accented by a white shirt and tie. A black mask edged in silver hid his face all the way to his chin. "Who's that?"

"You'd better find out."

"Why?"

"He's a knockout."

I laughed. "How can you tell?"

"He has a fabulous body, at least," she said. "I saw him hovering in your wake earlier. He moves like a cat. Go tell his fortune. If he's a stalker, you'll scare him off. If he's interesting, maybe you can make a date for later, with or without the mask."

"I definitely want to see him, first. Not a big *Phantom of the Opera* fan."

"It's the music of the night, baby," Wendy said with a smile before wandering off with her ukulele slung over her shoulder.

She was right. And I was bored. I threw back the rest of the punch, set down the cup and headed toward the deck doors with my crystal ball.

Is it my fault that I had Jace Edison on my mind? I was curious about Mr. Silver Suit, but that kiss, as insane as it had been, had haunted me all day. And I had a little fantasy about running into him. He could be here, hiding behind a mask. He could be here in a silver suit.

I slipped through a sliding glass door on the long, wide plank deck and closed it behind me. Another of our Bon Vivants was standing by the deck railing in the light of the tiki torches, playing a funny song on guitar. Out here, some of the guests had removed their masks, and they laughed along as they lounged in chairs and on benches; the atmosphere was more relaxed, more appealing. It was still warm, but not unbearable. Beyond the dunes, the waves rushed up the sand in their familiar hypnotic rhythm, simultaneously soothing and stimulating. I took a deep breath and watched the nearly full moon chase the foamy crests in silver.

"I was hoping you'd find me."

I turned, and there he was, the man in the dark silver suit. His voice wasn't quite as deep as Jace's, and he had an English accent. As appealing as that was, I couldn't help a twinge of disappointment. And puzzlement, too. Why did I so want it to be Jace, the man who kisses and yells and runs?

"Hello. I'm Penelope." I reached out and shook his smooth hand. "And you are?"

"No names," he said. "Isn't it that sort of party?"

"I don't know. Is it?"

"There are *intimations,*" he said in those dulcet, cut-glass English tones. "I like not having a name. But if you must call me something, try — Angelo."

"Because you're an angel?" I asked, dimpling at him. It was hard to see his eyes behind the mask, but I could swear they lingered on my lips.

"Or the devil," he said. "The devil would pose as an angel, would he not?"

"Then you should have donned wings along with that executioner's mask."

"Oh, it's not as bad as all that, is it?" His hands reached up to touch the mask's edges. "It's not a hood. It just covers my face. I thought it was rather dashing."

"Or rather sinister," I said, mocking his accent.

He chuckled. "Yours, on the other hand, makes it seem as if you'll take flight at any moment, with all those feathers."

"Aren't they angelic?"

"Oh, no," he said, reaching up to run one of the soft plumes between his fingers. "Sensual."

A rush of warmth went through me. Were my hormones working overtime this week? I'd had almost the same reaction to Jace. Clearly, I needed to get laid. But not by a guy wearing a freaking mask.

"Behave yourself." I reached into my bag and pulled out my crystal ball. "Would you like me to read your fortune, Angelo?"

"By all means."

"Let's go over here." I led him to the far end of the deck, away from the music and next to a tiki torch. "The firelight gives me visions," I said dramatically.

"You are a vision," he countered.

"If you don't stop flirting, I'll be too distracted to tell your fortune." I rolled the clear ball from hand to hand, watching the light change in its distorted heart, in his dark eyes as he watched. He moved closer as I held up the ball in front of the flames. "Give me your hand."

He instantly took my free hand. I didn't turn it over; I didn't read palms. I invented things. Or rather, I intuited them. With Angelo, I stared into the crystal ball and saw his masked, upside-down face mingling with the fire.

"You have suffered," I said.

His hand twitched. He said nothing.

I let myself spin the tale the light told me. Loss and travel, the bread and butter of fortune tellers. Though this time, the story seemed to shape itself without my conscious will.

"You have traveled far. You will travel farther still. You will not end where you think you will, but you must go back to where you began to find your path to the future."

"I can't go back," he whispered, his voice curiously flat.

"In your mind you will. In your heart. You must, if you are to succeed. The fire . . . " I suddenly felt lightheaded. "It will burn through the thicket."

"To Sleeping Beauty?" he asked, now sarcastic. "Penelope?"

I swayed, dizzy. He grasped my elbows with both hands, and I dropped the crystal ball. It hit the deck with a dreadful thud. He pushed me to a cushioned chair, and I fell into it. I felt hot.

"Are you all right?" he asked, rubbing one hand. "Do you want some water?"

"Yes, water," I said, lowering my head, trying to regain my equilibrium.

In a couple of minutes, I felt a little better and sat up. I'd almost passed out. It couldn't have been all that crystal ball nonsense, could it? More likely the rum punch, or my tight corset bodice. Still, my little fortune-teller act had felt like a dream, in a way it never had, when I'd held his hand and looked into the fiery refraction and spoke the words.

"Here's some water," Angelo said, getting down on one knee next to me. I sipped it. "Better?"

I nodded. "Much better. It was a passing thing."

"Just a little syncope between friends."

"What?"

"A fancy word for fainting."

"You're a doctor, aren't you, Angelo?"

He laughed. "Hardly, my dear. Your reading — it was very . . . interesting."

"Was I right?"

"Good psychics aren't supposed to ask if they're right. They know they are."

"I'm not a psychic," I said, trying to see his eyes in the shadow of the mask.

"If you say so."

"Oh, no. What happened to my crystal ball?" I sat up straighter, looking around.

"Don't move," he said. "I'll get it."

He came back a moment later with the ball. A jagged line ran through its heart.

"I'm afraid it's cracked," he said, handing it to me.

"That makes two of us," I said, dropping it into my wrist bag.

"Or three," Angelo said. Was he smiling under that dark visage?

"I think I've had enough of this party. I've put in my time." I thought for a moment. "Thank you. I feel much better. I — I suppose you wouldn't want to go with me? We could get a drink. Without the masks."

"Oh, I can't take off my mask," he said, his tone not as light. He took a step back. "But it was lovely to meet you, Penelope. And a little frightening."

"Thanks," I said drily. I stood and took a deep breath, almost back to normal.

I couldn't believe he'd blown me off. I'd felt a strong connection. Had he? He stood very still, staring at me, silent.

"I guess I'll see you in the next lifetime, angelic devil." I walked past him, feeling an unnerving spark as I brushed against him, and reentered the house.

DAMIEN WAS SCARFING crab dip at the refreshment table.

"How's it going?" I asked.

"I may have talked these tasteless people into coming to look at my art. That's something," he said. "You OK? You look paler than usual."

"It's the white dress. Have you seen Wendy? I'm over this party. I'm ready to go."

"It's not that bad. I have a feeling there's a lot more trouble I can get into. Oh, and there's Wendy."

Wendy strolled over and grabbed a mini cupcake off the table. "What do you guys think? Another hour?"

"I'm ready to go any time," I said, "but I suppose I can stay that long. Don't expect me to entertain anyone else, though. I'm going to be a wallflower."

Wendy's brown eyes scanned me through her dark mask. "How'd it go with the silver suit?"

"Strange," I said.

"Okaaaaay," Wendy said as a tall, paunchy man in black approached us with a swagger. "You'd better fill me in later."

"Damien?" The man removed his mask, revealing a round face, dark brown hair parted in the middle and an ingratiating grin.

"Yeah," Damien said. "Joe, isn't it?"

"That's right. Joe Stier, from *The Bugle*." His consonants slurred. A drunk reporter. Not exactly a novelty.

My friend Cali, who used to shoot photos for the local paper, had told me about this guy. He'd been an asshole to the women on staff after replacing the sweet, knowledgeable woman who was the arts columnist before him. She'd retired. He'd been promoted from one of the bureaus.

Joe, his face flushed, scanned Wendy and me with a little too much interest. "One of you wouldn't happen to be Penelope, would you?"

"Guilty," I said after a moment. Hiding seemed like too much trouble.

"I want to write something about the play the Chamberlain is doing. Do you have a second?"

I couldn't blow him off. Anne would have my head. They were always begging the newspaper for publicity, especially when the features department seemed more interested in covering reality shows and theme parks than the arts these days.

"It's not a great time to do an interview," I said, "but I could set something up at the theater."

"It'll only take a minute, I promise. Just a quick question or two so I can get oriented, and then I'll call Monday to set up an official interview. Can we go somewhere quieter?"

Out of the corner of my eye, I saw Damien grinning and Wendy crossing her eyes. I'd make them suffer them later.

"The kitchen?" I reluctantly suggested.

"How about the billiards room upstairs? That was pretty quiet, last time I checked."

Upstairs? I had no idea what was going on upstairs, but I didn't think I wanted to find out. He must have seen my hesitation.

"My wife's up there," he said. "She loves to play pool. I'm sure she'd like to meet you. She's crazy about clothes, too, and that dress is something else."

I sighed. I supposed it was safe if his wife was there, too. "All right," I said and followed him toward the winding staircase.

It ascended to an open sitting room with a few book-shelves and a TV. Hallways extended to either side, and he took one, swaggering down the corridor. I reluctantly followed. Where were all the people who'd been heading up here all night? And then I realized that, although there were many rooms, there were no open doors. Over the music drifting up the stairs, I heard muffled sounds. A moan. A slap? *What the fuck?*

I was ready to turn around and leave when Joe said, "Here she is." He opened the door to a well-lit game room. A tan, maskless woman in a slinky black gown and frosted hair, whose stretched face suggested an overfondness for surgery, played pool. I recognized her, but I'd never met her. She was a thrice-divorced socialite of known wealth who did the charity circuit. Joe must be husband No. 4.

"This is Marissa," Joe introduced us. "This is Penelope Locke, the costume designer at the Chamberlain."

"Nice to meet you," I said as the woman sunk another ball, then stood up straight to look me over.

"Sweet dress. So did Joe ask you yet?" Her voice was fuzzy. She grabbed the chalk and roughened the end of her cue stick. "We want to know all about Jace Edison."

My brow wrinkled in annoyance, even if they couldn't see it under my mask. "Is that what this is about?"

"We want to talk to you, too, of course," Joe said, pouring himself a glass of brown liquid from a decanter on the sideboard. Obviously not his first one. "And the director. I understand this is Jace's spin on *A Midsummer Night's Dream?*"

"That isn't really my place to say, but it's an original play. You need to set up that interview."

"Is he as sexy as they say?" Marissa asked, her eyes dewy like a cartoon cow's.

A groupie. Great. "I don't think I can help you. It was nice to meet you. I need to catch up with my friends now."

"Wait a minute!" Joe said as I exited the room and headed down the dark hall. Alarm bells rang in my subconscious. He caught my arm halfway to the stairs. I smelled whiskey on his breath. "Don't go, Penelope. You have to understand that it's a big deal to have an actor like him come to our town. It's just a little interview. But now that I've met you, I want to get to know you, too." He leaned closer and whispered in my ear: "I could get to know you a *lot* better. It could be really good for your career."

Now I was pissed off. "I don't do married men," I hissed and yanked my arm away.

"But what if I don't mind?" came a voice from behind me. I spun to see Marissa leaning against the wall. "Especially if I join in?"

"Are you people *serious?*" Maybe I'd had a daydream or three about being trapped in an elevator with a couple of choice movie stars, but these two drunken creeps weren't exactly what I'd had in mind.

"What kind of party did you think this was?" Joe asked, pressing against me. Thick in the waist and taller than I was, he was as immovable as a wall. I took a step backward and bumped into his wife.

"You're drunk, and this conversation is over," I declared, trying to push past him.

"This won't look pretty in my column next weekend," he said. It sounded like a joke, but its sinister edge made me balk. I pushed again, and he grabbed my waist. Before I could panic, another voice came from the dimness in the hall.

"Let her go. She's with me."

It was Angelo, Angelo with a voice of steel, deeper than it had been earlier. Angelo, my guardian angel.

Suddenly, I had the strangest feeling I knew who Angelo was.

"Chill, man, we were just playing," Joe said, stepping aside.

"Go," said Angelo, his mask like a messenger of death.

Jace.

Joe shrugged, put an arm around his wife's waist and pulled her back toward the game room. I watched them go with a shudder of anger and revulsion and didn't move until the door closed behind them.

I spun. "It's you," I said. *Angelo or Jace?*

"Are you all right?" he asked.

"Repulsed, but fine. It's lucky you were there."

"I couldn't get you out of my mind." His accent faded by the second. "I followed you."

"I'm glad you did," I murmured as he moved closer. I was transfixed by the graceful movement of his body, the eerie mask that hid a face I imagined as he stepped closer. All my senses fired. My nostrils flared with his scent. I hadn't noticed it earlier, in the ocean breeze.

It's him. It's Jace.

Did he know I knew? By mutual agreement, perhaps, neither of us admitted the truth.

He held out his hand. I looked at it, then at his face — no, the mask. It was forbidding, strange. But I could see the glint of his eyes, the man behind the mask. His gaze seared me. The little hairs raised on my arms and the back of my neck. Had anyone ever made me this crazy? Maybe. Almost.

I took his proffered hand.

Inch by inch, he pulled me toward him, effortlessly, as if I were drawn by a magnet and not his strong grip. My hip bumped his. I breathed him in. As we stood there, as he looked down at me, pressing against me in the shadows, I wondered briefly if it was too late to flee.

Muffled laughter rang from somewhere down the hall, behind one of those closed doors. I breathed in sharply. He pulled me closer and listened for a moment at the nearest door. He opened it and guided me inside, or maybe I followed. He closed it behind us. Locked it. My heart rate quickened.

We were alone. A dim lamp illuminated a desk, a sleeping laptop computer, bookshelves and a plush leather couch the color of a baseball glove. Sports memorabilia were barely visible on the walls — pennants, photos, glass cases with baseballs and autographs, a rich man's collection.

He reached over to the desk and shut off the lamp. The darkness was almost complete.

"I want to see you," I whispered, breathless now. The only light was the pulsing of the laptop's power cord, like a distant star in a black universe.

"It's just me," he said. "Your Angelo."

I reached up, feeling for him in the darkness, and pulled off his mask, dropping it to the floor. I ran my fingers lightly over the angles of his face, the rough hairs on his chin, the deep cheekbones, the strong nose, the exquisitely shaped lips. He grasped my hand, opened his mouth around my fingers and sucked.

My breath caught. I gave way as he pushed me toward the desk. My rump hit the edge and I stood still, my breaths shallow. He touched my cheek, his fingers gentle as he traced my jawline, moving up to the mask. He removed it carefully and set it on the desk. His hands moved to my waist; I felt him breathing, so close.

"Penelope?" he whispered. In my name, he asked for everything. Held in his arms, I lost my mind. The only force in the universe was this man who set fire to every molecule in my body, and I would have launched a thousand spaceships for him.

"Yes. *Yes.*"

He pressed his lips on mine, hot and sweet, sipping, nipping, supplicating, dominating. This wasn't like the ravenous kiss of last night; this was playful, decadent, assured. Because tonight he was someone else: Angelo, who had no history with me, no reputation to protect.

His hands roamed across my back and to my waist as he

tasted my mouth; then he slid them up until he cupped both breasts. He ran his thumbs along the edge of the boned fabric of the corset top. He kissed my chin, my neck; he licked my mounded cleavage, then blew on the wet skin. I shivered as he scooped each breast out of the corset top and latched his mouth onto one nipple, lavishly tonguing it while he pinched the other. I moaned, gripping his back under the jacket of his suit. He paused in his ministrations to yank off the jacket. I didn't see where it went. I closed my eyes and saw stars as he licked and pinched my breasts again.

"You're even more beautiful in the dark," he murmured as his hands wandered across my body. I unbuttoned his shirt as he caressed me, anxious to touch his skin; I savored the undulating landscape of his muscled torso under my fingers.

He gripped and squeezed my buttocks through the dress, then pulled up its fluffy skirt, groping through the crinoline. "Just how much material is under here?"

I giggled.

I stopped giggling with an "oh" when his hands found my thighs, the tops of my stockings, the garters.

"Someone's a naughty girl," he said, and I could feel him kneeling before me. I began to tremble. He kissed the inside of my thigh, and I almost jumped out of my skin. "I like your scent. I like everything. I want everything."

He kissed his way north until his lips pressed against my thong.

"God," I hissed as he used one finger to rub my clit through the satin.

"You like this?" he asked.

"Yes," I breathed, moving against his hand, all control gone.

"As soon as I saw you, I wanted to taste you." He kissed

me, tongued me through the fabric. "You look like a confection tonight," he said between kisses, "sparkling like sugar." He roughly pushed the slip of cloth down and tugged open the strings that held it to my hips, and then his mouth was on me, teasing me with his tongue in slow, exquisite torment. I was almost embarrassed at how wet I was. Almost. I could feel the hot slickness between my legs as he set my sensitive nub afire. I slipped my fingers into his hair and kneaded his scalp as he sucked and nibbled; I bit back a cry even as I writhed against him, silently begging for more. His tongue danced over me, and then I came hard, shaking and whimpering.

He stood and caught my cries with his mouth, and I tasted myself on him as he clutched me, as his tongue teased mine. The kiss deepened, his tongue sweet in my mouth, making me wonder what it might be like to wrap my lips around another part of him.

He paused, cupping one breast again, stretching out the nipple as we both panted.

"Do you want more?" he whispered, pinching the nipple harder, twisting it. With the pain came outlandish pleasure.

"Yes," I almost sobbed.

"Do you want me to fuck you?"

"Yes." *God, what am I doing?* Even I didn't move this fast. Or hadn't in a long time.

"Say my name," he whispered, pinching the other nipple.

I froze — melting, freezing, wanting him beyond reason. Him? His name? Was this a test?

"Angelo," I moaned softly.

"That's it, darling," he said, his English accent stronger for just a moment. He kissed my breasts and released them; I heard his pants hit the floor, heard a rustle and a tear, heard the snap of a condom. The tiny pulsing glow of the computer light seemed brighter now as my eyes adjusted, and I could just make out the shape of his gorgeous face as he leaned over me and hitched up my skirts again. He lifted me onto the edge of the desk, and I felt its cold edge against my ass.

Holding back the crinoline and skirt, he pressed against me. I felt his rigid cock slide against my oversensitive clit, my slick cleft. I wanted him between my legs, inside me, now, *now*. My craving became frantic. I opened my legs wider, reached down and grasped his length, hard and pulsing, and guided him to me, into me.

Jace groaned as he drove forward, seating himself deeply inside me in one smooth motion. My breath came in short pants. He hooked his arms under my thighs and pulled me closer to him, thrusting with a sudden urgency. I wrapped my legs behind his back, opening, wanting more. He filled me, stretched me, and waves of pleasure swept through my core. I clenched around him, and he growled in appreciation. Our coupling turned fast, hard, desperate. I held on to his strong shoulders and arched to take him, all of him, high on his strength and scent and passionate need. He bent over me as he plunged in and out, grazing his teeth along the skin of my neck. I almost laughed; in another world, in one of the movies I liked, he would have been a vampire. Instead, he was so much more — superheated muscle, strong and forceful and male, going deeper with each thrust until fire-flies twinkled in my vision. I came like a supernova, convulsing in ecstasy around him, and he pumped into me harder, once, twice, thrice. With a desperate sound, he clutched me close as his powerful spasms shot new waves of pleasure through my exhausted body.

At last, he stilled, and his breathing slowly eased as he

held me, his damp chest against my exposed breasts, his arms warm and powerful around me. I kissed his neck, licked the skin, tasting him, the hint of salt and still that scent that made me think of forests. He eased out of me, disposed of the condom and guided me to the couch, pulling me down with him. He lay next to me, half-clothed, kissing me with slow, light touches of his lips, bringing us both back to some peaceful, strange realm where two strangers who weren't strangers had just shared the most intimate moment imaginable.

"Are you all right?" he asked finally, nuzzling my neck.

"Oh, yes."

"It's a shame I'll never see you again."

A flutter passed through me that felt like emptiness. "You won't?"

"I can't. Remember, I have a long trip to make," he said, evoking the fortune I'd told.

"Oh, that," I replied, playing his game. "You can put it off for a while, can't you?"

"It's foretold in the stars, I'm afraid." He released me gently and stood. A few moments later, he'd donned his pants and jacket, found his mask and handed me mine. "I'll make sure you get safely downstairs."

My glow slipped away. How could this be a hit and run? I wanted to confront him. To say his name, his real name. But there was something about his role-playing that stopped me. There was a reason he was acting as Angelo, and it wasn't just fun and games. I sensed something behind his mask. Fragility? I didn't want to shatter it, him, this resplendent night. I didn't want to admit I'd made a mistake.

I straightened my clothes, smoothed the wig, freshened my lipstick. When we were put back together, I let him escort me down the staircase. At the bottom, he barely glanced at me as he squeezed my hand, and then he strode away, toward the front door. Angelo was gone.

So was Jace.

And, *holy fuck,* I would have to see him on Monday.

On the way home, I was quiet as Wendy and Damien joked about the people they'd met, the horrible columnist and the party's peculiar mix of sex and geekiness. I laughed along, not hearing half of what they said. Under my numb exterior, I seethed like lava, hot for Jace, wanting more, angry that he couldn't deal with me as himself, and aghast that I'd gone along with his ruse.

What have I done?

SOMETIMES THE JUNCTION Box felt like a bad habit. I'd get ready to go, thinking I should find a new bar, shake up my weekend. But then I'd walk through the door and see the friendly faces and hear Ez and the Emeralds playing, and I remembered why I always came back.

I took an Uber there Saturday night so I could drink away my anxiety. I'd slept late, then hit my favorite coffee shop to work on my costume designs for a while, then took a nap. And still I didn't feel right as I headed to the bar. Nightmares had plagued me, dreams of faceless men fucking me and leaving me cold. Or a faceless man fucking me and Jace coming to my rescue, friendly and open and not in disguise, making love to me. The Jace I'd met in real life had been none of these things. He was much more complex than my dream engine seemed able to process. I quailed at the thought of meeting him again, but I rationalized: If he wanted our encounter at the party to remain anonymous, I could play it off that way, too. For all I knew, he might think he'd fooled me. He might think he had a secret, that I'd thought he was Angelo, the mysterious, devilish Brit. But I doubted it. He'd asked me to say his name. He'd demanded suspension of disbelief, the theater's magical elixir.

The Junction Box was almost shaking with the beat when I walked in. It seemed as if the Emeralds were doing more rocking tunes these days, though they still threw in a few of Ez's heartbreaking ballads. She was up there now, banging on the baby grand piano and belting out a throaty tune. Her man, Gary, was at the Victorian-styled bar, watching her; nearby were Damien, Alex and Cali's guy, Wyatt, chattering over Neil's exquisite cocktails. I headed for the table where the girls sat. This is how these nights always started; the women had their conference, and the men drank and talked shit, and then the couples paired off and I went home.

"Penelope!" Cali said, standing to greet me with a hug. Her long blond hair was loose tonight, and she wore a V-neck T-shirt and a short skirt. No camera. The others greeted me, too: Sloane, a talented potter who was studying at the Bohemia School of Art and Design, demure with her dark hair and floral dress, and Thea, a redhead in jeans and a tank top who did graphic design.

"Have you lost weight, Thea?" I asked. She was taller than I was, and she'd always been a bit broad of shoulder and long of limb. Now she looked thin, maybe too thin.

"Stress will do that to you," she said as I sat with them.

"What's wrong?"

"Oh, you know, moving, trying to balance work and art, living up to my dad's standards, the usual crap." Thea shrugged with a tight smile and sipped her beer.

"Your new place is great, though," Cali told her before

turning to me. "She found an apartment in the industrial district. Someone's converted one of the old factories into big studio apartments. It's nice. Not far from Gary and Ez's place."

"Gawd, it'll all be gentrified before we know it." I flagged down a waiter and ordered a vodka martini.

Thea made a face at me. She liked to tease me about my fear of gin. Cali was having an Old-Fashioned, her usual.

"And what are you drinking, Sloane?" I asked. She was sipping from a dark green ceramic head that gazed at me fiercely.

"One of Neil's special concoctions. A Painkiller. Actually, he said it was a classic tiki drink, but what do I know? My brain is full of wine vintages, thanks to Alex."

"A Painkiller? Maybe that's what I should have ordered. I have *pain* to *kill*," I intoned, slipping into my dramatic voice.

"It wouldn't have to do with a certain actor at a certain theater, would it?" Cali asked.

My jaw dropped. "What do you know?"

She laughed. "I saw the way you stared at him during the bonfire, and you may have mentioned something at lunch."

Shit. That's right. I'd told her about the kiss. At least she didn't know about last night. Good God, I hoped nobody knew about last night except me and Jace. Damien was Cali's brother, but I didn't think he had any idea.

"Jace and I are working together, when he's not being openly hostile," I said.

"He's hostile?" Sloane asked. Her cheeks looked pink, maybe from the drink. "That's too bad, because he's pretty hot."

"Pretty *and* hot," I said. "Maybe too much of both. Whenever I'm near him — " I wondered how detailed I should get.

"Do tell, do tell, do tell!" Thea said, her red curls almost bouncing with enthusiasm.

I lowered my voice. "The man throws flames like a sun with a fever. And I get the impression that he feels the heat when I'm around, too." *Ha. Maybe because he fucked me sense-less at a party.* "But then he runs away." *Pretending to be someone else.*

"Not that I have your experience," said Thea — she was under the impression that my experience actually meant something — "but my understanding is that most guys run away *after* they get what they want. So maybe there's still hope. I mean, if you want your sunburn." She grinned.

Perhaps I took too long to answer. As I sipped my newly arrived martini, Cali's eyes grew wide.

"Oh, my God. Did you — ?"

The others, smelling blood, stared me down.

"No! No, no, nothing like that," I protested hastily. "He keeps running away, remember? Though there *may* have been a close encounter of the kissing kind before he blew me off."

Thea's dark blue eyes assumed a faraway look. "Tell us everything. Every second."

"That's about how long it lasted," I said, leaving out his hungry assault on my senses backstage — and Angelo. "I think he just doesn't know what he wants, so my goal is to keep it professional from now on."

"Bullshit," Cali said, and Sloane laughed. "I mean, it's not like he's a permanent employee of the theater, right? He's not writing your checks. Maybe you can have some fun with him. It sounds like he only needs a little push to jump into your pond. Make a little room among your water lilies."

"Stop making my privates sound like a fetid swamp," I intoned. The others burst into laughter.

"That's not at all what I meant," Cali gasped as tears of hilarity rolled down her face.

"You'd better not be laughing at the Emeralds." Ez had arrived at the table. Just behind her was a server with a tray and another one of those tiki mugs. He handed it to her and awaited her verdict. Bartender Neil always had a soft spot for Ez.

"You guys sound *wonderful,*" I declared as the others tried to get their guffaws under control. Canned rock music played from the speakers now. I hadn't even noticed the band going on break.

"Yeah, right," Ez said, taking a liberal suck from the straw. "Huh. Kind of fruity. Not sure I like that." She took an even longer pull. "Oh, wait. There's the rum. Get me another one of these, will ya? And tell Neil he's awesome."

The guy with the tray smiled and acknowledged my "one more" gesture with a nod, then headed off to the bar. Ez sat, pushing the long bangs of her short, mod cut out of her eyes. "What the hell are you all laughing about?"

"Penelope's theatrical drama," Thea said with a twinkle.

"I take it you don't mean the latest play."

"Of course not," I said, finishing off my martini.

"Enter, stage right," Sloane said cryptically. Thea's eyes widened as she looked beyond me.

No. No way.

We all turned, and there he was, Jace Edison, making his way from the door to the bar in a dark blue button-up shirt with the sleeves rolled up and nicely clinging jeans.

"Well, isn't that convenient," Cali said.

"He's not even looking over here," I said. "Don't stare."

"Is it me," asked Thea, "or did the temperature go up in here about ten degrees?" She fanned herself as the others chuckled.

"You might as well go for the best," Ez said. She was the only one still ogling him. "He's not just gorgeous. He can *sing.* I have the soundtrack to *Acid Candy.* His voice gives me goose-bumps." She shot me a wicked smile, and I tried to rearrange my expression into indifference. "Don't worry about it, Pen. I'm more than occupied these days with Gary." Her teasing expression melted into something soft and fleeting, a big change for Ez, as she glanced back at the bar and exchanged waves with her curly-headed guy. Maybe that's what love did for people.

I would never know.

Still, I drank my new martini and watched Jace until he got his drink, turned around, leaned against the bar and caught my eye. After that, I paid him no attention at all, except when I thought he wasn't looking, and even then, he usually was.

"He's going to burn a hole through that dress," Cali murmured at one point when she looked around and saw him staring.

"He hardly has to," I said. It was a low-cut white linen swing dress, and I hadn't worn a bra. I knew it left little to the imagination. It occurred to me that I was wearing white again, a color that rarely left my closet. Was I unconsciously reliving last night? "Ridiculous," I whispered, and the others exchanged glances.

"I've seen him give the cold shoulder to five women so far," Sloane said, "not that I'm watching. Though Alex is raising his eyebrows at me, so maybe I am."

The conversation moved on to other topics, but two-thirds through Ez's second set, and through three too many martinis, I couldn't stand the pressure of Jace's stare anymore. The power I'd dedicated to ignoring him was not as great as I'd hoped.

"Listen, girls, I'm going to call it a night. I had a Bon Vivant gig yesterday, and I've been working hard on these costume designs. You'll be hearing from me about the dress rehearsal. If any of you can make it, it always helps the cast to have an audience."

The others assented with good humor and turned back to the band. Except for Cali.

"Call me," she said, looking worried. She had a way of seeing through my little act.

"I'm fine," I murmured, putting down money for my drinks. "We can't all have hot surfers to go home to. But I will call you about taking photos of the actors in costume, OK? If I ever get them done. And the pinups are talking about doing a calendar for next year to benefit the humane society. Want to shoot it?"

Cali grinned. "I'd love to! Take it easy, Pen."

I nodded, presented my most dazzling fake smile and headed for the exit.

Outside, I took a deep breath of the warm night air and tried to ignore the feeling that Jace's eyes were still on me. I suppose a normal girl would be freaked out. Creeped out, even. But I'd felt his touch. I felt it again when he looked at me. He was more heady than the drinks Neil was slinging behind the bar. I was drunk on the memory of last night. I didn't care how foolish I was. I wanted another shot of him.

I needed to get out of here. Flee temptation. Usually I grabbed temptation with both hands, but this — this wasn't just intoxicating. It was insane.

The moon was even closer to full, and downtown Bohemia was abuzz with drunken revelers in the mood to howl at it. I fell into pace with the crowd, drifting toward my old neighborhood on the river, a tad unsteady on my heels. It didn't matter here; people were laughing, talking too loudly, staggering, practically skipping. The men were in crisp button-up shirts or tight T-shirts; the women in holey jeans or short dresses or even shorter hot pants. I had not yet made a judgment on whether sporting the lower curve of one's butt cheeks was a sexy trend or just ass. If I weren't wearing a dress like the one I had on tonight, I'd rather go for the high-waisted, high-cut shorts of a 1940s pinup model, but I was an exotic bird among Bohemia's pigeons.

This wasn't so bad, being alone in a throng of happiness. I let it seep into my bloodstream with the vodka. A wave of dizzy contentment swept through me, and I grabbed a lamp-post and paused to breathe in the warm night. I closed my eyes and listened: music from the bars; a honking horn; a shout and a giggle . . .

"Penelope."

Jace's voice.

My eyes drifted open. He wasn't a dream. Well, he *was*, but he was all too real, standing in front of me, his dark eyes hooded. No mask except for the one he projected, always the actor.

"Jace." I tried to sound neutral.

"Are you all right?"

"Absolutely fine. It's a beautiful night to be drunk." I stepped away from the post and swayed.

He grabbed my arm. "Let me take you home."

"Now that seems like a bad idea." *Or a very, very good one.*

Jace took a deep breath. He didn't meet my eyes. "I owe you an apology."

You mean for taking me in the dark while you pretended to be someone else? This was going to be good. I cocked my head at him, waiting for his confession.

"I shouldn't have yelled at you backstage the other night."

Backstage? Christ, was he talking about the kiss? After what had transpired since? Doubt flickered through my brain, a pulse of fear, wondering if it really had been him at the party — but I knew it had been. I knew his voice, his scent. I *knew.* And he was still acting. Did he really think I didn't know?

"Guys don't usually run when I deign to kiss them," I answered, playing along.

"I don't — I never should have let that happen."

"At first, I was under the impression that you rather enjoyed it." In my mind, the fevered kiss was eclipsed by the dark heat of that room last night, the way he held me, penetrated me . . .

"I can't get involved with anyone — "

"Anyone you work with?"

"Anyone," Jace said, finally meeting my eyes. God, those eyes. They said something entirely different. They said, *I fucked you, and I would do it again.*

I took a deep breath and tried to get a grip. Somehow, what he was saying hurt, much more deeply than it should. I was caught in his cobweb, layers of deception.

I pulled my arm away from his grasp. "Now that we've established your rules, I'll just be heading home." Damn it. My reserve was gone, and I could hear it in my voice. I whirled and started down the street. I'd made it two blocks before I heard him again.

"Wait!" He sprinted to catch up. It was surreal to have him walking alongside me, this beautiful creature, so exotic in Bohemia. He seemed entirely unattainable, even as he oozed sex. I laughed at the places my drunken mind was going.

"What?" he asked.

"Unworthy thoughts. Why don't you go back home, or wherever it is you're staying."

"I'm in a house on the beach. One of the theater's patrons is away for the summer, so they've lent it to me."

"Sounds nice," I said, not without sarcasm.

"It's beautiful. The pool keeps me sane. I like to swim."

And his body showed it. So we were having a normal conversation now?

"How's the play coming?" I asked. "Ready for read-through?"

"I've done a few rewrites. Costumes?"

"I've been working on designs for most of today. I thought I'd get out and have myself a little fun." I hoped my tone implied that this was not my idea of fun.

"Stop." He touched my arm, lightly this time, and I slowed my pace, then halted. We were on the edge of my neighborhood, darkly shaded by oak trees and thick foliage that shrouded historic riverside homes that dated back to the late 1800s, including my funky apartment house.

"Go home," I told him.

"Where are you going?"

"I'm going home, too." I pointed down the darkened street.

"You shouldn't walk down there by yourself. Not in your — "

"My dazzlingly drunk condition?" I shot him one of my

killer smiles, and something in his face, his dark eyes shifted. Hunger, there, then gone.

He moved ever so slightly closer. "I don't want you angry with me."

I stepped closer to him this time, lowered my voice to a purr. "Then how do you want me?"

I heard his breath hitch. So I wasn't the only one affected by this, whatever this was. An owl hooted deep in the trees as we stood there; another answered, closer.

"I want you safe," Jace said, taking a step back. "I'll walk you home."

I stood there for another second, shrugged and resumed my slightly uneven pace. He slipped his arm into mine. Maybe he thought he was lending me the support I needed. Mostly, he set me on fire, first as a lit match brushing against my elbow, then as a torch flaming up my arm, and then as a bonfire wrapping itself around my skin and burning its way in to places where it shouldn't go.

I focused on the sounds around us. It was quieter here than it was downtown. The owls hooted again, and I heard the distant drone of a boat on the river. In a few blocks, we were crossing the little gravel parking lot that led up to my door. I pulled away from him and dug into my purse for my keys, fumbling, finally finding them. Dropping them.

He leaned down and picked them up, handed them to me, his fingers stroking mine as I clutched the keys. His eyes roamed from the low cut of my dress, where I knew my nipples poked against the fabric, and up my long neck to my face, my lips, finally my eyes.

"You tempt me," he said hoarsely.

"Sure, blame it on the girl." I'd had it with his shit, as much as I wanted to kiss him the way I had backstage. I wanted him to own it, to admit he'd pretended to be Angelo, my rescuer, my lover. Damn it, I wanted more.

"I blame myself." He reached out and ran one finger lightly over my cheekbone, under my chin.

"I thought you were a man more sinned against than sinning."

"You're quoting *Lear* at me?" A small smile crossed his lips as his finger wandered farther, down my neck, across the low neckline of my dress, the pale curve of my breasts. I resisted the urge to lean into him. He needed to decide whether he wanted me or not.

"How else to reach the actor?" I asked. " 'One man in his time plays many parts.' "

Jace froze. His hand fell away, and his eyes met mine. Mixed with desire was something darker. Sadness. Bitterness?

"As you like it," he said softly. "Good night."

He walked away swiftly until the darkness swallowed him. The owls hooted, and a gust of wind rustled the oaks and palms around me, carrying the sweet scent of night-blooming jasmine. The night was drunk, too, velvety dark and soft and romantic.

And I was alone again.

MONDAY WASN'T USUALLY a rehearsal day, but given our tight schedule, director Dirk had ordered the read-through that evening. The Chamberlain might be on the stepladder to being a full-time professional theater, but it was still a community theater at its heart, and most of the actors had day jobs.

My hours would shift to coincide with rehearsals as needed, but I'd be working constantly in the next several weeks to make sure the actors looked as good as they sounded on stage.

Since I was still firming up my concepts and designs, I looked forward to hearing the play voiced by the actors. It would help me get a sense of what they'd bring to each role, as well as exits and entrances and the time they'd have for costume changes. The last thing we needed was actors having nervous breakdowns because they couldn't switch gowns or crowns in time for their next cue.

I stopped by the fabric store on the way in and picked up swatches I thought would work — damask rather than satin, which could look cheap under the lights; cotton over certain synthetics, for texture and movement. Then I browsed the racks in the costume shop to see if there was anything I could plunder. I found a few outfits to cannibalize, but essentially I was starting from scratch with *Midsummer at Midnight*. And that made me kind of excited. I loved the act of creating something from nothing — the beautiful phantoms of characters the actors would embrace and inhabit to bring the play to life.

I was putting swatches together with sketches when Millie popped her head in the door. Her brunette bob bounced with her motions; she exuded energy, just as she did when she worked at the Double Diamond Diner. I knew she'd taken one of Cali's photography classes, too. A woman of many interests.

"You had a message," she said. "A guy from *The Bohemia Bugle* called, said you were going to set up an interview with Jace Edison?"

"Hilarious," I said. "Was it Joe Stier?"

Millie checked the piece of pink paper in her hand. "Yeah, that's him. He said, and I quote, 'It will be worth her while to call me back.' I didn't like his tone."

"Can you pass the message on to marketing? I'm in no position to help that creep, and I wouldn't want to anyway. But I guess we can't afford to piss off the only daily newspaper in town."

Millie smiled. "He worked with Cali, right? She's mentioned him."

"She got out of *The Bugle* before he could get his claws into her. Speaking of Cali — are you still doing photography?"

"I might take another class, but I'm not sure it's where I'm meant to be. That's why I'm doing the summer gig at the theater. I have all these impulses — oh, this is embarrassing."

"What? Do you want to get naked on stage or something?"

Millie laughed. "No, I mean, I have creative impulses, but I just haven't found the right gig for me. I'm going to help out the costume shop, too, did you know?"

"I didn't. That's great! Sometimes it's more fun to shop around, you know. And not just for a career. See you at the reading?"

"Sure thing," she said, heading off to marketing.

Later, I dropped into the green room to raid the fridge for a ginger ale and looked around, enjoying the mad clutter, the flea-market detritus of hundreds of shows — shelves of props that hadn't found a home where they really belonged, or that had a sentimental place in the actors' hearts — the leg lamp from *A Christmas Story,* a gilded birdcage, a railroad lantern, a picnic basket, fake flowers, our version of Excalibur from *Camelot,* an old sign for *A Little Night Music.* Furniture that could be drafted at any time for a play was scattered around the room — a modern leather chair, a fainting couch and everything in between, offering a comforting, comfortable place for the actors to hang out before, during and after shows. A kitchenette and a craft table helped feed the herd on busy nights.

I caught sight of myself in a mirror hung between the doors to the dressing rooms. I could have walked right out of a play in my 1950s-style dress. Maybe *Cat on a Hot Tin Roof?* Holy shit. I was wearing white again. I wasn't as busty as Elizabeth Taylor, but I wasn't hurting in that department, and the sleeveless, V-necked bodice showed off my assets well. Of course, I tended to give dresses like this a Marilyn Monroe vibe, since my hair was blond (and pink).

I usually dressed up, sure. But I had to ask myself, with brutal honesty: Was I dressing for him?

On one wall of the green room hung a large, flat-screen monitor. It showed what was happening in the theater in wide angle, with audio, so the actors wouldn't miss their cues. The stage was visible at the center, as were most of the seats. I tensed as I spotted Jace and Dirk wandering around the corners, talking about blocking, while a couple of the stagehands set up a long table and chairs for the read-through.

I had to get over this thing with Jace. Or maybe it *was* over; he'd fled again. But we had to be able to talk. He had been given an unusual amount of input for a playwright in this show, no doubt because of his Broadway clout. If he was essentially Dirk's assistant director, I would have to deal with him at every stage of production. And I wasn't going to screw up this play. Maybe I wanted Jace, but I needed and wanted this job.

Jace was a mistake I couldn't afford.

My heart lightened by 6:30, as the actors began to arrive.

They brought with them a joyous energy that made me remember why I loved theater so much.

I took a seat in the first audience row of the main performance space, tablet in hand. Wendy bounced in, and I stood to give her a hug.

"Hello, gorgeous," she said. "So how's Mr. Devastating today?"

"And why would I care?"

"Ooo, that good, huh?"

I shrugged. "I haven't spoken to Jace today." And I hadn't seen him, either, since my moment of indulgence watching him on the monitor, when he'd moved around the stage with the grace of a lion. I simply couldn't grasp why he didn't want to perform in his own show. He would be magnificent, the box office would help the theater immensely, and he'd be guaranteed an enormous amount of attention for his first play.

"And Dirk?" she asked. "Stormy or sunny?"

"Partly cloudy, I think."

Wendy laughed. "Let me know how I do."

"You'll be great, as always. But you'll be better in my costume."

"Make me sexy!" she commanded with humor in her tone, then took a seat at the long table. It was really two long tables pushed together, topped with black cloths. A couple of water pitchers and cups awaited the actors, but no distracting snacks. Dirk was like a first-grade teacher in that regard. Nothing earned a faster smackdown than munching on anything in his presence while on stage.

The actors filtered in, among them Holland Ivey, the long-haired brunette from Orlando who'd been cast as Titania; and attractive, shaggy-haired Paul Terrimore, Wendy's counterpart as Demetrius. He was voluble and merry, but was he drunk? I'd give it even odds.

I knew most of the actors, including the handsome forty-something playing Oberon, a veteran of local productions. Puck, however, was new, a cute, elfin nineteen-year-old named Harry who'd just finished his first year in the theater program at my old college. Among other talents, he could actually ride a unicycle. I didn't remember seeing him at auditions, so Dirk must have done a search offline to find his special skill set. Dirk usually got what he wanted.

At last, there was one seat left at the table, and there was a nervous electricity among the cast as Jace made his entrance. Dirk might have been in charge, but Jace commanded the room. He had that charisma that only a few actors had. "Star quality" was an overused term, but I felt it, and it wasn't just me. Though maybe I felt it more intensely, knowing how he kissed, how he felt . . . He glanced in my direction, just for a moment, and I almost lost it.

I tore my eyes away from him to see Wendy watching me. A corner of her mouth turned up in a knowing smile that made my face burn even hotter. I raised a scolding eyebrow at her, and she grinned and turned back to Dirk, who was giving a pep talk.

Each actor introduced him- or herself in turn. Jace described himself with a self-effacing "I've been in a few plays and things, and I wrote this one" that made everyone in the room chuckle, including me. He was a charmer or a psycho, or maybe both.

"Why don't you do the honors and set the scene, Jace," Dirk said, and even from my place in the audience — there were a few others gathered around, theater staff, all anxious to hear the play in its entirety — I could see Jace relax. Here he was in his element.

"Setting: A large city in the near future, not unlike New York," Jace intoned in his mellifluous voice. I couldn't help my sigh. He set up the story the way he'd described it in our meeting, a modern re-imagining of *A Midsummer Night's Dream* in which the magical land of the fairies, rooted in nature, is threatened by the industrial world surrounding it. And then the reading began — a little rough, but glowing with potential, the proverbial unpolished diamond. It didn't hurt that Shakespeare provided the source material, but Jace had taken it and twisted it, run with it, and there were moments when *Midsummer at Midnight* sounded so fresh and eerie and exquisite, I forgot about good old Will altogether. Jace read the stage directions, and the actors read their roles, and I was up and soaring with them, caught up in the story, the humor, the romance, the gravity of it. Holland had a dark sexuality as Titania that came through even though she wasn't moving around the stage, and her chemistry with Oberon would be potent. The young couples would be hilarious as they played off each other, once they had their timing down; Wendy shone. I realized how important the clockwork baby would be, along with Bottom's donkey head. I began to see the head as much more than the goofy ball cap with ears. It was a product of Oberon's imagination, and as such, it had to have a hint of the mechanical about it, since the urbanization of society threatened the pastoral magic of the fairies. I started to see it as a metalwork contraption, steampunk style. I'd have to run it by Dirk later. And Jace.

There was a break, and then the shorter second act. The play drew to its close, and Puck had the last few lines. Harry would address the audience as he perched on his unicycle and the happy couples cavorted and faded, two by two, into the background.

"You — I see you don't believe. And how about you, pretty girls? And you, stern sir? You think I lie? Or is it possible I dream?" Harry's cadence had a rap feel to it, just right for the tone of the play — iambic, a nod to Shakespeare. "I *am* a dreamer. I don't lie. But still I see the cruel world. The serpent belching diesel fumes. The pills that put us all to sleep. Except now, you're all awake. The dream is a reality. And while I roll into the night, I'll take you with me to the woods, where all that's real still lives and grows. If you agree to walk with us, you will awaken with the truth. The sun will help our spirit thrive in green and blue, in land and sky. Give me your hands, my dearest friends, and let tomorrow mend this end."

"Puck moves up center. The baby cries," Jace said. "The clockwork baby has come to life, and Titania cries out in delight, holding it tight."

Holland made a dramatic noise, and I tried not to roll my eyes.

"Oberon puts his arm around her," Jace continued, his voice spellbinding, "and they walk behind Puck into the forest, upstage center, into the trees of the city park, which close ranks behind them. The lights go down. The End."

The actors clapped and made appreciative noises. Holland actually had a tear in her eye. She was committed to the role, no doubt about it. And I was moved, too. It was a zany journey to the end, but a weirdly beautiful one.

"Really nice job," Dirk said. "Jace — any thoughts?"

"Well, you've shown me my weaknesses," he said, to the amused murmurs of the cast. "I'll be working out a few rough spots. I'll try to have rewrites for the first rehearsal."

"Wednesday night," Dirk said as the actors picked up their bags and scripts, "6:30. Now don't leave before Theresa and Millie get your measurements!" He nodded at Theresa, our costumer's assistant, a quiet, attractive woman a couple of years younger than me who already had her tape measure and her tablet ready to go. Millie had a big grin on her face. The giddy actors lined up, joking with one another as the women recorded their dimensions.

Wendy gave me a wave as she left with the crowd, and I shot her a smile before turning back to my scribbles on the tablet computer — last-minute notes and sketches of how I wanted the cast to look at the end of the play, when they've given up their urban artifice and embraced love and nature. Dirk and the other bigwigs gathered and chatted, but after a few minutes of absorbed note-taking, I looked up to see the stage empty. The stage lights clicked off, leaving only a ghost light on. I stuffed my tablet into my bag and headed toward backstage to make my escape.

Jace was gone. I was glad. I was disappointed.

God, this was some kind of sickness. I'd thought one good screw was supposed to obliterate sexual tension, make the want go away. Instead it had sharpened my appetite, perhaps because he hadn't come to me as Jace. He'd been Angelo, my mysterious lover. And I wanted Jace, still, knowing how bad the idea was, how bad he'd be for me. I wanted to understand what drove him. I wanted that body, yes. But goddamn it, I wanted his mind, the organ that could conceive both this beautifully strange play and the seductive charade he'd conducted at the party — and afterward.

I cut again through The Attic, the room full of old stage pieces and props lit only by its own ghost light. I tried to get my mind back on the costumes and how I would share my new inspirations with Dirk and the others.

And the bulb went out.

"Shit." I halted, knowing my next move would to be trip over a papier-mâché tree stump or an old bicycle or whatever happened to be strewn around me. There were no straight paths in the Attic. I rummaged in my bag for my phone so I could use it as a flashlight, and then I heard someone moving in front of me.

Electricity shot through me. Fear — it could be anyone. Hope — wanting it to be Jace. Disgust — hating myself for hoping it was him, kicking myself for not wielding my keys to stab all comers in the eyeballs.

I stood very, very, very still, my hands on my bag, ready to swing it at anyone who came near.

"I thought I told my lady never to come to this part of the castle," came a stern voice in a English accent.

A thrill went through me, and still a stab of fear. And the instinct to run, no matter who it was.

He was closer now, his voice not the same as Angelo's the other night — deeper, if anything. "Have you nothing to say for yourself? This area is for the prisoners only. You won't find your lover here. He's betrayed you. He's a spy for the French. Is that who you want in your bed? A damned traitor?"

I had to give him points for creativity, but I was thrown by his games. I wanted to see him. He was almost close enough — and then, *yes,* I caught his scent, and my body both relaxed and tightened at the recognition.

"My — my lord, I was only trying to get a breath of fresh air," I said, calling on rusty acting skills to play along.

"You'll only get the air of the dungeon down here, my lady — or is that what you came for?"

A tiny light came on, silhouetting the figure in front of me. The light flickered. I realized it was one of the LED candles that were often used on stage. Real fire was verboten in the theater.

It was a man in black, wearing a black mask — a simple domino this time, over his eyes only, so I could make out more of his face.

His lips.

I dropped my bag.

"You aren't afraid, are you, my lady?" he said more softly, almost tenderly.

"No."

He chuckled softly. "Maybe you should be."

Before I could move, he'd grabbed both my wrists. I gasped.

"I'll set you free right now if you wish, but you'll lose my protection," he said in that deliciously evil accent, leaning over me, his breath against my ear. "And chances are you'll end up in the Tower for harboring a traitor. It's your choice. Do you want to face the court?"

"N— no," I whispered, tilting my head up, wanting his kiss. Wanting to taste this madness, to take it further.

"Then I'll be your jailer," he said, grabbing my arms, pushing them behind me, wrapping a long silken cloth around my wrists and binding them to the faux porch railing he pushed me against.

Oh, my God.

I couldn't believe this was happening. Jace Edison had just tied me up.

There were worse ways to go, I thought, as he sniffed around me.

"Where are your coat and boots, my lord?" I asked, scanning the silhouette before me. Modern pants, modern shirt, modern shoes.

"Your bloody lover stole them when he left the castle," he improvised. "You like a bit of villainy in your men, don't you?"

"I — " *Say no. Ask to leave. This is a mistake. A bad, bad mistake.* "Yes, my lord."

"Ah, *yes,* that's a word I like to hear from you," Jace murmured, close to me now. "Say it again." He clutched the skirt of my dress and slowly drew it up my leg. The fabric brushed against my skin, setting it tingling. "Say it again. Say you want me to punish you."

"I don't want to be punished, my lord," I said, breathless now. "I think you're the one who should be punished."

"You'd like that, would you? Only I'm not the one sleeping with a traitor."

"I'm not — I'm not sleeping with anyone."

He let out a low, knowing laugh, and I would have joined him if I weren't so aroused. "If you don't want to be punished, then perhaps you want something else? Is that why you dress like a wanton in my presence? These virginal white gowns showing off your harlot's wares?" In one motion, his hand slipped into the bodice of my dress and popped out one breast. I quivered as he popped out the other one, and I strained against my bonds, liking the feel of them, the feel of being exposed in the faux candlelight.

"I dress well within the realm of fashion, my lord."

"Fashion for a slut, my lady," he said, caressing my breasts, squeezing my nipples. The sensation was maddeningly stimulating. "Tell me, did you dream of me when you fucked your lover? Have you dreamt of me since you last opened your legs for a man?"

He was clever. I knew what he was asking me. Had I dreamed of him since he had me on the desk at the party?

"Yes, my lord," I said softly.

"Then you are a slut," he whispered in my ear. "That's fine, because I like my ladies a bit slutty."

At this moment, I liked being a bit slutty too. A lot slutty. I was breathing so fast, I thought I would pop my zipper.

No need for the zipper. He was pulling up my skirt. He pulled my thong down and off, then slipped a hand between my legs. I jumped at his first touch, before I started to melt. He fingered my clit in slow, delicious circles. My breasts brushed against his shirt, his warm chest. My nipples were erect and aching from his attentions. I trembled against him, unable to embrace him or push him away, my hands held fast behind me.

"Fear not, my lady. I want to give you pleasure."

"You want to torture me," I said in my best feisty maiden voice.

"In the best possible way." He pushed a finger inside me. "It seems my lady is not fully against my invasion. You're as wet as a London gutter after a rain."

I panted as he pushed his finger deeper, touching that part of me that begged for him. I rubbed against him, straining to increase the contact.

"Do you want me to take you, slut?" he asked, his voice breathy and excited. He slipped a second finger inside me, stroking my wet passage as he kissed my neck, licked the skin, which sparked with the sensation.

God, I wanted him. "Yes, my lord."

He pressed against me, pushing me against the railing, stroking me harder with his nimble fingers. "Tell me to fuck you."

I could barely speak. "Fuck me, my lord."

"Say it again. Tell me to fuck you. Tell me what you are."

"I'm a slut, and I want you to fuck me," I whimpered. I would have said anything.

His fingers slipped out of me, and there was that sound again, the familiar sound of the condom being opened and applied. He touched my lips first with the fingers that had been inside me; he slipped them into my mouth so I tasted my arousal on him, and I sucked, slowly, once, twice. Swiftly, he withdrew his fingers, pushed my skirts higher, grasped my thighs, hoisted me.

He took a moment to position himself, teasing my opening. I cried out with pleasure as he thrust into my slippery sheath. I should be protesting this, a little voice inside my head said. I should be running away, setting boundaries. But giving up control to him felt so good. I succumbed to the helpless ecstasy of being bound and fucked by this man I wanted so much.

His rhythm was slow and deliberate and mind-altering. He held me close and hard, pushed into me and pulled back, teetering on the edge of losing contact. Then he slid deeply inside me again, touching the bedrock of my lust, melting it into lava. I had never been tied up before, never fucked in this way, and never by someone I had longed for the way a parched desert wanderer yearned for water. I never knew how thirsty I was until I met Jace Edison.

I teetered on the brink as his breathing, his cadence increased in pace, as he clutched and squeezed me until I cried out again. The intensity was overwhelming. And then, for the first time in this crazy encounter, he devoured my mouth with his. The kiss drew me into a cave of darkness and desire as he slammed into me and held his cock inside me, swollen and hot and, *God,* I was coming, contracting around him with an unearthly cry he echoed with his guttural one. We shook and pulsed together, my orgasm milking him, and even before I was done I wanted more. More than this night. More than this masquerade. I shook against him, my head against his chest, as he stilled.

"Please," I said as he slid out of me, eased me down and let my skirt fall. I wanted to say his name. I wanted to say it so badly.

"Don't beg, my lady. It isn't seemly. I'm satisfied. I'll set you free." And I was free, the silk scarf already loose in his nimble hands. He stuffed it in his pocket. "Shhh," he said, putting a finger to my mouth. It was all I could do not to lick it. "Go back to your manor, my lady. My castle is too dark for one the likes of you."

"Wait!" I called out, but he slipped out the door just as the ghost light came back on, by switch no doubt, its bleak bulb casting eerie shadows all around me. I looked down at myself, my rumpled skirt, my bag and underwear on the floor. My legs ached from his rough treatment; my pussy felt gloriously sore. I rubbed my wrists, and a last pulse, a final whisper of orgasm, shuddered through my body as I remembered it all in perfect, terrifying clarity.

Was this what drug addiction was like? I knew I wanted more, even if the next hit might kill me. I didn't fear physical harm. But my emotions had never been set to boil the way they were now. I hadn't felt anything close to this in years, and then, oh, how I'd been burned. I wasn't sure my heart could stand another scalding.

∾

THE PRODUCTION of *Midsummer at Midnight* seemed to accelerate to light speed overnight. It seemed real, now, with the actors always around the theater, before and during rehearsals. The sets began to build and grow, and the rapping of hammers and the smell of fresh paint drifted through the building. Alan, the lighting designer, set about bending a grid of five hundred lights and gels and gobos to his will, and I made sure my fabrics would work with his vision. Sound designer Bill pitched in to help make the magic. There were more meetings. More plans.

It had been more than a week since Jace's naughty nobleman had cornered me backstage, and ever since, in medieval fashion, I'd avoided him like the plague. Or I'd tried. Unlike before, now he seemed to pop up wherever I was, but never in a way he'd have to engage me. I caught him watching me when I met with Karen on stage to talk about how my colors would work with her scenic design, which now included a city skyline behind the trees. Another day, he was loitering in the back parking lot with the carpenters when I pulled up on my scooter. He watched me all the way into the building, his eyes burning like coals, without ever saying a word.

And did *I* say a word? Hell, no. I had no idea what to say — not without potentially going supernova on him. Especially with all of his new attention. Frankly, the more I thought about him, the more I was pissed off. If he could seduce me in private, pretending to be someone else, why couldn't he deal with me in public? *Date* me in public? I was hardly an old-fashioned girl, but I wasn't about to be somebody's dirty secret, either. It's not like dating anyone would harm his reputation. The fans who loved unavailable men might feel a thud of disappointment, but after a flutter in the gossip rags — which wasn't terribly likely either, given that no one gave a shit in Bohemia — we could almost be normal together. At least for the summer. Until he left.

That is, if Jace ever *was* normal. There had to be a reason he behaved the way he did. I just had no idea what it was.

I prepared to pitch my new ideas to Dirk and get approval for my final designs. I had Millie set up the meeting and hoped Jace wouldn't show up. I could deal with him on a professional level, I told myself, but it would be a lot easier if I didn't have to.

When I arrived at the meeting room that Tuesday, a week after our last encounter, the door was closed. I knocked, expecting Dirk and maybe Millie. Either way, I'd worn black capris and a sleeveless pink shirt. For now, I'd sworn off white dresses.

Jace opened the door, sexy in jeans and a black, V-neck T-shirt. That's all some guys ever needed. Somehow, his bullet-proof looks made him all that much more annoying.

"Come in, Penelope. I understand you have some new designs?" He sounded cool, but as I brushed past him into the empty room, he swayed toward me ever so slightly, breathing me in.

Damn.

He closed the door behind me.

"Where's Dirk?" I sat at the table with my tablet computer and looked at Jace expectantly, trying to ignore his scent, the rumpled appeal of his thick, short hair.

"He's confident in your work. He'll look over your designs at rehearsal tonight, but he said that as long as I was happy, he'd be happy."

"It's not like him to give up so much control."

Jace chuckled as he sat across the table from me, fiddling

with that silver watch of his. "Oh, he's not. He's just trying to make me feel like I have some input. Everyone wants me to feel special."

"Do they?" I couldn't keep the sarcasm out of my tone.

"Apparently they think I'm a celebrity of some sort."

"I wonder where they got that idea?"

"I take it you don't want me to feel special?" His gaze held mine, superficially amused, but smoke roiled in his dark irises.

"You don't need my help. I think you already have a well-developed sense of entitlement." My mouth was running away from me. I'd meant to be chill with him, but the real me was taking over, the woman with the vengeful temper and the flaming libido. I already knew this conversation was off the tracks, and I didn't give a fuck.

"Is that what you think?" Jace asked, softly this time.

"You take what you want. You take everything except the responsibility."

"Ah," he said. He stood. He paced. "Then you really don't know me."

"How could I? You run away from me every time you get — close."

Jace stopped, turned toward me, his voice low and dangerous. "Don't push me."

"Why not? I think you've pushed *me*."

"I've done nothing of the kind. I apologized for my reaction to the kiss. I'm trying to keep it professional."

I barked out a bitter laugh in surprise. "Is that what you call tying me up backstage and fucking my brains out?"

"Penelope!" He looked around for the audience that wasn't there. "I have no idea what you're talking about."

"Oh, I've dated some shits in my time. I'm not even dating

you, and I've bought into your delusion, body and soul. It stops here. You can lie to yourself, but you can't lie to me."

I stood, fuming. He didn't move, either, but I saw a set to his jaw, a tension in his body — almost imperceptible — and reeled at the wave of emotion rolling off him. It confused me. I couldn't let him confuse me. I needed to make my dramatic exit.

Given his power around here, it might be the last exit I'd ever get to make at the Chamberlain Theater, and then I'd be hunting for a job.

I scooped up my tablet, designs be damned, stomped out and slammed the door behind me.

I was in the stairwell, heading for the second floor and my office, when I heard the door and the clatter of feet behind me. He caught me on the landing. Filtered sunlight shone through a wall of glass brick, giving the gray stairs a watery appearance. Appropriate, I thought. I was drowning.

Jace grasped my arm and turned me to him. He was breathing hard. I moved to break away from him, and he pulled me closer. He leaned into me, over me, diminishing my height under the shadow of his darkness, his desire. And then his mouth was on mine, needy and devastating, as he crushed me into him. I clutched my tablet between us and let it happen. My traitorous mouth opened under his, took in his tongue as he fucked me with it, and my walls tumbled down. I moaned under his pressure, his heat, his overwhelming desire — and as if awakening from a dream, tore my mouth from his and pushed him away.

I trembled, standing there on the landing a foot away from him — trembled with anger, with lust.

With steel I didn't know I had, I locked down my emotions. "So. Did that happen?"

Jace's eyes were wild. He was still breathing hard. He didn't say anything.

I turned and started down the next flight of stairs.

"Yes!" he called out.

I stopped halfway down, half in shadow, and looked up at him, a delicious, demented man aglow in the diffuse afternoon light.

"Yes, Penelope." He walked to the stairs, took each step slowly until he reached me. "It's just that I can't get involved — "

I turned and took the rest of the steps to the next landing. I had my hand on the door handle when he said, "Wait."

"Why can't you?" I asked, not turning from the door. "I'm not asking you to marry me. I'm just asking you to acknowledge me. Us. What we did. Unless you didn't — enjoy it."

"God, you know that's not true." He was down the steps in a flash, and this time, he touched my shoulder lightly and turned me toward him. "You don't want to know why."

"Maybe I do."

"I'm not a good person, Penelope."

"Ha. Like anyone is."

"Some people are." He looked almost ghostly, now, and decidedly unhappy.

"You're probably not as bad as you think." *Really? I'm defending him?* "Besides, that's about the worst excuse I've ever heard for a fuck and run."

Jace nodded. "Maybe."

I waited. It was his turn.

He took a deep breath. "Let me — let me see you."

"I think it's I who needs to see you."

"What do you mean?"

"I mean, not in the dark. In the light. Like normal people.

Where you are you, and I'm me."

Jace leaned closer and put his mouth next to my ear. "Not just in the light," he whispered. "There's something about you. I can't leave you alone."

"I guess we'll see," I said, trying not to give in to the instant arousal he engendered in me. "Plumeria Bar. Tonight after rehearsal. Or that's it, and your dream comes true, and nothing ever happened. OK?"

He nodded. Before I gave in to the need in his eyes, I went through the door and fled to my office.

Had I just agreed to the weirdest date ever? And would I grow to regret bringing Jace Edison into the light, where I'd have to face the fact that I wanted him so much, my bones ached with the craving?

I took the scooter home before rehearsal, ate a scant serving of leftover ravioli and changed. If I was going to see Jace on something resembling a normal date, then he was going to get Penelope on a date — not Penelope in a dark room. I chose a black dress with white polka dots, not unusual for my rockabilly tastes, except that it was a clingy sheer wrap dress I'd made myself, with a thin black underskirt and a ruffle at the plunging neckline. Under it, I wore a black corset and black stockings. I went tall on the heels and hot pink on the lipstick, to pick up the color in my hair. If it was our first and last real date, I didn't want him to forget what he'd be missing.

While I was wrapping up the primping, my phone rang. I glanced at the screen. *Ugh.* My mother. I put it on speaker and answered as I thickened my mascara. "Hello?"

"Penny, when are you coming home?" she asked in a voice coarsened by years of smoking.

"Don't call me that."

"Don't get snotty with me," she said.

"What do you want, Mom?"

"Why do I have to want something?" I pictured her in the trailer park, looking out the window toward the barest glimpse of the lake through the other trailers and the scrawny palm and pine trees, coming up with her next scheme. "Can't I just want to see my daughter?"

"I'm busy with a new play, Mom. I'll call you later."

"Wait!" she said, as I knew she would. I thought I heard her sucking on a cigarette. "I just need a few dollars, honey."

"So three would be enough?" I couldn't help my sarcasm. She'd asked so much, so often, after giving so little.

"Three hundred would do it," she said, deliberately not hearing my crack.

"Why do you need three hundred dollars?" I picked up the phone and wandered to the living room and the windows, where the evening light mellowed over the river, so calm, so beautiful, so utterly unlike my childhood. "Do you still have your job?"

"Of course I do. The tips just aren't as good as they used to be."

She waitressed at a strip club. At least she was working, but there was a reason the tips were getting smaller. She wasn't getting any younger.

"Why don't you switch to one of those restaurants over in Kissimmee?" I asked. "You'd make some real tourist dollars there."

"My clients would miss me." Again, I wondered if she still had *those* sorts of clients. The kind she occasionally brought home when I was a teenager dying to get out of that pit of despair. "You don't know what it's like to have men asking for you every day," she added smugly.

Ha. I knew what it was like to have them pawing at me when she brought them home. I'd babysat and saved up and bought a heavy-duty lock for my bedroom door to keep them out. "I've got to go, Mom."

"Just send me a check, won't you, honey? I've got this friend who's starting a business, and he wants me to be an investor. I'll get ten times my money back in two months."

I rolled my eyes. This was my mother — spending what little she had on get-rich-quick ploys, pyramid schemes and sweepstakes and then moaning when the rent was due.

"I don't think so, Mom," I said. "Maybe if you wanted to spend the money on something more practical? A chandelier for the kitchen, maybe? Or a new suit for the chauffeur?"

"I don't know how I raised you to be such a bitch, *Penny.*" The connection clicked off, and I laughed bitterly at her last words.

I knew how I became such a bitch — or, I preferred to think, a bitch when I wanted to be. I had the best role model in the world.

I TOOK my car to the theater — even I, the queen of heels, didn't want to walk too far in these babies — and got to the rehearsal just as Dirk was calling the break. I approached him with my tablet, relieved that Jace was nowhere in sight. Maybe he was debauching one of the cast backstage.

No. I didn't believe that, somehow. But it was just as well I didn't see him — I needed to pitch my designs to Dirk.

"Jace says your new costumes are great," Dirk said as I approached. Funny. Jace hadn't even seen my designs. Dirk looked me up and down with appreciation. "You ever think of going on the stage, Penelope?"

"Been there, done that," I said brightly. "But thanks. Would you like to look over the changes?"

"Sure," he said, his smile even warmer. He did have a taste for the ladies. And the men. There was something about the focused attention he gave them all that earned him welcoming responses in return, despite his unconventional ginger looks. I supposed it was his confidence. So far, I'd been immune, maybe because I was too easily distracted by tall, dark and handsome.

Dirk took the tablet from me and paged through my sketches as I described my changes. He made a few suggestions, then stopped and closely examined my drawing for Bottom's donkey head, which I now pictured as having big metal ears and a steampunk metal framework that suggested a large, equine nose. There was still a place for the stylized virtual-reality glasses all of the game-designer characters would wear, and I wanted to incorporate a bit of glow around them.

"I like this," Dirk said. "It looks a lot more involved. Can the costume shop handle this in addition to all the rest?"

"I'll do the head myself. I might need to get some help with the engineering, but I'm confident I can execute it."

Dirk nodded and looked up at me, handing the tablet back. "These are really nice, Penelope. I hope everyone appreciates them the way I do."

I smiled in confused thanks and walked away, wondering at the backhanded compliment. Did that mean that the artistic director, the executive director and God knows who else were finding me wanting? Hell. There was no use worrying about it now. I felt good about the designs, and there wouldn't be much more room for doubt as we plunged into producing them.

Chatter picked up as actors returned to the stage, Wendy among them. She gave me the once-over and shook one hand in the universal "girl, you're hot!" gesture, while mouthing the word "hot" just in case I didn't get it. I laughed and waved, eager to leave before Jace could see me. Then again, if he was in the green room and the monitor was on, he'd already seen me.

Maybe I wasn't ready to see him.

I left my tablet in my office and walked the few blocks to Bohemia's harbor, where Plumeria Bar occupied a spot on the waterfront. The plants the club was named for were all blooming now — yellow and pink and white and lovely combinations thereof, glowing and fragrant in the golden light just before sunset. The thick branches and deep green leaves surrounded the door and obscured the floral mural on the wall behind them. The art was nature's backup; in the winter, the plumeria lost their leaves.

Inside, the plush decor of Plumeria Bar remained eternal, and the air conditioning was a welcome relief from the sultry evening. I immediately felt more relaxed among the red walls, moody lighting, dark wood wainscoting and lush photos of flowers. Behind the horseshoe-shaped bar, dimly lit by red glass pendant lights, a wide window showed an exquisite evening descending on the boats of the harbor.

I opted for the plush seating instead of a barstool, choosing a soft armchair in a dark corner where I could watch the comings and goings without drawing undue atten-tion. That said, I politely declined the advances of a couple of men (reminding me again of my mother's infuriating remark) while I awaited the arrival of Jace. I was into my second Hemingway daiquiri, a pleasant change from my usual vodka martini, when he entered the room. Women's heads turned, but he didn't seem to notice as he scanned the bar, then took a few steps inside. I didn't move, waiting for him to see me, almost hoping he wouldn't. He'd taken so long to arrive, I'd started to chicken out, imagining it might be better if we really did pretend that nothing had happened. And then I remembered his urgency, his wildly creative seductions, and that now familiar yearning flared in my belly.

I knew the moment he saw me. His eyes widened. His nostrils flared. He stood straighter, in his stylish charcoal gray pants and black jacket over a crisp burgundy shirt, his watch winking at his wrist. So he'd changed, too.

He walked toward me with all the elegant control of a great actor who knew his body, who instinctively conveyed confidence and assurance. But the light in his eyes was nothing less than feral.

He held out a hand and I took it, letting him lift me so I stood before him. He leaned toward me, and I presented my cheek, which he kissed with a feather-light touch that hit me like a sledgehammer.

But I could act, too, and this was no place to lose it.

"You look beautiful tonight," Jace said, the slightest hitch in his polite tone.

"It's hard to match the hottest actor in Bohemia."

"You'll have to introduce me to him sometime," he joked, and I couldn't help but smile. "Why don't we sit over here?" He pointed to a love seat nestled behind a screen of tropical plants. It wasn't completely private, but at least it would cut down on the stares.

I nodded and picked up my drink. In a moment, we were in the arms of the comfortable piece of furniture, his warm hip pressed against mine. He sat half-turned toward me, sitting up straight only to order a Manhattan from the waiter.

"How appropriate," I said when the server left.

"You don't have to live in Manhattan to drink Manhattans."

"I know. I have several friends who enjoy them. I'm more of a vodka girl, with occasional trips to the islands." I lifted my rum cocktail.

"May I try it?"

I nodded and handed him the drink.

"Mmm, that's nice," he murmured. "What is it?"

"Hemingway daiquiri."

"I thought daiquiris were pink, frothy, icy things."

"Only at the bad hotel bars," I said. "This has rum and a little lime and grapefruit juice, and something else — I can't remember."

He took another sip and handed it back to me. "Cherry liqueur, I think."

"Aren't you clever."

"Just a part-time lush. I'm embarrassed I didn't know about this drink before now."

"And you being from the big city and all," I said, putting on my Southern accent that wasn't really a put-on, if you knew what I sounded like growing up.

"You know, I like talking to you," he said, taking his drink from the server, who vanished again beyond the plants. "I wouldn't be so — so interested in you if I didn't."

"So I'm not interchangeable with any random woman you happen to meet at a kinky party?"

His eyebrows lowered and his brow creased, giving his

handsome face a dark intensity I found all too attractive. "You are not."

"Go to a lot of kinky parties, do you?"

"Do you?" he shot back.

"My first one, actually," I said wryly. "We didn't know what it was before we arrived, and the rest of our group didn't, uh, partake, as far as I know."

"I don't go to a lot of kinky parties, no." Jace sipped his drink.

"What's 'a lot' in your fancy New York world?"

"Damn it, are you trying to piss me off?"

"Is it working?"

"I — I have been to a couple of parties like that one in New York. A friend suggested it. I never — I only watched."

I settled against the back of the love seat and lapped my cocktail, enjoying both the power of being his inquisitor and the way his mouth tightened when he saw my tongue flick the tangy drink.

"You never touched a woman — or a man — "

"I don't do men."

"You never took advantage of the more-than-willing women exposed to your imposing presence?" I goaded him. "You never let one wrap her pretty lips around your big, hard — "

"Stop it." His jaw, that exquisite jaw, was set hard. He was staring at my mouth. I glanced down. Something else was hard, too; the tent in his pants was all too obvious.

"How is it," I asked, even more quietly, "that the famous actor with the reputation for being a cold-blooded asexual goes out of his way just to watch other people getting it on at kinky parties in New York?"

He leaned farther over me, and I felt his warm breath,

took in that forest scent of his and wanted him to take me right there. But we had stuff to work out. A lot of stuff.

And he was angry. "I had my reasons." I waited for more. "It seemed like it might be a way to . . . You have to understand that I haven't been involved with anyone since . . . " He sat back and took a large swallow of his drink.

"Since when?"

"Since I graduated from college."

I did the math in my head. "You haven't been involved with anyone since — but that can't mean you haven't been with anyone in four years?"

"Five," he whispered, looking without focusing at one of the sexually suggestive flower photos on the wall.

Good God. I didn't know whether to be flattered or appalled. "You're putting me on."

His gaze snapped back to mine. "I'm not."

"Because you didn't want to get involved. Emotionally involved?"

"Yes. Not just, but yes."

"I suppose there's a reason for that?" I asked.

"There is." He didn't elaborate.

"And is there a reason you decided to end the drought with me? To use me as your fuck toy?"

He sported a laconic, wicked smile. "You seemed to enjoy the game as much as I did."

My temper was starting to simmer, but I put a lid on it. "What, you were just far enough out of town that you thought it would be safe to indulge yourself?"

"That wasn't it. It was you."

"But it wasn't *me* you were screwing, right? I was just an actor in your play. And it wasn't you, because Jace Edison doesn't get involved with anyone."

"Pardon me, but neither does Penelope Locke, does she? I know about you."

Like the wind changing in the path of a storm, the power suddenly shifted to him. My face heated. "What do you know about me?"

"I asked around." He tasted his drink again with an air of nonchalance, the actor back in control. "I always ask about the people I work with. 'She dates a lot,' they said, 'but never seems to have a boyfriend.' Online dating. One-night stands."

I was furious, not just at him, but at whoever had decided to share their insights with the Babe of Broadway. "So I'm some kind of whore?"

"No!" He looked uncomfortable, sympathetic even, which made me even madder. "But it's not like you're looking for a relationship."

"So you screened your co-workers and decided I was the most convenient fuck? Nice. And you have no idea what I'm looking for." I knocked back my drink, got up and walked out.

It was only a minute before he came up behind me as I stood out front, fumbling in my purse for my phone so I could get an Uber.

I clamped the purse shut and stared out into the quiet street. "I hope you paid for the drinks."

Jace laughed in surprise. "Yes. Is that foremost on your mind?"

"No, but I have to live in this town, unlike some people who just hit and run and leave."

"Penelope." His voice was gentle now. "I really like you. And, God help me, I want you more than I've ever wanted anyone. I just — I didn't go about this the right way, but I fucking lost my mind when I met you. The only thing I could think about was having you. I went to that party in Bohemia

Beach because I knew you'd be there. I'd heard about the Bon Vivants. I heard you were going. I thought maybe — I didn't know if you'd be, you know, involved in the party, but I wanted to find out. And then when I got close to you — "

He slipped an arm around my shoulders, holding me like a delicate doll, but there was so much tension in him, he was almost vibrating. I thought he might crush me at any moment.

I wanted him to crush me. I wanted him to smash into me and set me on fire and scatter my molecules in the air.

I looked up at him, into his face, half-shadowed in the street lights. "I wasn't looking for anything. I wasn't looking for you."

"But you found me, and I wanted you," he said. "I want you, Penelope. Let me have you. No games, not tonight. No masks. Just you and me."

"I can't imagine what you think of me," I said, pulling away slightly. "I'm not a sex toy, despite what you may have heard."

"No, you're not," Jace said. "You're a goddess. Let me worship you."

I sucked in a breath. Maybe it was a line, but as lines went, it was pretty damn good. And my body was telling my brain to forget all its questions and melt into this stunning man in front of me, to respond to his need. My own desire was an oxygen-consuming backdraft, wrapping me in flames, and I needed him to feed the fire.

So what if our connection was only physical? He wanted it with *me*.

"What do you propose?" I whispered.

He held out his hand. I wondered where he would take me, on what flight of the imagination, as I grasped it.

PART 2

*A*s it turned out, Jace took me to his car, opening the passenger door of the red Jaguar F-Type Coupe and helping me inside without saying a word. His light touch aroused me more than any of his fierce possessions of me had until now. I was aching for him as he drove the sleek car down the gloomy back streets of Bohemia, curving around the harbor and heading for the causeway that would take us to the beach. The soundtrack to a retro spy film thumped through the speakers. Was everything in this man's life like a movie?

A sliver of moon was setting behind us, and the water was black, an empty universe as we soared over the lagoon on the bridge, too fast, not fast enough. And then we were in Bohemia Beach, heading down A1A to a section where the retail dropped off and only large, lonely homes were nestled among the dunes in the dark.

Jace wheeled into the driveway of a modern white house, smaller than the one that held the party the other day, but impressive nonetheless. It was two stories high, with a peaked roof and rigid lines that belied the soft sounds all around us as we exited the car — the wind in the palms, the relentless ocean.

He pressed his hand against the small of my back as he guided me toward the side door and let us in. Narrow stairs took us up to the second level. Jace hit a switch that turned on subtle lighting that made two large, colorful abstract paintings glow, each on adjoining walls of an airy living space. At one end, to my left, was a roomy kitchen and dining area; at the other, a hallway led to more rooms. The furniture was modern, mostly black and white. A sleek little art deco bar sat in one corner. Two sets of sliding glass doors led to a deck, the perfect excuse for me to prolong this strange dream a few minutes longer. I wanted to see the ocean.

I strode through the half-darkness to one of the sliding doors, tried and failed to open it, and had to endure Jace's amused smile as he unfastened the tricky lock. But then the portal opened, and I was outside on the concrete deck among a veritable forest of potted plants, leaning on the white metal railing, breathing in the fresh, salty air of the Atlantic. Below me, a turquoise rectangle glowed in the night, surrounded by tropical foliage — an elegant pool.

Jace pressed against my back and kissed my neck. His hands slid from my waist to my hips as he tongued my sensitive skin, mouthing his way slowly up to my ear. I was hot and cold, chilled by the wind evaporating his kisses, and crackling with the fire he started every time he touched me. The roar of the ocean was as hypnotic as his touch, and the cocktails were doing their work, too.

Now that I had him, had him for now, as Jace, I didn't want to rush.

"Got a drink?" I asked.

"After," he whispered in my ear. He licked my earlobe.

"Now."

Jace's groan was almost drowned out by the sound of wind and waves, and he let me go. "Whiskey, vodka, gin or wine?"

"Vermouth?"

"Of course."

"Vodka martini then, please," I ordered, enjoying his discomfort as I drew this out. I still ached for him, but anticipation was a nice change from our previous wham-bam-thank-you-ma'am encounters.

I heard the sound of the cocktail shaker through the open door and sighed as I looked out toward the waves, barely glinting in the starlight. The lights along the beach were all off this time of year so as not to disturb the nesting sea turtles, and the nearest house was far enough away that it wouldn't have bothered us anyway. I was struck by the quiet privacy of this place. It was so different from my hectic daily life. The grind. The struggle to succeed, to survive. I wondered if Jace, at the top of his game already, could possibly know what it was like to make one's way as an artist in a small city like this.

I turned to the house. Jace walked toward me, carrying two martini glasses. He'd shed his jacket and his shoes and socks. God, he moved like a dancer. Well, duh. He'd done a little of that, too, in the musicals he'd been in, even if "dancer" didn't headline his resume.

"Make sure this is the right one," he said, handing me a glass. That silver watch of his flashed at his wrist.

"What do you mean?" I sipped it. "Ah. Ice cold. Divine. And with a nice, fat olive. Thank you."

"Of course. Mine's gin." He sipped as I frowned. "What?"

"Gin and I don't get along."

"Sounds like a story." He smiled. "Care to tell it?"

"No." I drank down half the martini.

"Secrets?"

"Look who's talking."

"Oh, Penelope," Jace said, his body brushing against mine, his hand caressing my waist as we stood at the railing, facing each other. "Now you're my secret, too."

"If that's what you think, I'm leaving."

"What?"

I downed the rest of the drink and set the glass on the railing. Liquid courage. "I'm not sneaking around. Unless this is just for tonight, and then we never see each other again." *Could I even do that?* "We would never mention it. And you would never touch me again, Angelo. Or should I call you 'my lord'?"

"No," he said softly, putting down his glass, too. "I want to see you again. I can't stop here. I want more of you. I want to taste all of you, touch all of you. As much of you as I can get, before — "

"Before you go. That's fine," I said, hoping he didn't notice the catch in my voice. "Then we acknowledge this, whatever it is?"

"You want me to announce it at rehearsal?" he said with a half-smile.

I couldn't help but dimple. "Of course not. But if I see you in the hallway, I don't want either of us to run in the other direction. I don't want to pretend."

"I pretend enough as it is." He grasped my face with both hands, rubbed my cheekbones with his thumbs. "I think what you're saying is that we should be friends. I can do that.

I'm sure I can do that." He sounded as if he was trying to convince himself.

"You are deeply fucked up," I said lightly, drinking in his dark eyes as he pulled me closer.

"And you need to be deeply fucked." He crushed my mouth with his. Gin didn't taste so bad on Jace Edison's lips. His stubble burned my cheeks; he pushed one knee between my legs and slid his arms to my waist, my ass, pulling me against him. I ran my hands down his taut back and surrendered to the fire as it swept through me, off and running, licking up my calves and thighs and triangle, circling my belly and heating my breasts and sweeping into my mouth, where my tongue met his.

I was spinning; we were spinning. He was spinning me back into the house, never breaking our touch, our kiss. He paused by one of the white couches and started tugging at my dress. He spun me again, tugged some more.

"How—?"

I laughed. "Let me." I untied the sash and slipped it out of its slot, unwrapping the sheer polka-dot fabric. He stepped back and watched. I was drunk now, for real, not just on the cocktails, but on his rapt attention. I slowly shrugged the dress to the floor and stepped out of it, enjoying the way his eyes roamed from my tall black heels to my garters and stockings, the thong and the black satin corset.

"Tell me again why you aren't on the stage?" he whispered, getting down on one knee to run a hand up my leg, along the silky stockings.

It was all I could do to stand still. "Because I love designing costumes. I do a little pinup modeling, just for fun."

"You are delectable." He kissed one knee through the

stocking, then my thigh, moving up ever so slowly, one kiss at a time.

"Men never were attracted to my brain."

"I like you, Penelope. I do. You're talented and smart. But you can't present me with this — with you" — he kissed my pussy through the triangle of fabric, and I trembled — "and not expect me to fall at your feet."

"I suppose the feeling is mutual, pretty boy." My voice was breathy as his tongue teased me through the thong.

He looked up at me and smiled. And stood, grasping my neck, kissing me hard. "Show me," he whispered.

Show him? Show him how much I wanted him? Too much. Show him how I would fall at his feet?

I kissed him back, a kiss that showed there was nothing equivocal about this moment. I had never been so sure of anything. And then I began the journey down his body, his neck, the hard chest, which I slowly unveiled as I unbuttoned his shirt and pulled it off his broad shoulders. Next I tasted the skin of his sculpted belly, outlining each beautiful ridge and valley of his muscles with my tongue.

I unbuttoned and unzipped his trousers, noticing the fine fabric, of course, and dropped them to the floor. His erection stretched his burgundy boxer briefs to a hard peak. I slipped them off, and Jace groaned as his engorged cock sprung free.

I dropped to my knees as he had done. I looked up at him with a wry smile and adopted the English accent he was fond of using. "Is this what you wanted, my lord?"

He could only nod as he watched me, rapt, his mouth open. I cupped his tight balls, caressing them until I felt a tremor pass through him, and then I grasped the base of his erection. It was long and hard and red, almost purple, a pearl of moisture hovering on the tip of the wide head. In one sweet, languorous motion, I licked it off.

"God," he hissed. "Suck it, Penelope."

I licked the head first, thoroughly, under and around the ridge, as I moved my hand up and down the base, guiding him to me. I snuck a glance or two at his face, at him watching me, enjoying his need, imagining what I must look like to him in my lingerie, kneeling at his feet, my pink lips, swollen from kissing, wrapped around his cock.

I was tingling and wet between my legs as I took him deeper, appreciating the velvety feel of him in my mouth, hot and big. I liked sucking cock, though I didn't do it often, because I wanted to really like the guy. And since I rarely saw a guy more than once, it was hardly a sure thing.

Jace was different. I loved tasting him. He slid forward, to the back of my throat, and I pulled away, drew him in again, tonguing as I went, my hand taking care of the rest. I sucked harder, faster, taking him deeper, and he groaned. He was pure sensuality in my mouth, silky on the surface, steel beneath. That feeling of power and powerlessness all at once overwhelmed me, even as all of my focus centered on his pleasure. Before I knew it, he was coming down my throat. I swallowed his hot seed and released him, licking my lips, looking up the length of his beautiful, naked body to observe his moment of ecstasy.

He lifted me up, pushed me down on the wide couch and fell on top of me, his naked skin rubbing against my satin and lace. He crushed me, and damn, it was marvelous, having his hard body pressing into mine. I wanted him to obliterate me.

He popped my breasts out of the top of my corset and kissed the curve of each white mound before working his way to the nipples, dark and pebbled and erect under his tongue.

One of his hands crept to my pussy, at first lightly touching my bud through the fabric of the thong.

Before he ripped it off.

Yes. I'd always thought thongs were made for ripping. It was just that no one else had been gracious enough to do it before now.

I gasped as he pushed two fingers into my slick slit, parting my thin strip of curly hair to get there, probing for the spot that would make me his. I went off like a boxing bell when he found it. I moaned under the magic of his lips, his fingers, and I started writhing under him, wanting more, wondering if he could give it.

And then I became aware of his member, already hard again.

"Fuck me, Jace," I murmured.

"Condom."

"It's OK. I'm tested all the time. I'm on the pill. And you haven't — just fuck me."

"No. Wait." His hands, his mouth were gone, and he was rummaging in his pants. I barely had time to process the odd moment before he had the condom in place, and then he was sliding against me, between my legs. "I love these stockings. I love this corset. God, please always dress like this for me."

"It wouldn't go over so well at the Chamberlain."

He let out a half-laugh, half-groan. "I'll be imagining it, then, whenever I see you. Here." He stood, half lifting me, flipping me, guiding me to the end of the couch so he could kneel behind me. "Like that," he whispered. "You're so beautiful." He caressed my behind with sweet attention, and, there, on my hands and knees, I shivered with a new sense of vulnerability. "Do you like being my slut, my lady?" he said in the English accent he'd used backstage.

"Oh, yes, my lord," I said, unable to keep a hint of a laugh out of my voice.

"You won't mock me after this," he said. He wedged his big cock into my wet cleft and plunged.

I made an incoherent sound as I clenched around him, as he held himself there, deep, a sword delivering sweetest death, and then he was pounding me, and I was crying out with the pleasure of it. I braced myself against the arm of the couch as he stoked my fire again and again. With a shudder, I came in crashing waves, like the ocean outside, and still he fucked me, taking me to a height I didn't know I could reach, until he, too, spasmed, shooting exquisite ripples through my already oversensitive sex.

We collapsed together on the couch. I toed my shoes off, and he turned me over and kissed me and held me. He disposed of his condom; I helped him unhook my corset and toss it aside, and his hands lingered over my belly and my breasts, a small smile playing about his lips. I caressed his face and arms and kissed him as he settled against me, his breathing slowly easing. The tension in his body was gone. He closed his eyes and his lips parted as he drifted off, a drowsy dream in my arms.

If this were anyone else, I'd leave. I'd never see him again. But not Jace. I'd see him again and again at the theater. Even if things went sour between us, I'd be forced to see him. The idea made me strangely elated. I shouldn't care what he thought or felt, but somehow I did. I wanted to know more about him — really know him, if that was even possible.

He wasn't in the dark. He wasn't in a mask. I could see all of him this time — handsome, exhausted, unguarded.

But I still couldn't see into the darkness of his heart.

I AWOKE ON THE COUCH, still in my stockings, the only clothing that hadn't been stripped from me the night before. Jace was gone, or, at least, not on the couch with me. The golden rays of dawn were pushing their way through the thin curtains on the sliding glass doors. I found a bathroom, and then slipped my wraparound dress back on, like a robe. A sheer robe, but still. I wasn't ready for the corset yet.

A clock in the empty kitchen showed it was almost 7 a.m. I'd have to think about getting to work soon, though our hours were flexible as they stretched into nighttime rehearsals. I padded in my bare feet outside to the deck, where the martini glasses still sat on the railing, proof the night before hadn't been a dream. The ocean sparkled, alive and blue-green in the light of early morning. The plants in their pots looked perky in the sun. A squad of pelicans dipped low over the waves. I saw a cargo ship on the distant horizon and no one else, until I looked down. Jace was swimming the length of the pool, in the briefest of swimsuits, the water shimmering on his back and arms, across his muscled skin. He just about took my breath away.

That's when the tickle of panic crept up my neck.

What the *hell* was I doing here with the Babe of Broadway? With Mr. Up and Coming TV and Movies? Of all people, a celebrity should be the easiest to have a shallow relationship with, and I specialized in shallow relationships. I should be perfectly pleased with this arrangement. Someone like Jace, whom everybody wanted, who moved from show to show, should be used to meaningless hookups, too.

Only — apparently — he wasn't. He hadn't been with someone sexually in five years. It was terribly difficult to believe — though I did believe him. Why had he waited so long, and why was I different? Maybe he was just way over-due. It was just sex. He'd wanted me. I supposed that was flat-tering. God knows, I'd wanted him. I still did, watching him crawl swiftly through the pool, his feet kicking up a low splash, his legs toned and beautiful as he did a neat turn at the wall and cut through the water, heading in the opposite direction.

I began to realize what scared me so much. He wasn't like my other hookups. He'd hooked *me* — drawn me in with his crazy contradictions, his angst and indecision, his coldness and passion, his kinky imagination and admiration. I was totally into the sleek, delicious puzzle box that was Jace Edison, and I wanted to figure him out. I didn't want a shallow sexual relationship. Not just that. I wanted to know him. And I had a worrisome feeling that he was unknowable.

He'd said he could be friends with me. He hadn't sounded too sure of it. Could I be friends with a man whose clothes I wanted to tear off constantly? Could I simply have sex with a man whose captivating soul I wanted to examine under a microscope?

It was too many paradoxes for my hangover.

I slipped back into the house, put myself back together, summoned an Uber and was gone before he could find me and make me confront my confusion.

I SHIFTED AT MY DESK, stretched, took another sip of water from the metal bottle I stored in my office. My muscles ached pleasantly from the exertions of the night before, but my head thought otherwise — headache mixed with something that might be called regret.

I'd hailed my ride to the theater, taken my car home and prepared myself for the day in a light cotton-print dress, black with little flowers on it, almost innocent, though it had a hint of décolletage. I wore cotton pettipants beneath it for maximum comfort. No fancy underwear. And sandals with barely a heel. I knew my choices reflected the feeling that I needed to pull back, throw a little ice water on the heat between Jace and me. If it was still there this morning. Maybe it had been just a one-night stand for him, despite all he'd said — if you could call our third fuck a one-night stand.

I had to get my mind off him and into *Midsummer at Midnight*. The problem was, Jace was everywhere in *Midsummer at Midnight*. The play had the same wit, contradictions and allure as its mercurial author.

Boris had sent out a reminder of our budgets for the production, and I'd crunched the numbers and figured out how much more I could buy in materials. I'd talked prop master Marty into letting me have a few more dollars for the building of Bottom's head, especially since it was so technical now, and he hadn't been thrilled about having to handle the piece during productions. The metal-framed donkey head was going to have lights incorporated into its fanciful virtual reality glasses, and he spent ten minutes bitching about batteries and maintenance before I could get away.

I made my way upstairs to the costume shop. It felt like home — not the crappy home where I grew up, but a place that nurtured me and let me grow. My happy place.

The big windows that faced the parking lot at the back of the Chamberlain were filled with light; the shades were hauled all the way up. The broad work tables were draped with fabric. The washing machines and racks of outfits awaited their next task, and the air hummed with the sound of sewing machines. Two of the stitchers were already at work on the minor costumes I'd sent over last week for Bottom's players, er, game designers. A few of their clothes — jeans and T-shirts — would come right out of a store, while others were made by us: geeky plaid pants and shirts in colors that complemented the production. The draper's patterns were at the elbows of these older women — brilliant seamstresses who'd retired from other jobs and decided to explore their creative side at the theater.

"Penelope, sweetheart!" called Midge, the shop manager, with her tight, almost-red curls, red lipstick, laugh lines, loose blouse and short jeans. As always, her neck was draped with the yellow ruler of her sewer's tape measure, along with a couple of lengths of ribbon and the beaded cord that held her half-moon glasses. A pencil was stashed behind her ear, and she had scissors, a rotary cutter and markers in a holster at her hip. She was like one of those pen-knife multi-tools, always with the right implement at hand.

We hugged. "How's Arlene coming with the first patterns?" I asked of the draper.

"She's at lunch, but they look beautiful so far. Of course, she's looking forward to the rest of your drawings, but there's plenty to keep us busy. I've got Theresa going for the rest of the fabrics this afternoon, at least the ones we don't have to order. And that summer hire, Millie, is awfully efficient."

"She and Theresa will get things done in half the time," I said. Theresa acted as both my and Midge's assistant as we cranked up for a show.

"Why don't you ask Millie to do our part of the show bible?" Midge asked.

"Great idea. I can have her start scanning samples today."
The show bible illustrated all of my designs with swatches of
fabric and color, along with all of the other blocking, scenery
and plans for the show — though we were just starting to
make it digital so everyone could see the specs on their
tablets.

Midge cocked her head and eyed me from head to toe.
"You look tired, honey."

"Gee, thanks."

She patted my shoulder. "Oh, even tired, you're gorgeous.
You know that. The makeup girls could take some hints
from you."

"So I not only look tired, but you're implying that I hide
my flaws with makeup?"

"There is no such thing as natural beauty," Midge said
wisely.

I laughed. "All the world's a stage."

"And we are merely costumers."

I stayed for a while, looking over the draper's interpreta-
tions of my costumes, checking in with the stitchers,
browsing through the fabrics we already had for Puck's
costume; his jacket would be a patchwork of styles and colors.
Then it was back to my office to eat a granola bar, polish more
designs and get them over to Arlene. I closed the door so I
wouldn't hear the hammering of the set builders, plugged my
phone into my speakers and cranked up my rockabilly
playlist. In a few hours, I made real progress.

My stomach was growling by late afternoon. I debated
skipping rehearsal tonight. There was no real need for me to
be there. I'd already put in a full day, though I'd spent more
of it than I wished thinking about Jace. And maybe that's why
I didn't want to go. I loved rehearsals; they helped me think

through details as I watched the actors speak and move. And I loved the people I worked with. But I never went to all of them, and —

Oh, who was I kidding? It was all about whether I wanted to see Jace. And had he come to see me today? No. I hated this post-game analysis. It wasn't my style. There was a reason I rarely went beyond one date. The ridiculous plotting, the who calls whom, the who does what when, the who feels what where — it was all bullshit. I wasn't in the market for love. So there was no need to put all that energy into a campaign that would lead only to defeat.

What I needed was a good dinner and a good sleep. Maybe takeout. Chinese? No, Thai. Some nice pad thai with shrimp and tofu. Or sushi?

Still thinking about dinner, I grabbed my backpack, opened the door and almost fainted. Jace was there, wearing jeans and a black T-shirt, his hand raised to knock.

"Good afternoon, my lady," he said with a sly smile. "Have you been avoiding me?"

"I thought you were avoiding *me,*" I said, moving to slip past him. He didn't budge. And then I was all wrapped up in his scent and warmth as he slowly pressed his body against mine, against the doorjamb.

"I said I wouldn't run away. Why would you?" he whispered. He leaned over me, and I tilted my face toward his as if my head were on a string, as if his very presence commanded control of my body. I opened my mouth to his kiss even before he claimed my lips. He sipped my mouth, his tongue dancing slowly with mine. We parted reluctantly, still holding on to each other.

"I thought maybe last night was just last night," I replied.

"I told you it didn't have to be. I thought we'd sorted all

that out. Though I wondered when I found you gone this morning. And I was hoping we might have breakfast." The light in his eyes when he said "breakfast" made me think he wasn't talking about pancakes.

I was panicking so hard, I told him the truth. "This is weird for me."

He ran a hand through my hair. "Me too. You have no idea."

"Maybe you can give me an idea."

"Maybe we shouldn't talk about it." He leaned in and kissed me again, and I moaned into his mouth, curled my hands around his neck, tilted my head to let him farther in.

"Ahem."

Shit. I pulled away and looked up, and there was Anne, the artistic director, in one of her colorful outfits, looking at us with amusement.

"Anne," I said, stepping back from Jace, whose face had become a neutral mask. "Can I help you?"

"I just wanted to check in with you, see if you needed anything else. I hear you've changed Bottom's donkey head quite a bit."

"You've been talking to Marty," I said. "Dirk likes it. We can make it happen, though I may see if anyone in the scenery shop has special skill with metal and wiring."

"I think Karen has someone."

"Great," I said. "I'm fine, then."

Anne's mouth quirked. "I can see that. I'll talk with you later." And she turned and walked the other way down the hall.

When she was gone, I turned to Jace, wondering if this was when he ran.

"Well, that's that, then. My sweet secret is out." He kissed me lightly, and his eyes twinkled. "Do you want to grab dinner before rehearsal?"

WE WENT for sushi in downtown Bohemia. I picked the place I figured was most likely to approach New York standards. We sat at the dimly lit sushi bar, where we could watch the chefs work. It was like the United Nations back there — with chefs of Latin, Asian, African and Caucasian descent — but there was only one woman. There must be some kind of seaweed ceiling I didn't know about.

Jace enjoyed the food, especially the yellowtail handroll, which I recommended. He talked me into trying eel, which I'd never realized was so delicious. Especially if I didn't think too much about the creature itself and whether it fit into my fishatarian diet. Jace talked about his preferred restaurants in New York, and I gave him recommendations for Bohemia; he made me promise to take him to my favorites. On the whole, dinner was — well, normal. Why wouldn't it be? Maybe because all the other time I'd spent with Jace was *not.*

At least, it was normal until a couple of cute teen girls came up to him and asked if he would take a selfie with them. He did so graciously, while I was careful to stay out of the photo, and they went away giggling, looking at their phones.

"You have the oddest look on your face," Jace said as he paid the bill. I didn't object. After all, he didn't even have to pay rent this summer.

"I've never hung out with a semi-famous person before."

"Semi-famous?" he asked, amused.

"You know what I mean. You're famous, but you're not the Pope."

"Thank God," he said, putting a hand on my knee and slipping it halfway up my thigh. "What's this?"

He'd run into the cotton pettipants.

"Comfy underwear," I said nonchalantly, sipping my water and getting off my stool. "Should we get back?"

"There's lace on the edge of that comfy underwear," he murmured in my ear as he followed me out into the lingering heat of early evening. It hadn't rained in days, and there was a kind of tension in the atmosphere that Jace's attention did not diminish.

"They're like petticoats, only with legs. Soft cotton shorts for under dresses and things. They're kind of nice when I ride the scooter."

"I can't tell you how many images are running through my head right now," he said, his voice low as we walked toward the theater.

"Try," I said, pretending, badly, that his tone didn't affect me.

"Petticoats. The idea of ravishing you wearing petticoats."

"But these are pettipants."

"An absurd word," he said, touching my elbow to steer me around a happy couple who refused to give up their side-by-side occupation of the sidewalk. "Are they tight or loose?"

"Loose."

"So underneath, you wear panties?"

"Another absurd word," I pointed out.

"Yes, but it makes me want to lick you."

"Jace," I hissed, remembering how he'd tongued me through my underwear. "For the record," I said softly, so passersby wouldn't hear, "I don't wear panties beneath my pettipants."

"So I could just reach up there and touch you?" he said,

still leaning toward me, his voice intimate. He had an arm around my shoulders now so he could stay close, and my body hummed with his touch.

"Not now, of course."

"Don't tempt me."

"You have an extremely dirty mind for someone who's out of practice."

"Oh, my mind has had to work even harder on dirty scenarios while I abstained. Now that I have you, Penelope, my imagination is working overtime."

I didn't want to tell him how wet I was. If I didn't feel special before, I did now. "So that's the only image running through your mind? Me in petticoats?" I goaded him.

"Oh, no. I'm picturing you on that scooter, wearing nothing at all."

"You can see me on it wearing some very nice lingerie if you go to Calista Goode's gallery. The scooter and I were featured in a photo shoot there a while back."

"Suddenly, I have an interest in the photographic arts," he said, and I laughed. "When do I get to see this underwear?"

"Certainly not now," I said. We'd reached the Chamberlain. We popped down the alley and entered through a side door used by the staff. "You and Dirk have a rehearsal to run."

We walked through the green room, where the monitor showed actors already gathering on stage. Jace abruptly pulled me into a dressing room and closed the door.

"I want to see them now," he whispered. The walls here were notoriously thin.

"Don't get your hopes up." I crossed my arms. "They're hardly worth looking at, anyway."

"Here." He took the backpack off my shoulders and ran his hands down my bare arms. He pressed his lips against my neck, and my body flushed with heat as he moved his mouth down to the curve of my breasts. "Show me," he murmured, applying his mouth to one nipple through the fabric. The peak hardened as he made the fabric damp with his tongue.

"All right," I whispered, "if only to cool your ardor." They really weren't sexy, the pettipants. They were essentially soft shorts trimmed with lace. Not everything I wore belonged in a pinup calendar.

Slowly, I lifted the skirt of the dark floral dress so he could see the garment in question.

"Black. Lace edge. Not bad, if you're somebody's Aunt Ethel," he teased.

"Shut up." I dropped the edge of the skirt.

"Take them off."

My mouth dropped open, and I closed it with difficulty. "You have rehearsal. We don't have time for — for whatever you have in mind."

"Take them off and give them to me."

"You're insane." I reached for my bag, and he was on me in an instant, pressing me against the door, his mouth on mine, his hand up my skirt — and, as threatened, inside the loose leg of the pettipants. His finger was inside me before I could protest, and I wilted against him as he stroked me.

"You're so wet," he murmured, watching me now as I started to come apart. "You're so wet for me, my lady."

I prayed no one was on the other side of the door, even as I started to grind against his finger. I was close — so close —

Jace withdrew his hand. "Take them off, and I'll finish you later," he murmured. He put his wet finger in his mouth and sucked it once. "I can't wait to taste you again."

I was thrilled and frustrated and crazy with desire. I slipped the pettipants off, and he folded them up small and put them into a pocket. The padding made his pocket pouf a little — but not as much as his crotch did at that moment.

I smiled at him, a knowing smile, and leaned back against the door. Slowly, I lifted my skirt so he could see my pussy. He froze, watching me. I touched myself, kneading my clit until I was on the edge again, and then I slipped two fingers inside my slit as he watched, entranced, his breathing rapid, his eyes almost glassy.

God, it was hot watching him watch me. That dark look brought me to the edge and pushed me over it as I fingered my sweet spot. A shock of pleasure swept through me.

I acknowledged my light orgasm with a barely expressed sigh and let my skirt fall. I picked up my bag and opened the door.

"I'll expect delivery of those later," I said in a husky voice. I made myself turn away from his hungry expression. I walked through the green room, through the actors' passage and into the theater itself, where I sat in an audience chair halfway up the rows. I pressed my legs together and tried to look cooler than I felt. My body was keyed up so high, my hair should have been standing on end.

Jace appeared on stage a few minutes later. I wondered how he'd used those few minutes. His bulge wasn't so visible now. Maybe he hadn't been able to wait, either. The idea of him getting himself off and then carrying around my underwear made me even wetter.

He walked around, greeted the actors, talked with Dirk, and then he looked up at me. Slowly, holding my gaze, he licked one naughty finger, then reached down and used it to turn the page of the script he was holding. A small, wicked smile crossed his lips at his microperformance, aimed at a rapt audience of one. He turned away from me, but he'd done what he intended. He'd told me he had me.

He made me want him even more.

THERE WAS something about a disastrous rehearsal that chilled the blood, even blood on the boil.

Mine cooled quickly as the actors stumbled through the blocking and lines of a painfully awkward first act.

"Paul, you're playing an investment banker. You're cool. You're arrogant. You're not some floppy skater out for a lark," Dirk scolded.

"It's hard to be floppy when I'm surrounded by such beautiful women," Paul said with a grin, putting an arm around Wendy and nodding at the redhead playing Hermia. He did seem floppy — relaxed to the point of sloppiness. I put the odds of him being drunk at eighty percent.

Dirk was not amused, and he was getting louder. "Wendy, maybe you *are* too pretty to play Helena." I saw my friend's frown, the fragile look in her eyes, and I wanted to kick Dirk. "You're supposed to be *goofy*. You're a geek. You love going out with Hermia for cocktails, but you know you can't compete with her for men. I want more comedy and more vulnerability!"

Vulnerability wouldn't be a problem. Wendy was clearly distraught as Dirk moved on to harangue most of the rest of the cast, until he got to his Oberon and Titania.

"Ambition," Dirk said to Oberon. "You want power. You're drawn to the dark side, to the city, to the technology. You're the king of your world. You want to dominate Titania. Don't be so fucking nice.

"Oh, and Holland, you're gorgeous," was all he said to the sultry brunette, who'd been consulting Jace all evening, much to my annoyance.

"Let me refresh your memory," Dirk thundered, addressing everyone, his usually pleasant demeanor now on the verge of terrifying. "We open in a month. That's four weeks. And in one week I want you completely off book. Do you understand? Half of you don't seem to know which lines are yours yet."

He was exaggerating, but only a little. The cast was clearly demoralized.

Jace stood on the edge of the performance area, where the stage floor transitioned into the first row of chairs at stage left. His arms were crossed, his face impassive. This is where the director took up his mantle of power, and Jace understood that. Right now, he wasn't the Babe of Broadway. He was a visiting, first-time playwright at the mercy of Dirk, observing the director's efforts to shape these actors into a real cast.

"Go home," Dirk bellowed. It was an hour before rehearsal usually ended. "And come back tomorrow ready to work."

He made a dramatic exit, as theater types were wont to do, and the actors said little as they gathered up their things and headed for the exits.

"Anybody want to get a drink?" Paul called out, but no one responded, and he, too, left.

Until only Jace was on stage. Behind me in the booth, Alan turned off the bright lights and switched on the ghost light near the back of the stage before he headed out. I donned my backpack and walked down the steps of the nearest aisle to meet Jace.

"Is it too late for me to get a sitcom?" Jace asked. Worry furrowed his forehead.

"Don't even think about it," I said. "Dirk always has at least one meltdown like this during a show."

"It wasn't unfounded. Everyone was off tonight. I cringed at some of my own lines."

"Your lines are wonderful."

Jace raised his eyebrows. "You probably say that to all the playwrights."

"Only the ones I'm trying to get into bed." I moved closer and slipped my arms around his waist.

"Bed would be a novelty for us," he acceded, one corner of his mouth turning up. "But I'm a little too agitated to fuck."

I let my arms fall away and took a step back. Was he tired of me already? Was this his way of telling me we were done?

He must have seen the look on my face. I might have done some acting, but I was too stripped of defenses to hide my dismay.

"Penelope, I just mean — "

"You don't have to explain. It was a rough night. I'll see you in the morning."

"Wait." He stepped closer and brushed my hair behind one ear. "Is there anyplace around here I can get some pie?"

I pursed my lips, perplexed, wondering if this was more innuendo.

He laughed, reading my mind. "I just mean, you know, pie. With crust and everything. Cherry. Coconut cream."

"You're talking about pie."

"Yes, *pie,*" he said, laughing. "I find it comforting, and it helps me think."

I let out a long breath and whispered so no one watching the monitors could hear. "Weirdo. I'll take you for the best pie you've ever had, but you have to give my underwear back first."

I ALWAYS RAN into somebody I knew at The Diamond. I should have thought of that before I brought Jace there. From the dark street, I saw busy tables through the plate-glass windows. The glass reflected the cursive "Diamond" scrawled in pink neon over the sign's two blue neon diamond shapes. "Diner" was spelled out beneath in pink capitals. The Double Diamond Diner was a treasure that had been feeding the hungry and the restless in Bohemia for decades.

It also attracted the late-night crowd, since it was open all the time. A group of actors from our play already occupied one table, and they looked us over and murmured as Millie walked us to our booth, fortunately far enough from them so we wouldn't be privy to their conversation or vice versa. But word would be getting out. Jace and I were, at the very least, friends.

"Millie, I think you need fewer jobs," I said as we took our seats.

"Someday," she said cheerfully, her curious eyes roving from me to Jace and back. "I quit the library job, except for the occasional Sunday, so mostly it's just this and the theater. Free food and rent money. It's not bad. What do you want to drink?"

After last night's drinking, I wasn't ready for alcohol, though The Diamond was known for its greasy hangover food. "I'll take coffee."

"Same," Jace said, perusing his menu.

Millie's pen was at the ready. "Do you know what else you want?"

He looked from Millie to me and smiled. "Not yet."

"OK." Millie looked flustered. Did Jace have that effect on everyone? "Be right back."

"I thought you wanted pie," I said.

"Man cannot live by pie alone. I wanted to look over the menu."

"You're looking at me, not the menu."

"Mm-hmmm."

Heat crawled up my neck, flooded my face. It was almost too hot in here for the underwear I'd reclaimed.

The diner lights were not designed to enhance patrons' beauty, but it didn't matter with Jace. He simply was all that and more. Maybe there was no such thing as natural beauty for women, given the impossible standards we were expected to meet, but with Jace, it was clear he'd been born with it, a gift from the gods. The smoldering gaze, however, was all his.

"Just how does one get to be Jace Edison, anyway?" I asked.

He smiled at my diversion. "I used to be Jason Edison, but the rhyme was too sing-song, according to my high-school drama teacher. So I became Jace."

"I don't just mean the name, though that's an interesting tidbit. I mean *you*. Super-successful you."

"Not you, too," he said, looking back at the menu.

"What do you mean?"

"I mean I'm not super-successful, and I'm bored with everyone's obsession with my purported accomplishments." His brusque remark concealed something brittle inside him, I thought.

"Sounds like false modesty to me, but for the record, I'm

not a fame whore. Though it's been implied I may be a whore of some other kind."

He lifted his head at my sharp tone. "No, you're not," he said softly.

Millie arrived with the coffee and asked what we wanted. After thoughtfully contemplating her recitation of the pies, Jace ordered cherry. I asked for the flan.

"I didn't mean anything by what I said," Jace said when she left. "Nothing against you. My story's dull."

"I find that difficult to believe, given your resume."

"Trust me," he said, and for the first time, I sensed he was lying. "How did you get to be *you,* Penelope?"

"Obscure costume designer? Obscure pinup model?"

"Fishing for compliments? Then yes, *you,* all that you are, lovely, talented you. How did you get into the theater?"

"Ms. Bellina, my English teacher in ninth grade. She liked the way I read out loud in class — "

"Shakespeare?"

"Of course. 'Romeo and Juliet.' And she referred me to the drama department. My theater teacher was like a mother to me. The theater became my escape, the home I didn't have. I was in all the plays."

"So you were an actor," Jace said. "What were you escaping?"

"Hell on wheels. Only the wheels were gone. My mother's trailer-park kingdom and her endless stream of eager knaves."

His brow furrowed at my tone. "Did they — ?"

I shrugged, but the memory of their groping hands turned my insides to ice. "I was cornered a few times. I learned to fight. Eventually I figured out how to hide when I saw the whites of their eyes."

His jaw had hardened. "Where was your mother?"

"Probably on a beer run. She liked to entertain."

"And your father?"

"Excellent question. She's never told me who he was."

A quiet fury burned in Jace's eyes. "Where is she now?"

"Still in her trailer in Osceola County, next to Skunk Lake."

He took a deep breath, and the lines in his brow smoothed. "Sounds picturesque."

I appreciated the joke after his grilling. "It's named for the Skunk Ape. You know it?"

Millie arrived, delivering a pretty piece of cherry pie accompanied by a scoop of vanilla ice cream, along with coffee refills and my jiggling puck of custard.

"What's a Skunk Ape?" Jace asked after she'd left. He stuffed a big forkful of pie in his mouth, and I smiled at the boyish grin that transformed his face.

"Kind of a stinky Bigfoot, Florida edition." I tasted my flan and sighed over the creamy smoothness of it, the way the dark caramel sauce coated my tongue.

"I could watch you eat that all day," Jace said.

"Eat your pie. I'm busy."

He chuckled. "Have you ever seen this Skunk Ape?"

"Not knowingly. Sometimes I wondered if my mother's dates might be a Skunk Ape in disguise. But that would be an insult to Bigfoots everywhere."

"Ouch."

"I take it there were no Bigfoots where you grew up."

He grunted. "I think in New Jersey they were hiding in plain sight."

I laughed. "You lived near New York, right? I read something about you going to see plays on Broadway from the time you were a little boy."

"My parents are well off. I'm lucky. My dad's a lawyer, my mom the owner of a successful florist chain, though she's also a frustrated thespian. They did some work in the city and took me in frequently to see shows. I have a brother and a sister with no interest in the stage, so my mother poured all her theatrical enthusiasm into me."

"She must be proud now."

"Now she just wants me to marry someone and give her grandchildren." He scowled.

"A fate worse than death," I agreed, but an image flashed in the back of my mind: Jace pushing a little girl on a swing. My little girl.

Ridiculous.

"It's not in my plan." He sounded so serious.

"So you do have a plan for the continuing ascent of Jace Edison?"

He barely reacted to my teasing tone. "I want to explore every avenue of my talent. Though lately I've been wondering where that talent lies."

"Everywhere, it seems. Acting. Writing."

Jace finished off his pie, not responding, looking thoughtfully at his plate as he mopped up the last bit of cherry juice. Finally, he looked up. "So when did you move from acting into designing costumes?"

I didn't remark on his blatant change of subject. "I loved history, and I sketched characters from past centuries from an early age. I made and dressed paper dolls. That's where it started, though I really transitioned from acting to design in college. But I learned to sew in high school and got into making my own costumes for the plays. And I'd make my own outfits. I had a certain reputation for the way I looked. Of course, in high school, that's all people cared about anyway."

"You sound bitter. From what I've seen, life isn't difficult for pretty girls." He sipped his coffee, watching me over the rim of his cup.

I added a little sugar to mine and followed suit. "That might be true, but I didn't become a 'pretty girl' until around eighth grade. Before that, people hated me for being a brain."

"What?" Jace looked startled. "I mean, not that you aren't smart, but really?"

"Don't sound so fucking shocked," I said. "I was a skinny, awkward kid, and I studied a lot in the library and after school so I wouldn't have to go home. And yes, I had a brain. I soon learned that brains got beaten up in the hallways and laughed at by other little girls. I learned not to answer every question in class. And then I learned to laugh along with them. You know how hard it is to pretend you're a ditz when you're quietly acing every test?"

"That's the saddest thing I've ever heard. No one should have to do that."

"I agree, but when the messages girls get everywhere are that being hot is more important than being smart, that's the culture you get. Especially in the suburban swamp where I went to school. My life got a lot easier once I appeared to be more pretty than smart — and when I found the theater kids. I filled out in the right places. I got taller. My clothes got way better once I started making them. I was kind of a punk-rock-abilly girl, but that didn't matter. People liked me, and I liked being liked."

"But you still got good grades?"

I snorted. "How do you think I got out of Skunk Lake and

into UCF?" Despite a detour he didn't need to know about. "It all worked out. Now I get to play in the theater, that is, if I still have my job when this is over."

He looked puzzled. "What do you mean?"

"Oh, uh . . . " I hadn't meant to tell him. "I've been told that since the Chamberlain is growing, they might want someone with shinier credentials for the new season, unless my costumes are above awesome for your play."

"But your designs are fantastic. I'll have a word with Boris."

"Don't. I can handle it myself."

Jace watched me for a moment and then, finally, he nodded. He reached across the table and put his hand over mine. "I was going to tell you how pretty you look just now, but I'm afraid you'll hit me."

I gave him a big, fake smile. "I'm so flattered."

He laughed, catching my sarcastic tone, and let go of my hand. "I'm sorry. I didn't mean to be like the others. I didn't mean to underestimate you."

"You barely know me. You have nothing to be sorry for. If anything, I'm sorry for being so eager to please the assholes in grade school." I took a sip of coffee and tried to tamp down my unruly emotions. "So did the pie help you think?"

Jace shrugged. "I think we just had a bad night at rehearsal. But I still might rewrite a couple of lines."

I chuckled. "You're going to drive Dirk crazy with that."

"He'll survive." Jace smiled. "Can I take you home?"

"I don't really want to leave my scooter in the theater parking lot overnight. But — "

"But what?"

"I'd kill for another ride in the Jag."

Jace grinned. "It is pretty, isn't it? And smart, of course. Almost as smart as you are."

"Now you're pushing it, mister. I think I'll just head home, but you can walk me back to the theater."

I insisted on paying for our dessert, and in a few minutes, we were walking through downtown Bohemia. It was late on a quiet Wednesday night, and I leaned into him when he wrapped an arm around my shoulders. I still hummed with the low sizzle of electricity between us, but there was something else, now. A kind of companionability that hadn't been there before.

"You'll still see me again, won't you?" he asked when we arrived in the dim lot. My scooter and his car were the only vehicles left.

I turned to face him. "Tomorrow morning."

"You know what I mean. You had me in a fever earlier tonight, Penelope. I had to go jerk myself off in the restroom when you left me there holding your underwear."

Ha. I was right. And hearing him say something so crass in his lovely, deep voice, with his perfect diction, made his words all the more seductive.

"I'm sorry I missed it," I said.

"Are you?"

My temperature skewed higher as he moved so close, our chests were touching.

He put his hands on my shoulders. "I enjoy talking with you, but I want to do more than talk." His voice lowered, though there was no one around to hear. "To tell you the truth, I want you right now."

Ding ding ding — bells went off in my head, in my belly, all over my body, and I pressed further into him. His hands slipped to my waist, and he pulled me in for a kiss so deep and lavish, I felt it in my toes. I reached up, curling my hands in his thick hair. I tasted hints of coffee and pie and hot, delicious man as I let him hold me tightly and ravish my mouth with his tongue. His erection pressed against me through our clothes, and only the greatest resolve allowed me to take half a step back. My heart was beating faster than a rabbit's.

"Tomorrow," I whispered.

"I'll pick you up at 9:30 in the morning and give you a ride to the theater," he murmured into my hair, breathing me in. "And then I'll give you a ride tomorrow night." He stepped back, and I spotted his grin.

"God, you vex me," I growled. I let him go, grabbed and donned my helmet, straddled my Vespa and got it started. I blew him a kiss and was off and buzzing out of the lot, toward my apartment on the lagoon.

It was a good exit. Always leave 'em wanting more, as the quote went. Only I wondered how he could possibly want more than I wanted right now.

The warm night air caressed me. The scooter thrummed between my legs. But all I wanted touching me was Jace Edison.

When Jace picked me up, he had two cups of gourmet coffee, one for each of us. I'd been so busy primping and assembling my outfit — a hip-hugging pink dress with white polka dots and white belt, a pearl choker, and pink heels with white bows — I hadn't made coffee. So I was grateful.

As I eased into the car, I handed him a chocolate biscotti, and we both smiled. And maybe, I thought, panicked a little.

We'd been thinking about each other. It was awfully sweet and maybe, terrifyingly, just a tad domestic.

The Broadway channel played on his satellite radio, and after several seconds of coffee-sipping, biscotti-munching and listening to a Sondheim tune, a song from *Acid Candy* came on.

I grinned at him. "You didn't plan this, did you?"

"I swear." He held up a hand in protest. "I usually turn the channel when I come on. It's just too weird."

"You don't sing along with yourself?"

"Never. Well, almost never. Sometimes I sing the old songs in the shower."

That admission brought an image to mind that I wasn't ready to handle this early in the day.

"Well," I said, "I've been known to sing along with this one a time or two."

"Get out. How do you know it?"

"Duh. I saw you on Broadway a couple of years ago. I bought the soundtrack."

His sunglasses hid his eyes, but I spied a tiny smile. *"You sing it, then."*

"Really, Jace, if anyone should sing it, it should be you."

"We could sing it together, I suppose," sounding bored, but somehow, I knew he wasn't. He glanced over at me and picked up the song as the chorus started.

A pure, geeky thrill ran up my spine as I joined him. *I'm singing with Jace Edison!* OK, I wasn't a fame whore, but *damn!*

When the song was over, we both laughed.

"And that was Jace Edison and the cast of *Acid Candy,*" the DJ said in her warm, low voice. "Can't wait to see what he does next on Broadway. It's been a while. We hear he's *writing* something." The sarcasm was evident. "Stay tuned!"

"On the Street Where You Live" from *My Fair Lady* came on. When I glanced at Jace, his smile was gone.

He caught me looking and tried to recover it. "You have a lovely alto, Penelope."

"Just as well I went into costumes." I still had a buzz from singing with him. "So when will we see you on Broadway again?"

"My agent says I have a couple of offers. Right now I'm focusing on the play." There was a strange note in his voice.

"Is something wrong?"

He shook his head and put on a broader smile. I knew, the way an actor knows, that it was entirely fake. "Just hoping the cast turns around tonight so Dirk isn't a bear."

I said nothing and looked ahead, wondering what was bothering him. Most actors would love having their ego buffed by hearing their own performance on the radio. Instead, Jace seemed disconcerted — if not by the song, then by what the DJ said afterward.

We pulled into the back parking lot. Jace was swift to come around to my door and help me out, under the curious eyes of the four carpenters who were outside having their morning break.

"One of the footmen should assist me, my lord," I murmured in my lame English accent, gazing up at him under my eyelashes.

My attempt at flirtation seemed to jar him from his funk, and a real smile crossed his lips before he lowered his eyebrows and assumed his villainous role. "My lady, my motives are not pure for helping you return to my castle," he said so only I could hear.

And then he laid a hard, hot kiss on my lips.

I was still catching my breath when he closed the car door

and took my arm. He escorted me inside as the carpenters watched us. The slack-jawed looks on their faces showed they were not unmoved by his little performance. Neither was I.

He left me at my office door. "I'll see you at rehearsal, if not before," he said. He kissed me again, this time more softly. But I was still caught up in the fire he'd sparked moments before.

"Yes, my lord," I said without thinking, and he laughed and kissed me one more time before heading down the hall and around the corner to his office.

I went into my own, closed the door and flopped into my chair. Using the mirror in my compact, I dazedly touched up my mussed lipstick and tried to catch my breath.

It was going to be a long day.

Once I got over my surge of hormones, the work took over. I finished detailing more designs and consulted with the costume shop. But what I really wanted to do was talk to a friend, someone I didn't work with.

I called Cali. "What are you doing for lunch?"

"As it happens, Thea and I are supposed to meet with Ez and talk over the website we're doing for Melodeon." That was the musical instrument company where Ez worked. Most of us had only just realized she had a day job other than playing and singing for Ez and the Emeralds.

"OK. I don't want to intrude on a business meeting."

"It's just an excuse to get together. Business is going to take five minutes. Join us. Sloane's going to watch my gallery for me; Wyatt's shooting some surfers. We'd love to see you."

It didn't take much arm-twisting to get me to agree, and at 12:30, we met at Beso de Queso, a Mexican place downtown. Its orange and turquoise tile and paint gave it a vibrant energy. Old-time Mexican cowboys looked out at us from sepia-tone photos on the walls, judging me as I ordered queso and savored the creamy cheese dip while figuring out what else I wanted.

Cali was right about the business meeting.

"So how far along are you guys on the site?" Ez asked the others. Her attire was surprisingly businesslike, though her modern haircut, short with long bangs, gave away her rock-and-roll attitude.

"I have the architecture down," said Thea. Like Cali's blond hair, Thea's unruly red curls were pinned up with a clip, reflecting the growing heat outside. "My software guy is working with your sales manager on the e-commerce part. The rest of my design and the copy should be done by next week."

"And I just finished editing the photos I shot," Cali said, "so you can pick out the ones you like best and let Thea know."

"Great," Ez said, opening her menu as our waitress returned. "I'm getting a beer. A Corona and the enchilada special."

Cali laughed. "I think I'll stick with Pepsi. Could I have the burrito lunch?"

"Taco salad," Thea said. Her dark blue eyes appeared large in her thin face. She really had lost weight.

"I'll have the fish tacos," I told the waitress, who went back to the kitchen. "You doing OK, Thea? You mentioned stress the last time I saw you."

"I'll be OK," she said, dismissing my concern. "Just not getting enough sleep. Hey, are you guys going to that fair and car show at the history museum on Memorial Day weekend?"

"Funny you should mention that," I said. "My pinup friends are all going to be there, and they were thinking it would be a great place to shoot that calendar we were talking about."

"Right! The one to benefit the Humane Society. I love it!" Cali said. "I've been talking to the girl in charge of the project — Betty Lane?"

"That's her pinup name, anyway," I said. "Never call her 'Betty.' She always goes by two names."

"Uh, OK," Cali said. "She says she'd like to feature some guys posing with the girls. In fact, she talked Wyatt into it. They've got an old woodie wagon, and he's going to bring a vintage board."

"And he will look incredibly hot in a swimsuit," I said. "I love this idea."

"Yeah?" Cali looked at me funny. "Because she wanted me to ask you if you could talk Jace Edison into doing it. She thinks he might be a big selling point for the calendar."

"I guess." I sipped my iced tea. "Why didn't she ask me herself?"

"I don't know. Maybe she thought it was a big ask and it was better if I asked you. Do you have an 'in' with Jace?"

I choked on my tea. Cali patted my back, and Ez started laughing.

"Just what kind of 'in' do you have with Jace Edison?" Ez asked. "In? Out?"

"Oh, my God," Thea said. "You aren't — ?"

I took a deep breath or two and faced them all down. "You are *sworn to secrecy.*"

They grinned and leaned in.

"Both the in and the out," I said, and they busted out laughing.

"So he can do the photo shoot?" Cali asked, as always focused on her next assignment.

"Oh, lord, I don't know," I said. "I'll have to ask him. He's kind of kept himself out of the spotlight here, so I have no idea what he'll say."

"That's cool," Cali said. "But just tell him it's for a great cause. All the doggies and kitties. He doesn't hate puppies, does he?"

Thea smiled. "Oh, that would be terrible."

"Shut up," I said. "I came here for support, not to hear y'all give me shit."

"What's wrong?" Cali asked. "What could possibly be wrong with dating Jace Edison?"

"It's complicated." I bit into another queso-smothered nacho chip.

"It doesn't matter. You're fucking Jace Edison," Ez said.

"Shhh!" I hushed her and looked around. "I don't think he wants his sex life bandied about."

"I think it will come as a shock to most of the world that he has a sex life," Ez said. "Is this a secret affair or something?"

"Not exactly. It's just not something we're advertising. And it hasn't been — conventional."

"Whips? Chains?" Ez asked drolly.

I scowled at her, and Thea, briefly shocked, started giggling.

"Not that there's anything wrong with that," Ez added.

"No. I'm not telling you those sorts of details, but no." Images flashed through my mind of the encounter in the dark at the party — the scenario backstage at the theater — and that luscious evening at his house. "You all know I've had a string of men in my life."

"Yes," Thea said with a sigh.

"Well, they haven't exactly been boyfriends, and they

haven't been all that great. Most of them have been much less than that. And I've been perfectly OK with it. But this thing with Jace — which, if I understand it, is purely sexual and should be just what I want, has me — confused."

"Holy shit," Cali said. "You're falling for him."

"No, no, no. I haven't known him long enough for that." Had I? Of course not. We all fell silent as the waitress delivered our lunches. When she left, I continued. "It's just that I'm actually spending more time with him than I've spent with other guys, and it's — weird."

"This is how it starts," Cali said in hushed tones.

"Oh, please." I took a bite of fish taco — seared tuna. Fresh cabbage. Wasabi aioli. Delicious. It was so much easier to focus on food than it was to think about that very notion.

Ez, to my surprise, was nodding. "Just don't rule out any possibilities. That's my advice."

"Is this what relationships start out like?" I asked abruptly. "All mixed-up crazy feelings? I haven't had one in so long — a real one — and that one, *oy vey,* I'd rather not go there again. Not that this is real . . . "

"When you are completely confused and questioning the rules you live by," Cali said, "it's the universe telling you to pay attention."

"Or maybe it's just telling you you're nuts." Ez took a swig of her bottle of Corona.

"I haven't had as much experience as all of you," Thea said, "but if I were with someone as dreamy as Jace Edison, I wouldn't think too much about it at all. I'd just — just *feel.*"

Cali nodded.

"And that," Ez said, "is the scariest thing of all."

⌁

I WENT straight to rehearsal from the costume shop that evening, anxious about seeing Jace. Would he be moody? Happy? And what had bothered him this morning? I had so many more questions about him, but the more I knew, the more I wanted to know. And that impulse was dangerous.

If I'd had any plan when I first kissed him, it had been to enjoy him the way you enjoy a box of chocolates, savoring each sweet bite until it was gone. Because it would end up empty, and he'd go back to New York, and I'd still be here in Bohemia.

The chocolate box scenario wasn't so very different from Thea's suggestion — except that enjoying a chocolate wasn't the same as really feeling something. One didn't get emotionally attached to a sea-salted caramel, unless one was having a very bad week. But getting emotionally attached to the man who was touching you, talking to you, possessing you on a regular basis was far too easy. It was chemical, the way my reaction to chocolate was chemical, only, somehow, much more of a loaded gun.

I enjoyed reveling in pleasure. But I was deathly afraid of letting myself *feel*.

I sat in the third audience row, a little closer to the actors than I had been, so I could take notes about how they would move during the play and make costume adjustments accordingly. Jace arrived after most of the actors were already there, with a stack of papers under his arm.

"Rewrites!" he said, handing them out.

Holland lingered as he offered her a copy of the script. "I can't believe you're rewriting a word of this. It's *genius.*"

"Thanks," said Jace, with the slightest smile. He turned away from Holland before she could keep gushing and shoving her cleavage in his face. That was the public Jace, the one who didn't engage other people emotionally. I knew he was different with me.

And I was especially happy he wasn't different with Holland, whose eyes held mischief as she turned back to the rest of the cast.

Jace, meanwhile, was walking toward me. I moved to the aisle to meet him as he climbed the steps. "I thought you might want a copy of the latest version," he said, handing me the script.

"But the last one was *genius*," I murmured archly, beaming at him.

He laughed out loud, a sound so out of character for him that people all over the stage area turned and stared. He didn't seem to notice as he brushed a lock of my hair behind one ear.

"Later," he whispered, heading back down the steps to the stunned cast. They immediately went back to what they were doing, but not without sneaking a few glances at Jace and me. I felt the change in the air. They'd seen us together last night, and they'd seen us today. It was more than enough fodder for gossip.

Dirk walked in at 6:31 as if he hadn't left blood all over the stage the night before. "Let's do it from the top," he said. "Alan will be playing with lighting cues, so don't freak out if you're suddenly in the spotlight."

"Or the dark," Jace said, glancing at me for the slightest of moments. Just long enough to send a wave of warmth through my body.

Oh, he was so *bad* in the dark.

When I tore my eyes away from him, I saw Holland staring in my direction. I acted as if I didn't notice and turned back to the script as Mr. Duke — Theseus in Shakespeare's version — opened the play with his happy talk of marrying Hippolyta under the full moon. Not only did Jace reverse Shakespeare's moon phases; he made the Duke guardian to Hermia, eliminating her original father figure. Mr. Duke was also her boss, CEO of a massive corporation. So in Jace's modern setting, his power over her seemed even more convincing when he ordered her to marry Demetrius, despite her love for Lysander. Hermia's friend Helena — Wendy was killing it tonight — was goofily in love with Demetrius, who wanted the reluctant Hermia.

Paul was less jolly and more focused as Demetrius tonight; maybe last night had scared him. I put his odds at drunkenness at forty percent. His talent shone through, as did that of the other actors, as the lovers planned their flight, as Oberon plotted to trick Titania, as Titania hovered over her clockwork baby, as Puck made a mess of things with the administration of magical lattes, as the lovers loved the wrong people, and as the players — virtual-reality gamers — bumbled about in their virtual-reality glasses.

Despite its intrinsic madness and unpolished moments, *Midsummer at Midnight* was — finally — a play.

We all felt it, I think, and there was cheer in the actors' faces as Dirk made minor criticisms and told them to go home. I grabbed my bag and went to give Wendy a hug and tell her how great she was.

"Thanks," she said. "It really worked tonight, didn't it?"

"I can picture it now. I really can."

"There was only one thing that seemed a little weird."

"What?"

She leaned in to whisper in my ear. "What the fuck is up with you and Jace Edison?"

I stepped back. My face heated. "What?"

"Everyone in the green room was talking about it tonight."

"About what?" I hoped, really hoped, no one had heard us in there the night before.

"About seeing you at The Diamond. And then that little exchange earlier? Come on, girl, spill."

I shook my head. "What happens at the Chamberlain stays at the Chamberlain."

"I wouldn't be so sure. Some people will talk about anything to get their name in the paper."

We both looked to where Holland had cornered Jace again, touching his arm as she asked questions about her role. Questions I was sure she already knew the answer to. She caressed his forearm, looked up into his eyes, said something — *what?* — and jealousy shot through my heart like a shard of ice.

Uh-oh.

"I really can't, but thank you. I'll see you at rehearsal tomorrow," Jace said sharply. He turned and strode backstage.

Holland laughed, a stage laugh, and shrugged at the few remaining witnesses. "I thought he was available," she said in a lilting, offhand way, and she turned to me. Her smile didn't reach her eyes. She pivoted and left with the actor playing Nick Bottom, who'd taken a shine to her. Hell, half the men in the cast had taken a shine to her. Why did she need Jace?

Wendy watched me with one of her knowing smiles. "One of these days, you and I are going to have a talk. Or I'm available now, if you want to go get a drink."

"I'm — not available now."

Her smile broadened. "I didn't think you were. I'll see you later." At my nod, she winked and followed the rest of the cast out.

Alan had emerged from the booth and was exchanging notes with Dirk, so I walked around them and headed for the back — the green room exit, not backstage. As much fun as it might be to run into Jace in the dark — although maybe not in his current mood — I suddenly felt the prickle of prying eyes all around me.

The green room was empty, but just in case, I slipped into a dressing room and closed the door. I pulled out my phone and texted the number Jace had given us in that first meeting. "You OK? Ready for me?" And then I added " — Pen," just in case he had no idea who was texting.

"Car in 5," he texted back. A second text came a few seconds later: " — Jace :-) " With a smiley face!

A stupid little bubble of relief lightened my heart. The forbidding Jace Edison had sent me a smiley face.

A FEW MINUTES LATER, I exited and headed for the back lot. The heat of the day had barely eased, and still it hadn't rained. I walked past a few actors chattering by their cars under the street light and got into Jace's Jaguar. There was no point in sneaking around. If they wanted to talk, let them talk.

Both of us were silent as we cleared the parking lot. Then Jace startled me with a whoop as he drove through the lights of downtown. "What a night!"

"It was? I mean, it was!"

"This was the first night I really thought my play might work as a play. When it really came together. When I felt like Shakespeare wasn't laughing his bones apart in his grave."

I smiled to see him so happy, plus I was thrilled that nonsense with Holland wasn't at the top of his mind.

"It had a good feeling about it," I agreed. "Pace. Emotion. There's still a lot that needs to happen with the rest of us, but your play is great."

The smile on his face was a revelation, like the sun, not erasing the brooding handsomeness but creating a new version of him, Jace 2.0, that was appealing on a whole different level. I'd never seen him this happy.

"I wasn't sure I could do it," he said, "but now I feel like I can totally do this. We can do this." He threw another smile at me. "Though I want to tweak a few lines where Oberon is mixing up the potions in the coffee kiosk."

"You have to do something for Dirk to complain about," I joked.

"He was pleased, too. I could tell. But getting everyone off book by next week is going to be a job, even if I do write shorter than Shakespeare."

The Jag hugged the curves as Jace wound through the streets in a seemingly random pattern.

"So, thanks for the ride," I said. "Though I'm not exactly sure where you're taking me."

He laughed. "You know, neither am I."

"Are you hungry? Thirsty?" I cocked my head. "Sleepy?"

Jace shot me a sly smile. "Definitely not sleepy."

My skin tingled. I loved being near him, being in contact with all that electricity. And being wrapped up in this effusive mood wasn't bad, either.

I returned his smile. "Then maybe we should have some champagne."

"Oh, I totally agree," he said. "Do you have any?"

"Ah, no."

"Good, because I do. My place it is."

I chuckled. "Almost like you planned it."

"Not exactly. I had no idea how well rehearsal would go. But I always have champagne on hand. And I *may* have stocked some brie and crackers," he teased.

"Be still my stomach!"

He took the causeway at an excessive rate of speed again, and I was relieved to see no cops hanging out near the end, where the fishermen parked. A speeding ticket in Bohemia Beach would be just the sort of thing to get Jace in the gossip rags.

In a few minutes, we were at the beach house. Jace let us in, insisting I go up the stairs ahead of him.

"I just wanted to see how you walked in that tight dress," he said when we got to the top.

"How'd I do?"

"Magnificently."

My face warmed with pleasure. He was good with a compliment. And I *had* gone to that extra trouble this morning.

He prepared a tray with the brie and crackers and a bunch of grapes, and I opened the chilled champagne. We carried it all, plus a couple of glasses, down the stairs off the deck to the pool. Large and rectangular, it fronted the beach but was so surrounded by palms, sea grapes and other foliage that one could hardly see the ocean, at least in the dark. I could hear it, though, restless and wild. The only light was the ethereal turquoise glow from the water.

"The pool light changes color," he said. We set our repast on a table between two cushioned teak lounges in a secluded corner. "But I leave it on this setting. It seems more restful."

"Unless you get in one of your frisky disco moods."

"I don't think I've ever had a frisky disco mood."

"We should work on that," I said, slipping off my heels and curling up on one of the chairs. He sat in the other chair. I glanced above us, where three or four blooming orchids were secured to the palms. "Nice orchid collection."

"Not mine, of course. I wish it would rain. I'm watering them, because I was told in no uncertain terms that I wasn't allowed to let them die. I think the main reason they loaned me the house was so I could water the damn plants."

I laughed. "Shall I pour?"

Jace smiled and held out a glass. In a minute, we were enjoying the snack and the delicious fizz of the champagne, going over the minutiae of the rehearsal.

"Holland is an amazing actor," he said, and I stiffened, anxious to hear what he'd say next. "But she seems like such a manipulative bitch."

I guffawed. "She seemed to be set on you tonight."

"She saw me with you. She smelled blood in the water."

"Some actors — not many, but some — "

"I know," he said. "They're on an endless quest for approval, on stage and off."

"But you're not like that."

"I'm not sure." His face was mostly in shadow, but his dark eyes seemed to glow in the strange aqua light. "I don't need my ego stroked, but . . . oh, let's not talk about actors anymore. We're so boring."

He was holding back again.

"But what?" I asked.

"The time for talking is past," he said in a grand voice. "The time for swimming is nigh." He stood and pulled his black T-shirt over his head, making me almost lightheaded with his beauty.

So not fair.

"Are you coming in?" he asked.

"It *is* a bit warm, and a dip would be refreshing. I suppose I'll have to get undressed." I sighed dramatically.

"I hope so." He grinned as he kicked off his sneakers and pulled off his socks.

I stood and removed the white belt first. "I could use some help with the zipper."

"There's a zipper? I thought someone poured you into that dress."

"Oh, yes. My dresser, Jean-Paul."

"What?"

I smiled. "Kidding. I can do it myself, but it's easier with help." I presented my back to him.

"I do enjoy this side of you," he said, cupping my buttocks and squeezing. "So tight in this little pink frock."

His touch sent all the blood rushing to my lady parts.

"Zipper," I said hoarsely.

"Oh, yeah." Jace grabbed the tab at the top and pulled it down ever so slowly. Then he pushed the dress off my shoulders so it crumpled to the ground at my feet. I stepped out of it and turned around.

He blew out a low whistle at my retro underwear — the high-waisted underpants with garter belt, the stockings, the pointy bra, all in white. "You're some kind of virginal 1950s temptress in that."

I laughed. "Good one." And as he watched, I unhooked the bra and dropped it onto the lounge chair. "Now?"

"Now I want to do unspeakable things to you."

"Take off your pants first."

He grinned and worked on his jeans while I unsnapped my garters and rolled down my stockings, adding them, my pearls and the dress to the pile of clothes on the chair. And then we stood there in our undies, our last defenses, staring at each other with admiration.

"Do you need my assistance?" I whispered, trying not to stare at the tent in his black briefs.

"Soon," he said softly. "You?"

"Very soon." I hooked my thumbs in my waistband and slowly worked off the underpants. I stood naked before him and let him look his fill.

He took his time. He'd seen me before, but really just the once, and there had been such an urgency to our coupling. Now, as he regarded me, slipping off his briefs as he did so, I admired him — the enticing shadows cast on his torso by the subtle light; the legs and arms muscled from swimming and who knows what else; those hungry eyes and thirsty lips, and his member, so hard it pointed up toward his narrow waist.

I couldn't stand the tension anymore.

"Time to get wet," I teased. I turned and made a shallow dive into the water. The rush of sensation over my skin was delicious, but it couldn't cool the heat that had infused my body.

When I came up for air, he was already underwater. I felt him slide past my legs, a thrilling touch.

"Shark!" I exclaimed when he surfaced.

"I have a taste for mermaids tonight." He chased me to the shallow end, where we could both stand, and imprisoned me with his arms against the side of the pool.

His erection brushed against my clit in the water. I made a tiny sound of want. The intensity in his face reflected my desire. He cupped my chin with one hand and covered my mouth with his.

This was a slow, deep, ravishing kiss, all about his tongue

and his lips teasing and tasting mine. The rest of our bodies might as well not have existed, the kiss was so immersive, but I was all too aware of his cock pressing against my pussy, his chest against my nipples. My peaks were so hard, his touch was painful. I couldn't get enough of it. I wrapped my hands around his waist and pulled him toward me as his mouth devoured mine. I wanted him inside me. More than anything, I wanted to be joined with him.

Now. I wanted him now.

And then he was breaking off the kiss with a gasp and pushing off the wall. "I need a condom."

Talk about throwing water on the situation. "You don't need one, Jace. I told you, I'm fine. Birth control. Fully tested. You told me you haven't had sex in years, so — "

"I can't."

My body chilled pretty fast without his arms around me, and with that look in his eyes — *crap.* "You don't — I mean, is there something you want to tell me?"

"I've been tested, too. I'm fine. I just like to be safe."

I breathed a little sigh of relief, and then I realized what he was saying. "So you don't trust me?"

"I do. Look, you're completely safe. I'm safe. Everything is fine." His voice became more strident. "This is just something I have to do, OK? Can you deal with it?"

I stood very still in the water, confounded by the anguish in his face. I didn't understand it. But I didn't want to turn away from him. I wasn't ready to walk away, because if I walked away tonight, I knew, somehow I knew, that I would never be with him again.

"It's OK, Jace," I whispered.

He nodded, overwhelmed with emotion I didn't under-stand. He walked up the steps and out of the water and plopped onto one of the lounges. He leaned forward, elbows on knees, his head drooping, his face hidden by his hands. My heart went out to him as he sat there dripping, naked, vulnerable.

I stayed in the water for a minute, and then I walked out, too. He remained immobile as I picked up his jeans and felt around in the pockets. I found the foil square. Standing by his chair, I pressed my belly against his head and ran one hand through his hair, stroking him as I rested my other arm across his shoulders. Gradually, his breathing eased. The tension leaked out of him.

He lifted his head and pulled me down to his lap. He suckled my breasts with sweet, slow devotion as he caressed my back. I smoothed his hair, and then I pushed him back against the cushions, tore open the packet and rolled the condom on his towering erection. There was a strange gratefulness in his eyes that haunted me, as well as desire, the same fierce want that burned inside me.

I straddled him and grasped his cock, rubbing it against my wet sex until his eyes hooded, and then I slipped down onto him.

He gasped as I moaned — he was so big inside me this way, piercing me so deeply, the pleasure was a kind of agony, too. I rocked against him, and he reached up to squeeze my swaying breasts. I moaned again, moaned his name, lifted myself and settled again on his cock. He shifted and went deeper, harder; he reached out and rubbed my nub with his thumb, and every buzzer in my body went off. I began moving faster against him, up and down, forward and back, pushing against his hard chest for leverage. No one had touched me as deeply as he had, physically. He should have been too big, too intense, but this was everything I wanted —

even the ache of my body as we sped up our rhythm and crashed into each other again and again.

Jace suddenly reached out, grabbed my behind and yanked me hard against him, stopping my motion as he cried out, jerking into me even more deeply than I thought possible, tripping an explosion of throbbing pleasure that ricocheted through my body. I pitched forward and collapsed against his chest. He held me tight, and I held him there, too, treasuring the feel of him inside me.

Oh, Jace. How can we be so intimate and know so little of each other? I hoped he could find a way to tell me what stood between us besides that thin little sheath.

There under the stars, wet and spent and shaken, I knew something now with painful certainty. I knew I couldn't be satisfied with less than all of him.

DIRK HAD SCHEDULED an abbreviated rehearsal for Friday, if two hours could be considered abbreviated. During the season, scheduling got complicated when one show was on and another was in rehearsal, so we had a large studio space upstairs that rehearsing casts often used. It could double as a black-box theater for those wee gems that wouldn't lure large crowds.

But right now, we had unlimited use of the big space, and the actors came in chattering and energetic. Not only were they high on the way the play had gelled the night before, but they were about to start a weekend.

I was high, too, but for a different reason. It was sort of a melancholy drunk, because my intoxicant was Jace Edison. After our fraught evening by the pool, I'd had him take me home. He was quiet and calm, and he'd walked me to my door and left me with a sweet kiss goodnight, a dramatic change from the intensity I'd come to expect from him.

Now I wasn't sure *what* to expect from him. Without realizing it, I'd pushed him into a red zone last night, and I still didn't understand the boundary I'd crossed.

On my desk this morning, I'd found a small potted orchid, its blooms a happy pink. I knew it was from him, but a note would have been welcome, something to keep me from analyzing what it could mean. I decided to thank him in person and find out, but I didn't run into him all morning, and a knock on his office door yielded no results. He wasn't there. Finally, I'd texted him with a "Thank you."

To which he replied, "Sweets to the sweet."

I'm not sure it was ideal for him to quote Hamlet's mother talking about a dead girl, but I tried not to read too much into it.

After working in the costume shop most of the afternoon, I'd come to rehearsal hoping for more, hoping for answers. But really, just jonesing to see him.

And now the actors were here, pumped up and happy (someone had left doughnuts in the green room, which also helped). I was in the third row, thinking that we had to start fittings next week so we could get everything done in time. Paul was especially giddy, loudly telling jokes that had the men in the cast roaring and the women rolling their eyes. Wendy came over to see me while we waited for Dirk to finish consulting with Alan, Anne and even the rarely seen big boss, Boris, in the booth.

"Where's Jace?" Wendy and I asked each other simultaneously before breaking into laughter.

"I guess neither of us know," I said.

"But I'm guessing you would know better than I?" Wendy's eyes twinkled.

"I've seen him around once or twice."

"Uh-huh. Don't be coy."

"I think the rumor mill is more involved than we are," I said. "But I'm not going to deny there's something. At least not to you."

Wendy shook her head and sighed. "If anybody had to bag him, I'm glad it was you and not Holland. What was that all about yesterday?"

"The working theory is that she saw he could be had, so she had to have him. Perhaps she's proving her fertility to the tribe."

"All of a sudden you're an anthropology major? And I don't think she has to do much proving, not after half of us watched her practically eat Doug alive on the back patio of The Junction Box last night."

Doug was the smitten actor playing Nick Bottom.

"Glad I missed it," I said.

"I bet you are, given what you have instead."

"What I have is a lot of questions. Among them, how drunk do you think Paul is tonight? Eighty-five percent?"

"I put it at about ninety," she said. "He can barely stand."

Or sit. He was giggling and struggling to stay perched on one of the chairs they'd set up temporarily to represent Mr. Duke's office. A few wooden trees, yet to be painted, had sprouted upstage, but the scenery was far from finished.

"I'd better go," Wendy said as Dirk descended the steps to our left, heading for the stage. He had a strange look on his face.

"Nice of you to join us, Ms. Lilac," he said to Wendy as she caught up with him.

"Happy to be here," she said to Dirk, then flashed me a *what the hell?* look.

"I want to start with the scene where Helena is following Demetrius into the woods," he announced. "Everyone else, please step aside and be quiet or head into the green room and stuff yourself with doughnuts for a few minutes."

There were chuckles and murmurs as the stage cleared. A few actors sat near me so they would have the best view. When Dirk really started to break down performances, it was always a treat to watch — but rarely a treat to endure. I suspected Wendy was more than a little worried, especially after Dirk's criticism of her earlier in the week.

Paul, however, seemed bulletproof as he assumed his place.

"Quit following me around," he told Wendy as Helena. "I don't want you. I want your friend. Go back to whatever martini bar you crawled out of."

"But you called me," said Wendy, carrying her script but barely looking at it.

"Never!" Paul bellowed. To his credit, he had no script at all, though he was insanely loud.

"You may not know it, but you always call me. You're a magnet pulling on my heart. You should know by now, Demetrius — my heart is pumping iron for you."

"I want to marry Hermia, not you."

"But I love you."

"Tell you, I do not, nor I cannot love you?" Paul said.

Murmurs arose in the theater. The actors looked at one another. Dirk crossed his arms and let them continue.

Wendy's brow crinkled, but she continued. "Are you just playing hard to get? Do you despise me that much? I'm as loyal as an old dog, and I love you. Tie me up if you must," she said flirtatiously, "only pet me, Demetrius."

"Tempt not too much the hatred of my spirit; for I am sick when I do look at thee," he said, and then he laughed out loud.

"What is he doing?" one actor near me whispered.

"He's quoting goddamn Shakespeare," answered another.

Maybe it was better that Jace wasn't here to see this.

Dirk looked at Wendy expectantly. God, this was like watching a train wreck. He chose not to stop it, and we were all along for the ride.

"How can you be sick of me when you never see me?" Wendy recited.

"You're a fool to follow me here," Paul said. There was an audible sigh around me as he returned to Jace's script, but his recovery was short-lived. "To trust the opportunity of night and the ill counsel of a desert place with the rich worth of your *virginity.*" He giggled maniacally and almost fell over one of the chairs as he circled Wendy.

"I came to the park to find you," Wendy said, somehow maintaining her composure as the buzz rose in the theater. "It doesn't seem dark when you're around. I'm not alone when I'm with you."

"I'll leave you to the mercy of wild beasts!" Paul said, and as soon as Wendy tried to respond, he yelled. "Let me go! I shall do thee mischief in the wood!" He plopped onto the stage, laughing so hard, tears flowed from his eyes.

Wendy stood still, her eyes wide, clutching the script tightly.

"He didn't even get the Shakespeare right," one of the actors near me said under his breath.

"That's all I needed to see," Dirk said. "You're fired, Paul."

"You can't fire me. I'm a *volunteer!*" Paul screamed from his seat on the floor, still laughing. He flopped onto his back and hiccupped.

"Fuck," one of the actors said, and a couple of the guys went down to the stage to drag him away.

"Very nice work, Wendy," Dirk said. "You should consider improv. All right, let's move on to Titania saying goodnight to the fairies. Holland, have you practiced that song?"

Wendy moved offstage, clearly rattled, while Holland moved onstage, sashaying in the briefest of miniskirts and carrying a banjo.

I slipped out of my row and through a side exit, hastening to the green room. Wendy sat on a tapestried chaise lounge that had probably last seen action during *The Importance of Being Earnest,* hugging her knees. I waved away the actors who were hovering around her, and they headed back into the theater as I sat next to her.

"You OK?"

"What the *fuck* was that?" She looked at me, no longer freaked out. She was pissed.

"It was sort of Shakespeare," I said helplessly. "At least Paul didn't do it during a performance."

"Why did Dirk let it go on like that? I'm about to go in there and tell him to suck it. I don't need this stress in my 'fun' time."

"Don't!" I squeezed her arm. Wendy was my friend, but I couldn't help but think of the production first. We couldn't lose two major players on the same day. "Please stay, Wendy. Dirk loves you."

"He has a funny way of showing it. I want to kick his ass." Her eyes flashed with fury. "And I want to make Paul *suffer.*"

"Remind me never to piss you off," I joked.

"That's exactly right," she said. She took a deep breath. Then another. "I feel a little better now. Did you know they tried to bring Paul in here?"

"Um, and?"

"I told them to take him somewhere else or I was going to rip his balls off."

"That seems fair." I choked back a laugh.

"It's not funny."

"Of course not. Why don't you have a doughnut?"

"Where are they from?"

"Sugar Shack."

"OK," Wendy said. "But only if there's cinnamon sugar."

I got her the doughnut in question and grabbed a glazed for myself. We ate and watched the flat-screen monitor that showed the action on stage. Holland was singing with the fairies — teens from one of the local high school drama departments who would move around by skateboard and in-line skates, while Puck rode his unicycle.

"This is one wacky show," I said idly.

"Uh-huh."

"But in a good way." We turned to each other and grinned. "You ready to go back in there?"

She nodded, and we stood and hugged.

When rehearsal finally ended, with no Jace in sight, I let the cast leave before I approached Dirk. Anne and Alan descended from the booth.

"Well, that was an interesting rehearsal," Anne said. She didn't look happy.

"Paul drank two-thirds of the vodka in the green room freezer tonight. It's been getting worse. It was time," Dirk said.

"So you'll use the understudy?" Alan asked.

"You don't use an understudy with this much time left

before we open," Dirk said. "You get a replacement. The *best possible* replacement." Dirk gave us all a meaningful look.

There was a beat while his implication set in.

"He said he didn't want to be in the play," Anne said. "He was adamant about it in all of our meetings, even before he came here."

He?

"It makes perfect sense," Dirk said, confirming my fears. "Casting Jace will ensure that we sell every ticket to every show."

"It will do wonders for our budget," Boris acknowledged with enthusiasm. He had that executive director look in his eye.

"But he won't do it," I said. "You can't make him do it."

They looked at me askance. It was not really my place to say anything about casting, and Anne, who'd seen us making out in the hallway, raised an eyebrow.

"He'll do what's best for the play," Dirk said with confidence.

"Where is he, anyway?" asked Anne.

"He said he had to work on rewrites," Dirk said, "so he skipped tonight."

"He can't pull the play, can he?" Boris asked.

"Not according to our contract," Dirk said. "If he's outraged, he can leave, but we still do the play. Anyway, I'm sure it won't come to that. He chose not to be on stage because he didn't want to steal the spotlight from the other actors. It was generous of him, but this will be better for everybody. He'll do it."

That wasn't at all the impression I got. Jace had other reasons for not being on stage.

There was another moment of silence before the bomb

dropped.

"I think Penelope should ask him," said Anne.

"*What?*" I gaped at her. The others looked at me as if I were a bag of popcorn fresh out of the microwave, with avaricious glee.

She shrugged. "You seem to have a special relationship with him. And a lot is hanging on this play for you, too."

Blackmail? What the fuck?

Now, like Wendy, I wanted to do violence to someone. Instead, I kept my voice cool and steady. "You know it's not my place to ask him. And he's been very clear that he doesn't want to be on stage for this. He's trying to prove himself as a playwright."

"That's sweet," Dirk said drily. "Let us know what he says."

And they walked off, the hive mind, leaving me standing there.

Special relationship, my ass. I didn't even know where he was.

I wished for my quietus with a bare bodkin as I opened my bag. "Who would fardels bear?" I declaimed in my best Hamlet voice and pulled out my phone.

"Where are you?" I texted Jace. "Interesting rehearsal tonight."

I waited for a moment, then began my walk through the building to the back lot, where my car was waiting. The phone buzzed just before I hit the back door.

"Meeting room," he texted back.

He'd been in the building the whole time?

I spun on my rather tall heel — today I wore a flouncy yellow dress — and took the stairs up to the third floor. I was a tad out of breath when I pushed open the door.

Jace was sitting at the table, a laptop computer in front of him, surrounded by sheets of paper, empty coffee cups and Chinese takeout containers. He looked terrible, or at least, as terrible as someone that handsome can look. His hair, normally sexy when rumpled, just looked rough. Dark circles under his eyes suggested he'd slept little or worked too hard or both.

In front of him on the wall, the big TV screen was on, showing the empty stage. After a moment, it showed Alan crossing the stage; the house lights went off, and the ghost light came on. Alan crossed again, on his way out. I heard his footsteps.

I opened my mouth and closed it again.

Jace had seen it all. Heard it all.

"Do you have something to ask me?" he inquired in a mordant tone, looking at me from under those dark eyebrows of his.

"It's not my idea," I said. "I'm not going to ask you. You can do whatever the fuck you want."

"Good." He sounded resolute, even agitated. "Because I'm not going on stage."

He still hadn't said why, and I didn't ask. But I would, eventually. I needed to know, especially if his refusal got me into deeper shit with management. I needed to know a lot of things.

I sat opposite him, much as I had during that meeting that had become a fight, the prelude to our first real date.

"It's OK," I said. "I'm about ready to quit on these assholes anyway."

He waved off the idea. "They're not going to fire you if I don't go on stage."

Not expressly for that, I thought. *But maybe it would give*

them just one more reason, because they want to hire some hotshot
with a fancy resume.

"They're manipulating me," I said. "It's disgusting."

"It's the theater. Though I'm used to less drama at the New York level." Jace started gathering his scattered script pages, tapping the stack against the table to straighten it up.

"You're not angry?"

"I'll be angry later. Right now, I'm just tired." He stood, grabbed a trash can and swept the cups and containers into it, then closed his laptop.

"Didn't you sleep?"

"A few hours. I was thinking about — things."

"You had time to get me an orchid. Thank you. It — it made my morning."

His face brightened a little. "I found it in the grocery store. I hope that's not too cheesy. The pink reminded me of you."

"It was sweet." No one ever gave me flowers. "Did you have any idea they might tell Paul to walk?"

"Dirk told me he was worried. He said he'd talked to Paul about AA and counseling, and Paul had laughed it off. I had no idea Dirk would do what he did tonight."

"Wendy was pissed."

"I don't blame her, especially since Paul was quoting that hack Shakespeare at her."

I laughed.

"You want to grab some dinner?" Jace asked, stowing his laptop and papers in a leather satchel.

"I thought you had Chinese."

"That was lunch."

I laughed again. I couldn't help it. He'd been working his

ass off on his crazy play, and now my ungrateful bosses
wanted him to star in it, too.

"Do you like to suffer?" I asked.

"Bearing fardels builds character," Jace joked.

"Oh, yeah. You heard that, too."

He smiled. "What do you think?"

"I think Thai food."

"I concur. I'll drop this in my office. Drive or walk?"

"We can walk," I said. "Let's get the hell out of here."

WE ATE inside a tiny place that mostly did takeout, under
fluorescent lights, on a crappy little lacquered table, eating off
paper plates with white plastic utensils. Despite the lack of
amenities, it was the best Thai place in town. I had pad thai
tofu; Jace had the red curry, which he ordered at maximum
heat level. It seemed to revitalize him.

He wiped away a tear.

"Are you practicing for a scene?" I asked.

"Spicy," he explained hoarsely, chasing the bite with a
swig of beer.

I giggled. He could be a regular guy, even funny, given the
chance. I regretted I'd have to spoil the mood with more
questions, but I waited until we'd finished and were walking
through the busy sidewalks of downtown Bohemia in the
warm evening.

"What's this?" Jace asked as we came upon a dimly lit area
between buildings. We weren't far from the Bohemia School
of Art and Design.

"You haven't been here yet? This is Ponce De Leon
Square. It's a pleasant little park. Come on in."

We strolled under the wrought-iron arch toward the center, a wonderfully quiet space among the bustle of Friday night. The glow of a few streetlights filtered through the trees, and a couple of small lights lit up the two tiers of the bubbling fountain. At the top, the statue of Ponce de Leon pointed toward the east.

The fountain was surrounded by a low stone wall. Jace grabbed my hand and tugged me to it, and we sat. He didn't let go, but he didn't look at me, either. Instead, he stared into the falling water while his thumb idly rubbed the back of my hand, shooting sparks of heat across my skin. It would be so easy to fall into a simple physical friendship with him and not ask him any more questions.

Maybe I was through with doing things the easy way.

"Why don't you want to go on stage, Jace?" I asked softly.

He turned his head toward me. "You heard Dirk. I'm thinking of the other actors."

"I don't think so." I pulled my hand away from his and laid it against his cheek.

He pushed it away and crossed his arms. "I don't need to talk about this with you."

"Don't you?"

Jace's poker face seemed to have deserted him. Emotions ran across his features, turbulent, like a stormy sky. He shook his head.

"What?" I asked.

"Are you going to report what I tell you back to them?"

"Of course not."

"Good, because I'm still working it out."

He shifted closer, and confusion gripped me. My body reacted strongly to his, but my mind was alert to something greater at stake than my need.

I stayed still as he murmured, "This — this could ruin me."

What on earth could ruin Jace Edison? "Tell me."

"I can't go on stage."

I smiled. I couldn't help it. "I've seen evidence to the contrary."

He still looked as serious as death. "I have what some people call performance anxiety."

That brought an entirely different image to mind. "Again, I don't see — "

"Stage fright."

"Oh."

How was it possible? Jace had appeared in so many shows, not to mention TV and film. And then I remembered that he hadn't done anything particularly public for months. Even when he'd recited the sonnet at Gary's mom's wedding, the night I'd met him, he'd seemed nervous. I'd thought it was all part of the delicate act of performing a love poem.

"That obscure off-Broadway play — that was the last thing you were in," I said, almost to myself. "Six months ago."

Jace nodded. *"Piece of Work*. It was smart. Maybe a little obscure, but I like doing projects like that sometimes. Mind-benders."

"What happened?"

"That's a simple question. But the answer is not so simple, as I'm not a hundred percent sure myself. Actually — that's not true. I have an idea where it's coming from. But I haven't been able to beat it. I've tried biofeedback. Cognitive therapy. I tried beta blockers, too — it's the dirty little secret of some performers — but they just made me feel like a robot."

"So maybe you have to go to the source and get it there. Where it's coming from."

"If the therapy couldn't do it, I don't think talking about it now will." He stood and put a few steps between us. He looked up at Ponce de Leon.

"But it might make me feel better."

He turned to me, one corner of his mouth tugging upward in a hint of a smile. "I got a bad review for *Piece of Work.*"

I shook my head at the idea that one bad review could take down the Babe of Broadway. "That show got good reviews."

"But one particularly well-known New York newspaper took issue with my performance. I still remember whole phrases. 'Edison is as pretty as a picture, but a picture can rarely express more than one emotion.' And, 'It's performances like this that make us wonder whether our love for him in the past was nothing more than infatuation.' "

"Ha," I said. "That sounds bitter. Like you're being judged for being good-looking, not for your performance. Like the critic is resentful of your success. You can't possibly take that to heart."

"Oh, but I can. I did. It's not what he said." Jace kicked an imaginary pebble. "It's that he articulated everything I've believed about myself for a long time."

I went to him, slipping an arm around his waist. "I don't believe it. You're incredibly talented. You've had a career most of us would kill for, and you're only — "

"Twenty-six," he supplied.

"Right. Twenty-six. Forget the reviews if you must, though most of them have been stellar. People fucking *love* you. In fact, I can't believe I'm counseling a guy who's had more of a career in five years than I'm going to have in my entire life."

He slid his arms around me. "Don't believe it, Penelope.

I've seen your portfolio. You're only just getting started. I've had lucky breaks, is all."

Now that he was so close to me, I was muddled. I pushed him gently away and kept talking.

"That's nice of you to say, but forget about me for a minute. What do you mean by 'lucky breaks'? Maybe you have good genes, pretty boy, but your talent has proven you've transcended them twenty times over."

Jace smiled. "You almost make me believe it."

I rolled my eyes. "How can you not believe it?"

"Because I know how I came up. I got cast in a big show right out of college. I'd gone to an audition on a lark to support a friend of mine who was trying out, and they cast me in the lead. The *lead.* There were articles and buzz. Everybody loves a winner. My next role was even better. Since then it's been a torrent of good fortune. Great roles. Awards."

"This is what we call evidence," I said.

"Evidence that I'm a *fraud.* People love a good story. They want to believe in the fairy tale. That critic just came along and pointed out the truth: It's all bullshit."

"A million Broadway geeks can't be wrong. Jace Edison, if you don't believe them, believe me." I pushed down the unfamiliar rush of feeling that tightened my throat and stung my eyes. "You're wonderful."

His expression softened, and he closed the distance between us again, slipping a hand behind my neck and tilting my head for a kiss. Oh, it was a thorough, lovely kiss, five stars at least, and for a moment, I forgot all about his troubles and my bemusement and opened to his sweet ministrations. When he released me, I swayed a little before bringing myself back to reality.

He grabbed my hand, and we walked out of the park and

back through downtown, through the revelers celebrating Friday night. It was warm. The guys dressed lightly, the women wore even less, and laughter was in the air. But I didn't want to while away the evening with them. Suffused as I was with waves of warmth from Jace's touch, I was still bothered by something. How could Jace have so much insecurity about his career when there was so much proof of his success?

And then there was last night, which neither of us had talked about — the weird moment when he'd insisted on the condom. Safety first and all that, but we'd already talked about it. We'd both said we'd been tested. So why was he so adamant about it? Was he just obsessive-compulsive or something? His issues all seemed mixed up together.

I followed him to his car and got in without even thinking about it.

"I think we need ice cream," Jace said as he started it up.

"Now that's the first logical thing you've said all night."

"Where to?"

"I have some nut fudge ripple in my freezer."

"Nut fuck nipple, did you say?"

I laughed as he got on the road. "You are so bad."

"That's why you like me," he said with a smug smile.

At least he was confident of that. And damn it, he was right.

My neighborhood was quiet as always. My few fellow apartment-dwellers were either out or asleep. The sweet old lady who lived in the front half of the ground floor went to bed early. I figured Rock was out, because his motorcycle was missing, and the guy in the other apartment upstairs often didn't come home on weekends at all. The attic studio was empty.

"I should warn you," I said as I unlocked the door, "it's always a little warm in here. The air conditioning is primitive."

"That's OK," Jace said. "You have ice cream."

We entered the living space, and I shut the door. "Nut fuck nipple. How could I forget?"

I dropped my bag by the kitchen counter as he looked around. I felt self-conscious, suddenly, about how small it was and how lacking in amenities.

"It's not much," I said.

"It's still bigger than my apartment in New York." Jace poked his head into my megacloset/sewing room, bathroom and bedroom before returning to the living room.

"It works for me," I said, getting out the ice cream. "The view is great. I mean, maybe not as great as your beach house, but the river's beautiful in the morning."

"And it's not *my* beach house. This is perfect, Penelope." He looked closely at the framed movie poster on the wall above the couch. A photographic version of the *My Fair Lady* movie poster from 1964, it showed Audrey Hepburn in her iconic black and white Ascot dress and enormous hat, with a tiny Rex Harrison in the background. I adored Cecil Beaton's costumes.

"Ah, she was a vision, wasn't she?" Jace noted. "But I still lean toward Julie Andrews, given she actually sang the part on stage."

"Audrey tried," I said, bringing out two bowls of nut fudge ripple, a phrase I might never be able to say with a straight face again. "They brought in a ringer anyway. But you simply can't *not* look at that fabulous dress."

"Or the woman in it," he said, taking a bowl. We sat

together on the couch and spent a few minutes enjoying the cool sweetness of the ice cream.

He set his empty bowl on the coffee table when I was only halfway done.

"Slowpoke." Jace took my bowl from me and grabbed my spoon.

"Hey!"

He took a bite and grinned. *Oh, that grin.* "What?"

"That's mine."

"Oh, you want some of this?" He dipped out another spoonful and held it out for me, wiggling it.

"I'm not a child, you know."

"And I'm immensely grateful for that fact."

I opened my mouth, and he pushed the spoonful in, ever so slowly. I closed my mouth on it, and he pulled out the spoon as I savored the flavors of chocolate and vanilla — and the hungry look in his eyes.

"Put that down," I whispered.

"Why?"

"Because I don't want you to get it on my dress."

"That wouldn't be a problem if you weren't wearing it."

"That's what I was thinking," I said.

Jace put the bowl down carefully. In an instant, he grabbed me and shoved me down hard against the couch, his lips slamming onto mine. We were tongue deep in a hot kiss, our hands roving, mine over his back, his up my skirt. He touched me, my damp underpants. I made little whimpering sounds under his kiss as he pressed a finger against the fabric and my clit. It became extremely urgent to get my damn dress off. I did it with his help, and we kicked off shoes and yanked off clothes with abandon until we were both down to our underwear.

I got up and pulled him by the hand, tugging him around the corner to my bedroom.

I switched on a lamp on my nightstand, then grabbed a scarf from my dresser and draped it over the shade. Dim light in soft patterns of blue and green illuminated his face, serious and sexy.

"Perfection," he whispered, returning my unspoken compliment. He slipped the straps of my satin bra off my shoulders, then reached around back, deftly unhooked it and dropped it to the floor. He covered both breasts with his hands and squeezed until I gasped.

I eased my hands into his briefs, cupping his buttocks, and slid the underwear slowly off, getting an eyeful of his erection as I dropped to my knees. I ran my tongue once down the hot length of it, and a tremor passed through him.

He lifted me and slid off my satin underpants, tossing them on the floor. We stood against each other, touching, exploring. We sipped on each other's mouths until it seemed our over-stimulated bodies wouldn't hold us upright, and we fell naked into the bed. The window air conditioner rattled, but it was no match for our heat as our lips sought out every inch of skin we could taste. As I licked my way down his chest, he subtly changed the angle of our bodies, touching, squeezing.

I had made it to his belly button when I felt him nibble my clit.

Oh, God.

I grasped his erection and slid my mouth over the head, tasting him as he stirred the fire between my legs with his nimble tongue. I'd tried this position before, once. It had been awkward. But Jace and I just fit — his mouth on my pussy, his tongue making me crazy; my mouth on his cock, coaxing terse thrusts from him, an intoxicating invasion.

Damn, the pleasure was distracting. I'd start to get lost in the feel of his tongue flicking at my nub, and then I'd stir from my lazy dream, from the slow savoring of his tip, and suck him hard. I took him to the back of my throat and drew out again, writhing as Jace moaned against my sex, working his magic. Finally, the stimulation was too much; I twisted around and knelt in front of him on the bed, taking care of his magnificent cock with my hand and my mouth with deep, languid sucking. I slid his length between my breasts, then back to my mouth, and sucked again and again. When I tasted the first drops of come, I slid him out of my mouth and guided his spurts onto my breasts and belly. His face was flushed, devastating, unbelievably sexy in his abandon. I loved seeing him come undone.

I slid up next to him. I kissed him and tasted us mixed up together, musky, salty arousal.

When we paused for breath, Jace got up and came back from the bathroom with a towel. He carefully cleaned me and tossed it aside, then wrapped himself around me.

I'd seen a hint of Jace's fears, but now all I sensed was his strength. I felt safe in his arms, though somewhere in my soul, a warning bell was ringing. I told it to hush. Talk of worry and fear could wait until the morrow.

"She hangs upon the cheek of night like a rich jewel," he whispered in my ear, kissing my neck as he held me closer.

I almost answered from a different play, "But love is blind," and stopped myself. That word didn't belong in my bed.

Still — Jace did.

It was weird to wake up with someone under the sheets with me. I couldn't remember the last time a man had stayed over. Of course, I usually tried to push those nights out of my mind. They hadn't been worth remembering.

I remembered everything with Jace. He seemed to sense my wakefulness, but I didn't think he was awake. He shifted against me, and my body reacted with want. What was it about him that fired me up every time he was near? I'd never had this with another man — well, only once, and not with this much power, this much feeling.

Ugh. Feelings.

The trees outside cast shifting shadows on the window blinds — the window that didn't have the noisy air conditioner — and I could tell it was mid-morning. I could make breakfast. I had eggs and bread. Maybe French toast?

I gently tried to free myself, and Jace's grasp tightened.

"Where you do think you're going, my lady?" he murmured.

"How you can do that gorgeous British accent first thing in the morning is beyond me."

"Gorgeous, is it?" He opened his eyes, so dark, outlined by lush lashes, crinkling a little at the corners as he smiled.

"It's absolutely divine, darling," I said, echoing his tones.

"Mmm, darling." He kissed my neck.

"It's — I, uh . . . " I failed to explain the "darling." I was distracted as I let him tongue the sensitive skin at my throat.

"My lady, you have given yourself to me," he said, continuing with the accent between kisses — my chin, my cheek, my ear, which he teased with a flicking tongue. "You'll never be accepted into society again. I'm afraid you have no choice but to become my mistress."

I relaxed into the game as my body heated. His hands skated across my body under the sheet.

"I have to go back to my manor. They depend on me there," I said, doing my own version of the accent — not as well as he, but I wasn't Jace Edison.

"Oh, no, my lady. I'm going to treat you like the strumpet you are."

God, I was wet. "I confess it. I am but a slut for you, my lord."

"I knew it. Ah, I should have had my servant bring me my supplies." He moved to get up.

"Try the drawer next to the bed, my lord."

Surprise fleetingly crossed his features, and he rolled over a bit, opened the drawer, rummaged around and tossed a wrapped condom onto the bed — and a pair of pink leather cuffs.

"You say you weren't a slut before you met me, my lady?"

I suppressed a giggle. "They were a gift from a suitor, my lord. I turned down his advances."

"I find that difficult to believe, given your supply of French letters." He'd pushed off the sheet, giving me a full view of his long, elegant body as he rolled the condom onto a raging erection. "I'll have to punish you for your wantonness."

"But I'm a lady and above such things."

"I believe you have been a slut long before I came along, if the contents of your chest are any indication." So he'd seen the vibrator, too.

"Just evidence of my unwillingness to share myself," I joked.

And then I gasped as he grabbed one wrist and slipped it inside a cuff. He tightened it, and I didn't object as he slipped the short chain around a vertical slat in my headboard and secured my other wrist in the other cuff.

"My lord, you must free me," I intoned, but my humor was undercut by a wave of lust. I wanted to give myself over to him, this man I knew so little about. But maybe I knew enough. I had a sense of his goodness that went to my heart. My body had no fear, only anticipation. I wriggled against the bonds. "This is no way to treat a lady."

"No lady has a cunt as wet as yours," he said, dipping a finger into my slit.

I gasped at the word and got even wetter. It was so wrong — and so delicious in that English accent. His finger probed until it found a spot that made me tremble.

"My lord — I — I surrender."

"You have no choice, my lady," Jace said with delightful wickedness. My, he played the villain well. Someone should alert a casting director.

I opened my legs further. His eyes darkened. He withdrew his finger, grasped my hips and probed my entrance. His tip brushed against my clit, and I arched, straining against the cuffs.

"Is my lord afraid to take me?" I asked in a breathy voice. It wasn't much of an acting job, as I was suddenly desperate for him.

"Judge for yourself." With that, he entered me halfway, slowly, and then thrust hard. I cried out as he hit an exquisitely deep, sensitive place and held himself there.

"Oh, God," I hissed, my body wound up like wire, straining against the headboard, full of his cock, my muscles tense and aching for release.

" 'My lord' will suffice," he joked, but his face showed he felt far more than amusement. His lips were slightly parted, his eyebrows lowered, and his gaze took in all of me as his voice lowered, hoarse. "You are beautiful, my lady."

He pulled out halfway and pushed into me, starting to build a rhythm. He was deliberate at first, letting me feel every inch of his hot sex. He built up his speed, punctuating his thrusts with the occasional pinch or suck of my nipples, or a flick of my nub, until I was moaning with every move-ment, every touch. The cuffs, despite their fuzzy lining, were an annoyance at first; I wanted to touch him, too. And then they were thrilling, as I gave up all control to his desire, would have given up everything for his next plunge.

Finally, he came, holding himself hard inside me, his spasm triggering waves of mind-numbing pleasure that swept through my body and made me pant, almost sob, with my release. He let out a primal noise as he shuddered against me, and when he finally withdrew, his breathing was ragged. He released me from the cuffs, threw out the condom and gath-ered me in his arms.

"Did I hurt you?" Jace asked softly.

"Only in a good way," I murmured.

He chuckled against my ear. "I haven't — I haven't been with anyone in so long, and there's something about you that carries me away. I've never been so . . . "

"Dramatic?"

"Hmm," he said. "That's one way to put it."

"You mean — before?"

"Yes. Believe it or not, I used to have a lot of sex."

"I didn't think your prowess came from nowhere," I said, wanting to know more but not eager to shatter this bliss I felt with inconvenient truths.

"Mmm, prowess. That's the best review I've ever had."

I smacked his ass, and he laughed. We lay there for a few minutes, touching, enjoying each other, and I started to think that I needed a shower, and then I started to think about him and the condom.

And then I felt I couldn't go much further without hearing some inconvenient truths, because I was — feeling.

"Jace," I said, kissing him.

"Yes?"

"I need you to talk to me."

"I told you, I like talking to you."

I touched his cheek. "Tell me why. Tell me what happened."

He extricated himself from me gently, but the sudden distance between us was palpable. He stood and grabbed his clothes and went into the living room. I waited for the door to slam. Instead, after a minute, he reappeared in the doorway.

"Let's go for a walk," he said. There was pain in his eyes, and I was sorry I'd put it there. Or reawakened it.

"OK," I said. "Five minutes in the shower, and I'm there."

I left my hair wet and skipped the makeup, though I did put on sandals with a short heel; cute, very short denim shorts; and a clingy white T-shirt with a translucent bra beneath. When I emerged from my room, he had on shorts, sneakers and a *Rent* T-shirt, and he carried a water bottle.

"Where'd you get those?" I asked as we stepped outside and I locked the door.

"Workout clothes. I always keep some in the car. You look different," he said. "I like you without the makeup."

"Thanks, I guess. But the truth is, men *love* me with it."

"They love the Pinup Penelope," Jace said. "Maybe you should let them see the real you."

"Please. Look who's talking."

"Hmph," was all he said as we walked through the small gravel parking lot to the road, the River Road. It wound among the Victorians that made up the historic section of Bohemia. Some of these magnificent old houses were on the water, as my apartment building was. But most were across the street, meaning all the runners and cyclists out this Saturday morning had a beautiful view of the sun glinting off the lagoon, framed by elegant oak trees and swaying palms.

I grabbed the front of my T-shirt and flapped the fabric, trying to make a breeze. The heat had really taken hold, typical of late May, and the sun, while still not directly overhead, was brutal. I was glad I'd at least made time for sunscreen.

"I don't know why I bothered with a shower," I said. "I'm sweating already."

"I like you sweaty," Jace said.

I chuckled. "One-track mind."

"One track with a train going into the tunnel?"

Now I laughed. "Did you not get enough choo-choo this morning?"

"What an odd name for it." He leaned over and kissed my cheek.

I closed my eyes at the peck. When I looked up, there was Sloane, running toward me in her jogging shoes, her hair up in a ponytail.

"Hey, Penelope!" she said, popping out her earbuds. She stopped, breathing hard, and we did, too. "Uh, hi." She reached out a hand to Jace. "Sloane Abbey. I'm friends with Penelope."

"I saw you at the Junction Box. I should have introduced myself then. Jace Edison."

"Oh, I know who you are." She blushed. Sloane had a cute blush. Her relationship with Alex fascinated me. He seemed strong and quiet, while she was a talented potter with a demure side — and a not-so-demure side, if a recent photo shoot at Cali's studio was any indication. When Sloane and Alex were together, something potent happened between them; the sparks were almost visible.

"I thought you were living beachside now?" I asked.

"I am," she said, "but I still have a studio in my old place about a mile up the road. I thought I'd get in a run before I did some work. I'm so busy during the week at the school that I don't ever seem to have enough time for my personal projects. And this way Alex can focus on his writing." Sloane turned to Jace. "How are you liking Bohemia?"

"It's been even better than I'd hoped," he said, and unbidden happiness rushed through me. "It'll be tough to go back to New York."

And there came the crash. When had I become so invested in Jace being in Bohemia Beach?

"Well, enjoy," Sloane said. "If I stop now, I won't get my miles in." She shot me a subtle wink, then resumed her route amid the other runners and bicyclists in their colorful clothes.

"She's adorable," Jace said offhandedly after she left.

"Shopping, are we?" I asked drily.

"Not at all. Besides, I briefly met her boyfriend at the bar. Definitely a territorial vibe."

"Probably because you were so distracting."

He smiled. "I only wanted to distract you."

"Just the hazard of being you, I guess."

I was wondering when to press him with my big questions when he said, "Let's hang out here for a minute. Pelican

Park?" He regarded the single bench and the sign with skepticism.

"Oh, there's a development up there, Pelican Ridge" — I pointed to the street that intersected the river road — "and some wag thought it would be fun to label their river access."

We sat on the shaded bench, facing the river. "Not much of a ridge, either," he said.

"It's about fifteen feet above sea level up there. The Bohemia Alps."

"Florida is so different from what I'm used to." Jace watched a sailboat glide by. "I get so crazy in the city sometimes. Here, there's this subtle atmosphere of well-being. It's hard to describe, but I think it comes from nature. Everyone here seems so relaxed."

"The sun helps. It can be harsh in summer, but all winter, we have bright, happy weather. Life is still stressful sometimes, but a beach walk can cure a lot."

"Or a river walk?" He took a sip of water and handed the bottle to me.

"Maybe." I drank and passed it back. "Not quite as exciting as a walk in New York."

"Don't get me wrong. I love the energy there. I love the feeling of being at the center of everything. I went to school there. I made a career there. But sometimes, it's still not enough." He paused. "You must think I'm completely neurotic."

"But sexy," I joked, trying to ease the pain that crept into his voice.

Jace allowed a small smile. "This time with you has meant a lot to me." *Damn, that sounded like the prelude to a blow-off.* "You probably deserve to know a little bit more about why I am the way I am."

Pshew. "Probably," I quipped.

He held my hand, threading his fingers through mine. "I dated a lot of women when I was in college in New York. They liked me, for some reason."

"Can't imagine why, pretty boy."

"I deserve that. I took full advantage of being a pretty boy. At least, I did until I met Lauren."

I almost sensed her there, a third person on the bench. It was as if his memory had come and taken a seat. I withdrew my hand and shifted so I partially faced him. "You fell in love."

He nodded. "She was in the theater program with me, and it all seemed so easy. We did a play together — "

"Romeo and Juliet?" I tried to keep the snark out of my voice. Jace and his true love in *Romeo and Juliet* was the worst thing I could imagine.

"No." He chuckled ruefully. "We were seniors, and we did a production of *Streetcar,* which takes some nerve when you're that young. To our credit, an advisor chose the play."

"So you were Stanley and she was Blanche?"

"Oh, no. She was Stella. I loved calling her name on stage."

"Give me a minute. I'm comparing you to the young, hot Marlon Brando."

Jace shook his head. "Please don't. I wasn't that good. I mean, I wasn't bad. But we fell for each other during the play. It wasn't long before we were sleeping together. We starred in more plays together. We were the golden ones. Everyone predicted we'd both be incredible successes. We took it for granted, all of it. She was a radiant actress, an incredible talent. I've always thought she was better than I was. When we were on stage together, it was like great sex. And offstage — I couldn't get enough of her."

I nodded and took the water from him, took a sip, gave it back. "Did you break up? Or is she still in New York?"

"She died."

My hand flew to my mouth. There was nothing I could say. And in the face of that memory, I suspected there was nothing I could do if I decided I wanted him, really wanted him.

"I found her," he continued. "She was bleeding. I called the ambulance, but it was too late."

"Bleeding?" Images of violent death flew through my head.

"Ectopic pregnancy."

"Oh, my God, Jace." I took his hand again. "Did you have any idea?"

"Not until she died. She was barely conscious when I found her in her room. She kept saying, 'I'm sorry.' "

"But why? It wasn't her fault. Or yours."

"But it was. My fault, I mean." He paused, getting his emotions under control. "She had told me she was on the pill and couldn't get pregnant. Her sister, who was also her room-mate, told me later Lauren had never been on the pill, and she was in a position to know. Lauren was kind of wild. She liked the idea of seeing nature take its course. That what's her sister told me. I don't know why Lauren never discussed it with me. Some-times she would talk about the kids she wanted to have with me, and I went along with her happy talk, dreaming about names and the apartment we'd have and the Broadway shows we'd do, not realizing she was actually trying to get pregnant. But it doesn't matter. It's still my fault. I should have used a condom."

I let his story sink in before I spoke. "You can't blame yourself. I won't allow it."

He actually laughed, though the laugh was bitter.

"I mean it," I said. "First, she chose to roll the dice on pregnancy while leading you to believe otherwise, but second, the ectopic pregnancy was something she couldn't have foreseen. She could just as easily have had a normal pregnancy, and you would be a dad now." I didn't want to picture Jace in this alternate reality, with his happy family, because then he never would have come to me. But I still didn't want him to have suffered the way he had. If I could have magically restored Lauren to life, I would have in an instant.

"I know you're using logic, but logic can't get to what I feel," Jace said. "I failed her. I made her die."

"You made her love. That's not such a bad thing. She took a risk, maybe, but more to the point, she had terrible bad luck, and so did you." I lifted his hand to my lips and pressed a kiss there. He was still looking out at the river. His face was stoic, but his eye glimmered with an unshed tear.

"Don't be nice to me, Penelope. I don't deserve it. Just like I didn't deserve all the success I had when I got out of school. It all came to me so easily."

"When really they should have made you be a waiter for a few years in penance for your terrible deeds."

He looked at me, shocked.

"Did it ever occur to you that your stage fright may have its roots in more than just a bad review?" I asked. "Or, to be more accurate, that your belief that you're a fraud goes back to what happened to Lauren? Maybe it's all tied up together, Jace."

He shook his head again, but his eyes flickered, as if he were processing what I said.

I squeezed his hand. "Let me tell you something. I've never seen a talent like yours. It doesn't matter that you're a pretty boy. Lauren's loss was a terrible thing, but it doesn't change the fact that you are deserving of every role and honor you get. I think you know that, deep inside, but it's easy to get muddled when you've had something like that happen to you. It wasn't your fault, and shifting your guilt to your career isn't going to help you get over her."

Because maybe I did want him to get over her.

Jace looked back at the river, both eyes wet, his face stony. I released his hand. I felt as if I was setting him free. But I didn't really want to let go.

"Are you mad at me?" I asked softly.

He let out a long sigh. "No, I'm not mad at you. But I don't know how to feel if I'm not mad at myself."

"Come on," I said. "It's so hot, I'm sweating through my bra. Let's go back."

I didn't want to suggest anything beyond that. I didn't know if Jace was ready for anything else. But he got up with me, and we started our walk. The sea breeze had kicked up, fanning our faces with its warm touch. Out in the river, a pair of dolphins flashed their backs as they arced through the low, twinkling waves.

A few minutes later, walking under the oak trees in silence, he took my hand.

BEFORE HE LEFT, Jace kissed me goodbye, a friendly kiss, a kiss that made me wonder if our affair was over. He told me he had a lot to think about, and he said he wanted to buy me breakfast — tomorrow.

I figured tomorrow was better than never, so I smiled and told him I was looking forward to it. And then he was off in his sleek car, and I remembered that I'd left my own crappy car at the theater.

Oh, well. My fault for not insisting on a ride. The walk wasn't bad, and it offered an opportunity to work off some of my angst. I usually walked on the weekends, anyway, and I tried to do a yoga class sometime during the week, though I'd been forgoing them since we started prepping for *Midsummer at Midnight.*

When I got to the Chamberlain, it was nearly noon. I used my key card to get inside and went up to the costume shop. A couple of the volunteer seamstresses who only worked weekends were there, and I joined them for an hour, pinning patterns and sewing seams. I felt a lot more grounded when I left. Crazy guys may come and go, but at least I had my costumes.

By the time Sunday morning came around, I was reasonably rested and ready to take Jace in stride, in whatever form he arrived. He picked me up at 11, and I directed him to one of my favorite new brunch spots, the Heckled Hen. It was a couple of blocks off the main drag, but it was obvious people had found it; we had to wait ten minutes before we were seated.

"What's so great about this place?" Jace asked as he perused the menu, which was glued to a piece of wood.

"The chef goes for locally sourced ingredients when possible, and he puts a tasty twist on just about everything."

"Such as?"

"Well, I don't eat bacon, but this place has a sriracha

maple candied bacon that my friends can't stop talking about. Oh, and booze."

He chuckled. "Booze is special?"

"Great cocktails and mimosas."

"Sold," he said, ordering a smoky whiskey drink that came with a piece of bacon, along with a crab cake Benedict and a side of — yes — the maple bacon. I asked for a grapefruit mimosa and the Captain Crunch French toast.

"I know it's not health food, but it's so good. Kind of like all that bacon," I said with a smile as our drinks and the generous helping of meat arrived.

"This isn't good for my boyish figure," he said, biting into a piece. "But who fucking cares? It's delicious."

"It kind of makes me wish I wasn't a fishatarian, but I have to have some standards."

"Then I'm surprised you're seen with me," he joked. Knowing his insecurities, the joke wasn't as funny as it should have been. I looked around. In the crowded restaurant, he drew more than a few stares. I hadn't even thought about the attention he garnered wherever he went, I was so wrapped up in the idea of seeing him again.

And then I saw a face that made me want to walk out.

Too late.

"Jace Edison?" the columnist said, swaggering, as usual, up to our booth. "I'm Joe Stier, with *The Bugle*. I'd love to interview you for the paper."

Jace had seen him before, of course, when Jace was masked as Angelo, but he didn't let on.

"Nice to meet you," Jace said, reluctantly taking Joe's hand in a brief shake, then glancing at me.

"We've met," I said darkly.

"And you haven't put in my request for an interview? Tsk,

tsk," Joe said in his smarmy way.

"I forwarded it to the marketing department," I said. "Haven't you heard from them?"

"Oh, they said they were working on something for the play, but I was hoping for more access. After all, you're in town. It's a great opportunity," Joe said to Jace.

Jace's talents as an actor were never more in evidence, at least to me. He was polite and utterly untouchable. "I'll look forward to the interview that marketing sets up," he said. "Have a nice brunch."

Joe, flummoxed by the cordial brush-off, took a step back. "Uh, OK. I'll see you then." He turned toward me and scanned my outfit — tight navy blue capri pants and an off-the-shoulder navy and white striped shirt, with a broad band of blue at the neckline trimmed with an off-center bow. It hugged my curves and let about an inch of my midriff show. He smiled his sleazy smile. "I hope I see a lot more of you, Penelope."

My skin crawled as Joe went around the corner, presumably back to his table. "Creep. He has no right to be so familiar with me."

"Angelo should have kicked his ass," Jace said, sipping his whiskey drink. His expression was bland, but there was something close to fury in his tone.

I lowered my voice. "Angelo was busy fucking some slut. At least, that's what I heard."

"Disgraceful." A smile tugged at the corner of his delicious lips. "But Angelo told me that evening was the best he'd had in years."

"Really?" I couldn't suppress my genuine surprise.

"Of course." His foot bumped mine under the table.

"Are you doing OK after yesterday?" I asked after a

moment, heartened by his touch, even if it was sneaker to sandal.

"I've been thinking. Even if I can't rationalize my fear, I need to face it anyway."

"You're going to be Demetrius?" I cursed the trace of excitement in my voice, but to have him feel game enough to do it — and to have Jace Edison on stage in Bohemia, in one of my costumes — was thrilling on multiple levels.

He smiled. "I think so. I'll tell them tomorrow. But it's still going to be like walking a tightrope."

"I believe in you," I said simply as the rest of our food arrived. His eyes darkened with emotion, and then it was gone, and he was raving about the food. I tried his, and he tried mine, and for a few minutes, it was easy to forget the tragic past in favor of the pleasant present.

"You OK to drive?" I asked when we stepped out of the restaurant, stuffed.

"One drink versus all that bacon? No problem," he said, patting his belly. "Though I feel a need for a walk."

"How about a beach walk, if you don't mind driving us to your place? It's been forever since I walked on the beach, and I like to look for shells. Someday I'm going to make a costume that's entirely encrusted with shells."

"For what character?"

"Oh, I don't know yet. I'll know her when I see her."

"Sometimes you just know." He smiled, and my heart fluttered. "Let's do it, then."

Jace changed into swim trunks and nothing else (for which I was more than thankful), while I left my heeled sandals on his deck before descending to the sand.

"Ouch, it's hot." I led the way as we picked our way to the cooler, wet sand where the tide was just starting to go out.

The waves had left a thin, undulating line of colorful debris, a universe of little shells, along the sloping beach.

"You could take your shirt off," Jace suggested.

"I could, but there's nothing underneath, and Bohemia Beach isn't exactly the French Riviera."

"Now I'm going to think of nothing but your breasts for the next twenty minutes."

I grinned. The morose Jace of yesterday was gone. This was fun Jace, sexy Jace. I enjoyed his company, even as I wondered if I — if any woman — would ever find room in his heart after the way he lost Lauren.

It doesn't matter. I leaned down and scooped up a couple of colorful scallop shells, hiding my face from his scrutiny. *Pretend it doesn't matter, because it doesn't. He'll be gone in a couple of months, and you don't have any use for long-term boyfriends anyway.*

With that decision made, there was still something I wanted to ask him as we walked and waded, chasing tiny shorebirds that ran through the surf ahead of us.

"You know I do the pinup modeling, right?"

"I do, and I'd love to see you at work," he said, scanning my body.

"That's great news, because I'm doing a shoot next Saturday at the vintage car show, and it would be great if you came."

"Antique cars? That sounds cool."

"Only, there's something else. It's for charity, and — " I raised both eyebrows at him, hoping he'd catch on.

"And you want me to donate?"

"No, not exactly. It's for a calendar that will benefit the Humane Society, and we're recruiting guys to pose with us for certain months. We've got a couple of firefighters, a soccer player, a guitar player from a local rockabilly band, a hunky historian who's going to do the geek thing, and Wyatt Brooks, the surfer, and . . . "

"And?" He seemed to be enjoying my discomfiture.

"OK, I'll just come out and say it. It's the opinion of all involved that having Jace Edison in one or two photos would do wonders for sales of the calendar. And for all the homeless puppies and kittens," I added in a pleading voice.

He laughed. "You don't have to put on the big sell. I'll be happy to do it."

"Really?"

"I've done some modeling. This can't be as bad as some of the shoots I've done. Though I got this watch out of one of them." He pointed to the silver timepiece on his wrist, a thing of beauty.

"You're going to get a terrible tan line."

"Oh, hell, you're right." He immediately unfastened the watch and dropped it into his pocket.

"See. You're already thinking about how you're going to look on stage."

"I guess I am. That's probably a good thing, right?"

I stopped in front of him and embraced him, reassured him, enjoying the feel of his warm skin. I leaned into him and sucked on his bottom lip, then touched his upper lip with my tongue. His response was immediate. His mouth opened and slanted over mine. His hands slipped to my buttocks and pulled me against him, where I felt the stirrings of his arousal beneath his swim shorts.

We kissed, losing ourselves to our bodies in the hot, dreamy sun as the waves roared in our ears, until Jace broke it off. "I need you back at my place right now, or something very naughty is going to happen on this beach."

"Something unacceptable even on the French Riviera?" I whispered.

"Not sure. They're French. But probably."

I laughed and took his hand, hanging on to the moment, and we ran back to the beach house.

IT's funny how Mondays were still Mondays, even in a job you loved. After a weekend that wavered between mind-blowing sex and overwrought emotion, settling into my little office was almost agony.

I'd spent the night with Jace, and he'd dropped me at my place this morning. I took the scooter in, wondering how his conversation with the directors was going. I knew they'd be thrilled. I didn't care to wonder whether they were thrilled with me. I had nothing to do with Jace's decision to take the stage. I only wanted what was best for him.

Though I did delight in the idea of costuming his lithe body.

I'd already done the sketches for Demetrius, but I wanted to make the costume even darker for Jace's coloring and the jacket more dramatic for his profile. I called back my design and worked on it all morning, and then I called Jace, office to office.

"How'd it go?" I asked when he answered.

"Oh, it's you. Thank God. If one more theater person drops by my office to gush at me, I'm going to throw up."

"Hang in there. I'm not going to gush at you, but would you mind terribly coming to the costume shop so we can take your measurements?"

"Can I be naked?"

I laughed out loud. "As much as we'd all enjoy that, given how many people are likely to be there, no."

"It would be more accurate. Am I going to have a codpiece?" he teased.

"No! You've seen the designs. They're more modern than that, though I've tweaked yours. Demetrius's, that is."

"Will I be carrying pink handcuffs?"

"Hush, you rascal!" My face — and other parts — heated as he chuckled. "Just come to the costume shop, OK? Do you have time now?"

"Of course, my lady," he said in that put-on English accent, and I wished I were meeting him somewhere a lot more private.

I got to the room just before he did, and his arrival caused a sensation among the three stitchers on duty, along with manager Midge, draper Arlene, and assistants Theresa and Millie. Jace charmed them all, and soon they were almost fighting to measure his shoulders and waist and, be still my heart, his inseam.

Millie seemed flustered when she got to that point.

"Perhaps Penelope can do that one," Jace said, and the women tittered and stepped back as I took the tape measure, raised an eyebrow at him and knelt in front of him. He watched me with interest as I stretched the tape measure up the inside of his leg and barked out a number to Millie.

"He's a tall one," Midge said with approval.

I stood next to him, more embarrassed than I should have been. "And he has an enormous head."

Jace murmured in my ear as they laughed: "It's always nice seeing you on your knees in the middle of the afternoon."

I leaned in and whispered, too: "All you have to do is ask,

my lord." I smirked as he quickly took his leave and headed back to his office. I wondered if any of them noticed the hint of a bulge at his crotch.

"You're a lucky girl, Penelope," Millie said, a dreamy look in her eyes.

I looked at her, then looked around at the other smiling women. "Oh, shit. Does everybody know?"

Midge laughed. "Of course they do, honey. Do you want to answer a couple of Arlene's questions about Hermia's dress?"

And then it was back to business. Rehearsals this week were Monday through Thursday, since Dirk was letting the actors off Friday for the Memorial Day weekend, and there was a renewed sense of urgency in the cast. I didn't see much of Jace as the week wore on, except at rehearsal. We all worked long, exhausting days.

Then again, maybe I had put him off once or twice when I could have easily said yes. As much as I wanted him, and as much as I usually valued no-strings attachments, we were getting to know each other in a way that made me want to feel more valued than a typical e-date. I wanted to be more than a lay at the end of the day. Sure, I was being irrational, but feelings weren't rational, were they? I promised him that once we got through this crazy week, I'd see him again, hoping by then I'd have my expectations under control.

Besides, rehearsals were demanding for Jace, too. He had a whole new mountain to climb as Demetrius. In his version of the play, Demetrius was a bigger role on which many of the themes turned, even though it wasn't as major as Oberon.

The rest of the cast was unsettled on the first couple of nights, one, because they seemed to miss Paul's familiar if drunken presence, and two, because they were acting with a two-time Tony nominee. But Jace was gracious, and more than that, he was damned good. His professionalism seemed to elevate everyone in mood and performance. He appeared to have no fear on stage. But one night, when a dozen board members poked their heads in after a meeting to see the rehearsal, he had a coughing fit and exited backstage. I intercepted him among the props in the dark Attic and hugged him. And kissed him. And then we groped each other for a bit until we started laughing at the foolishness of it all, with the theater full of people. He went back on stage; the visitors were gone, and he did fine.

By Thursday, everyone had dispensed with their scripts, though there was a lot of frantic cribbing in the green room between scenes. Jace subtly prompted those who forgot their lines; he practically had his whole play memorized.

I spent part of my days working on shaping Bottom's donkey head. I had Doug's measurements and started constructing a base, the inner layer that would serve as his cap. I used heavy leather straps that would support the metal. After an hour in an ancient hardware store downtown, I came up with thin copper tubing and fine copper wire for the horse head. Both would take a dent out of our budget. I also found bits of metal that would add to the funky look of the piece, and at a computer repair shop, I asked for and got some old logic boards I could cut up and add for texture.

I still had the problem of the virtual-reality glasses. I knew I wanted them to have one lens, but a two-eyed frame, and I wanted the frame lined with LED lights. They would essentially be see-through, so the actors' faces were visible, because all of the players would don similar glasses for their video-game version of *Pyramus and Thisbe,* the play within the play. If I could get a special control for Bottom's head that

Doug could hit at certain moments in the script, making the glasses sparkle, that would be even better.

Unfortunately, engineering was a little outside of my skill set.

Karen was busy with the sets, but she agreed to set up a meeting Friday afternoon in the busy scenery shop with someone she thought could help me. I laughed when I saw it was Damien. I dropped my bag of metal tubing, leather and accents onto a work table and gave him a hug.

"So you're the helpless creature I'm here to save," he joked. He was in black from head to toe, though since it was summer, he'd acquiesced to a T-shirt and long shorts. His eyeliner was more elaborate than mine today, and his puff of long, spiky black hair seemed untouched by the humidity.

"I just need a little engineering help," I said. "You're not an engineer, are you?"

"It seems like it these days. You saw my piece last fall at the regional show at the art museum? The monitors and the software component? I'm building something right now on commission that's twice as elaborate."

"Nice. This should be cake, then." I explained to him what I wanted to do with the donkey head. I'd already shaped the main pieces of tubing, and when I held the head up, it indeed had an equine look. Before long, Damien was soldering the joints, and I was creating small sleeves to attach to the leather to hold the straps and tubes together.

"As for the glasses," he said, holding the bare bones of the donkey head, "I have some ideas. Give me a week, OK? All I need is a piece of copper, and I'll come up with something to match your drawing."

"Are you sure you have time?"

"Since my love life is a barren desert at the moment, yes," he said grouchily.

"Just hang around the theater some more, and that will change," I joked.

"It worked for you, or so I hear."

I put my hands on my hips. "What have you heard?"

"That you're dating the Babe of Broadway. I guess you didn't need my gaydar after all. What am I missing?"

"Shut up. It's not exactly dating — it's more like, um . . . "

"Fucking? Even better."

"Shut up!" I looked around to make sure no carpenters were listening. Most of them were at the other end of the big room, beating an innocent park bench with hammers, trying to weather it.

"What? He's no good?"

"Damien, don't be impossible." I lowered my voice to a whisper. "He's fantastic."

"And you know that from one time?"

I looked at him askance.

"Well," he said, "you usually do 'em once before you hang 'em out to dry. Not that I blame you."

"It's not like that. I don't know what it's like, honestly."

"That's a good sign," he said mildly, turning the headpiece over in his hands. "Can I have the whole head? I promise I'll get it back to you in time to add whatever gewgaws you find necessary. Sometime next week. If you let me take the wire, too, I'll fill in just enough to give it body. Like your drawing. Or I could really work it up, if you give me everything. You want me to do that?"

"I would *love* it if you did that. You're awesome."

"I know," he said, sounding bored, but his blue eyes sparkled. "Tell my sister hi tomorrow."

"Will do." Cali was shooting the calendar shots at the car show Saturday. I'd almost forgotten.

"And don't wear out your actor before he graces our stage with his presence."

"Not possible," I muttered, and Damien let out a whoop of laughter.

Once Damien was on his way, I went to find Jace. He'd been on my mind even before my goofy conversation with Damien, not to mention he'd given me a ride to work this morning. He'd brought coffee again, and I'd offered him a biscotti, along with a bag that contained the outfit I wanted him to wear for the car show shoot. And since I wasn't riding my scooter, I'd dressed up, in a retro dress in black with big white polka dots and a halter neckline that beautifully showed off my assets. He'd given me the once-over and practically growled.

"I've missed you this week," he'd said.

"You see me every night," I'd answered.

"Rehearsal doesn't count. Tonight, I'm making up for lost time."

I couldn't wait, either.

Now, Jace's office door was open, and he was on the phone. "Yes. All right. June the fourth is fine. Thanks."

He hung up with a sigh.

"What's June 4?" I asked.

"Media day. They're setting up several interviews in the theater with me and Dirk. I insisted they involve Titania and Oberon, too."

"Holland is going to love that."

He grinned. "I know. I wondered, would you mind running a few lines with me after dinner tonight? I know my own play, but I just don't feel like I've been able to deliver the nuances of Demetrius's speech to Helena, and that needs to be perfect. And I've rewritten it, like, ten times."

"Even this week?"

"Especially this week," he said.

"It was beautiful before."

"The core is there, but it's shifted to better show his change of heart. Anyway, Dirk has declared that rewrites are over, so we're stuck with this version."

I chuckled. "Unless you sneak one or two more in."

"Right." Jace smiled and let his gaze rove from my shiny black heels to my red lips. His eyes were full of mischief. "Ready to go?"

I nodded with pleasure, and we headed out to dinner.

"I'M NOT SURE the gnocchi was a good idea," I said as we slipped back into the empty theater after dinner. We'd had fantastic Italian food, and the gorgonzola cream sauce on mine had been delicious, but now I was as full as a tick. And the bottle of red wine we'd killed wasn't helping.

"But it was so good," said Jace, who'd had a bite of my pasta. "And my veal was excellent. Are you not up for this?"

"I'll be fine. I just need to grab my water bottle, and I'll be ready to go." That and a couple of the antacid tablets I kept in my office.

When I entered the main stage after downing a bunch of water, I felt better, if a tad apprehensive. Jace had already switched on a couple of lights, just enough to make a glow in the middle of the performance space. It was eerily quiet: no hammering, no yammering actors, just us.

"We could have done this in the black box," I said.

"What's the fun in that? Besides, the more I get used to being on this stage, the better."

The acknowledgment of his continuing stage fright made my heart soften. OK, it was already softened; it was threatening to turn into pudding. I took another long drink of water and set down the bottle with my bag.

"Are you worried about this?" I asked him. "You've got this."

"I'm working on it. It's not just being on stage that's worrying me at the moment. I'm wondering if all my modernizations are going to make the Shakespeareans run screaming. Making the Duke Hermia's father, the game designers, all that."

"It takes balls to rewrite Shakespeare, but Shakespeare would have approved. He twisted other people's stories constantly for his own ends."

"True."

"Do you have your new pages for me? You didn't do any rewriting while I was upstairs, did you?"

Jace passed me a handful of papers. "Rewrites are good for the soul."

"And bad for the trees."

"Ready to get started?"

"I'm not sure," I said. "Can I look these pages over? Do you want me to read the stage directions, too?"

"Fair Helena, wouldst thou focus?"

"Oh, geez, they're not talking in thees and thous now, are they?" I glanced over the pages; this modern Helena had more lines than Shakespeare had given her, and Demetrius's dialogue was ten times as long in Jace's version.

"Nervous?" He raised an eyebrow at me. "Babbling is often a sign."

"Of course not!" I exclaimed, but he was right. I was about to read a scene with a real stage star, and as well as I knew him, it still seemed an otherworldly moment. I tried to find a calm center, the heart of my character, the way I had back in school. I took a deep breath. "I await your cue."

"I'm not going to go through all this preamble, but if you'd read Mr. Duke's lines after Hermia and Lysander exit, and then read Helena's, that'd be great."

"I can do that." I hoped.

With fascination, I watched his posture subtly shift, the muscles in his face change as he became Demetrius, ready to plead his case. He had no script; he was completely immersed in the part.

His voice resonated in the empty theater. "I came here because I wanted Hermia, Mr. Duke."

"And I wanted you to want her," I said, putting on a deep Mr. Duke voice. "No reason why you shouldn't want her. I wanted you to marry her."

"But she wanted Lysander."

"What do wants matter? We had a deal, Demetrius."

"A deal that would have broken not one heart but, as I realize it now, two," Jace said.

"Or three," I said in Helena's voice, and then in the Duke's: "I thought you loved Hermia."

"So did I," Jace declared, "but now I realize that I only wanted her the way a boy wants a shiny toy. She's beautiful, but she was just a trophy, a symbol of the deal I wanted to make with you. She's a worthy woman, but she's not the one I want."

"What do you want?" I said in Mr. Duke's voice.

"Something's happened to me out here in the woods, and now I want more."

"Well, I want a drink," I said as Mr. Duke, "and Hippolyta. Come to the wedding, Demetrius, and we'll talk. *Duke, exit stage left.*"

I walked in that direction, then spun around and trotted back to center stage.

"Go after him," I said as Helena. "You can save your deal."

"The only deal I want is right in front of me. All I see is you." Jace's gentle intensity almost knocked the wind out of me.

"You see me as a joke," I read from the pages. "You and Lysander have mocked me all night, chasing me around the park, telling me how much you love me. And now that you've had a good night's sleep, you want to make fun of me again."

"But it wasn't a good night's sleep," Jace said, his eyes earnest, his brow creased with anxiety. "Last night I dreamed, and in that dream I loved you. But now I'm awake, truly awake, and I see you for what you are."

"I know what you see. A woman who's always the last to get sent a cocktail or asked on a date. Hermia's wing-woman. A girl who hasn't been able to get your attention in years, except when it was to answer the question, 'Where's Hermia?' The truth is, you've been cruel, Demetrius. I know how little I'm worth in your eyes."

The words sucked me in. Maybe I'd been the pretty Hermia much of my adult life, but I'd also been Helena, never hoping for more. Never believing in myself when it came to men.

"I can't change the past," Jace said. "But the past has changed me. Last night showed me that all my years of ambition were misplaced. I've wanted the wrong things. I didn't know that I really wanted you, Helena."

"You're just trying to save face now that Hermia and Lysander have found each other."

"No. I'm trying to save my chances with you, so many wasted chances. Oh, Helena. If you could see yourself through my newly opened eyes — eyes that can see all of you, inside and out. The brains I never gave you credit for. The heart of a loyal friend. The persistence that kept you after me until today — Helena, don't turn away from me now," he said as I faced the nonexistent audience. "I was sick before, and I didn't realize that you were my medicine. Look up."

He stepped behind me and put his hands on my shoulders, leaning close to deliver his next lines. "Look at the moon. It's beautiful. It's the end and the beginning of something new. Before I only saw time marching on. Now I see beauty." He spun me to face him and clutched my arms.

I glanced at the script. "My heart can't be broken again. It's already in too many pieces."

"That's not true. You're whole, like the moon," he said. "You're filled with the same light. Your eyes are filled with starlight. Your heart is the sun. I need your guiding light, your heat to live. You will be my constant, always, the northern star that guides me home, the sun that every morning lights me to my happiest days. You're the dream I want to keep. I'm sorry it took me so long to realize that you were what I wanted, but now I know. I love your light. I love you."

As Jace said these words, he moved closer and closer to me, looking directly into my eyes. I was transfixed; I'd read some version of the words before, but the passion he gave them set me trembling.

I dropped the pages and burst into tears.

"Helena?" Jace asked, his eyes still far away. And then, after a minute, "Penelope?"

He slipped his arms around me in a gesture that should have comforted me, but he was a stranger, Demetrius. Or was he Jace?

I broke away from him and ran into the darkness beyond the proscenium arch, back among the half-finished wooden trees, and flopped onto Titania's bower. It was a round wooden bed softened with blankets and pillows, still not dressed with the fabrics and flowers it would have in the production. Like everything on the stage, it was a simple reality that awaited the lovely lies of stagecraft.

Lovely lies like Jace's play.

It took me a minute or two of crying before I could get my burst of emotion under control. I sucked in a deep breath or two and opened my eyes.

Jace stood there amid the trees, silhouetted by the oblique light from center stage.

"Are you all right?" he asked softly.

I sat up. "I guess I was touched by your art," I croaked, trying to make a joke of my outburst.

He moved toward me in that graceful way he had and sat next to me. "I'd take that as a compliment, but I don't think it is."

"It moved me, is all." Jace didn't need to know how much, or why. How he'd struck at my empty heart. How the sound of the echo still reverberated through my body and soul.

He looked off into the darkness of backstage and spoke. "It's interesting to the writer in me that this scene is about waking up from the dream of the fairies, from the potion."

"The magical latte."

He chuckled. "Right. Because when I wrote that, even when I revised it, it *felt* like falling into a dream. Like it expressed something that I can't express in my own life. But the thrill of writing is that you channel another persona, so you can express those thoughts. And the beauty of acting is that your body believes the lie. It doesn't know that you're acting. If you tell it you're scared, or angry, or in love, your body follows, if you're doing it right."

"So," I said, "right now, you're in love with Helena."

I could barely see his face as he leaned closer to me and cupped my cheek, rubbing away a lingering tear with his thumb.

"That must be right," he whispered.

And he kissed me.

I tasted him and the salt of my own tears and the beautiful lie on his lips. Tender anguish filled his kiss, Demetrius's soul, or Jace's, or something that only happens in that veiled, magical place where imagination and acting meet. He pressed me gently against the pillows, and I slipped my arms around his neck, letting myself imagine. Letting myself believe. Love? Why not? Here, in the land of the fairies, Demetrius loved Helena, and I loved him.

Jace kissed my neck and slipped a hand under the neckline of my dress, twirling his fingers around one nipple. He drew the breast out of its hiding place and closed his mouth over it, suckling. Heat bloomed in my center, the familiar heat I always had with him, only different, more mystical as Helena let Demetrius make love to her. In slow motion, he reached under my skirt and slid his hands up my legs. I grasped his thick hair as his fingers found the lacy edge of my stockings and then the delicate thong. This time, he just pushed it aside, and then he was unzipping his pants and pushing down his underwear and rubbing his cock against my nub, my wet slit. It was all so inevitable, so fast.

With a low groan, he slid inside me.

I opened to his deep glide, wrapping one leg around his hips and arching to meet his thrusts. I moaned as the warmth became fire, as the gentleness was outstripped by need, as we crashed into each other with animal ferocity. When he came inside me, sweet lightning branched through my body, bright in the darkness, igniting sparks of pleasure that sizzled through my veins — along with a shocking realization.

He hadn't used a condom.

We'd already had that conversation, of course. The one about safety. And then the conversation about the love he'd lost, the loss he blamed on himself. And still, after that, he'd used a condom.

Until now.

Until our lie of love.

I clutched him tighter as he jerked against me twice more, breathless and hot, triggering a new spasm inside me. He caught my sigh with a long kiss, needful and scorching, bittersweet as burnt sugar. He kissed my neck, nipped my earlobe, licked the seam of my lips and kissed me again, his touch now tempered by sweetness, tenderness, making me want to believe. Here in his arms, enveloped in the dark dream of *Midsummer at Midnight,* I tasted love in his kisses. I'd never known what that was like, not really, and maybe I still didn't. Jace was a consummate actor, immersed in a role.

He made me hate myself for wanting so much, so much he couldn't give, when I knew I would only get burned.

With one last, sweet kiss, he withdrew, leaving me wetter than before and even more overwhelmed with emotion.

We still had most of our clothes on. We quietly put ourselves back together. Jace gathered the discarded pages, went up to the booth and turned out the lights, leaving only the ghost light on. I got up to get my stuff and join him. Casting long shadows, we headed for the exit.

He was courteous and quiet, his arm warm around my waist as he guided me outside to his car in the shadowy parking lot. My legs were shaky. But the more alarming quake was in my heart.

Was he *that* good of an actor? Was this was just one more of Jace's roles, one more way to have me without making it mean anything?

But it did. It did mean something. *Shit.* Even if it didn't mean anything to him, it meant something to me.

Without asking, he drove me to my place. We sat in the car and faced each other.

Jace reached out and took my hand, his face impassive. "I'd like to come in."

"I don't think so," I said with difficulty. His hand was warm, real. Even if what was happening between us — wasn't. I needed to process tonight: his passion, sans condom. My emotional reaction. I knew I was in trouble. I was building myself up for a fall. A hard one. I squeezed his hand once and let it go. "Can you pick me up in the morning for the car show? Nine o'clock?"

He was quiet for a moment, searching my face. "All right, my lady."

"And wear your costume."

"Am I going to like it?"

"You'd better," I teased, trying to make light of the moment.

Jace smiled, but his dark eyes were cloudy. "Thank you, Penelope."

I nodded, got out and watched him drive off, wondering exactly what he was thanking me for.

PART 3

J had two ensembles lined up for the pinup shoot. Betty Lane, who was organizing the calendar, had told me to prepare for a photo with a 1950 Oldsmobile. I needed a knockout outfit to go with the suit I'd prepared for Jace, so I chose a dress I made a couple of years ago, based on one Marilyn Monroe had worn. It was a scarlet wiggle dress that hugged my curves, with cap sleeves that almost fell off the shoulder; a wide, low-cut V-neck; and a bow that tied the fabric between the breasts. Below that was a diamond-shaped opening. Over my belly, matching buttons allowed for two more keyhole gaps in the fabric, almost down to my belly button. This dress revealed a tad more skin than Marilyn's, though it stopped just below the knee. Shiny, precipitously tall black heels and red rhinestone clip-on earrings completed the outfit.

I also had a swimsuit for a to-be-named scene. Although I did my hair and made up my face to perfection, I packed a kit in case anyone needed a touchup during what looked to be a beastly hot day.

For now, I wore vintage, high-waisted shorts, a halter top and wedge heels: comfy retro until I had to change into my stuff. I was standing in front of my Victorian apartment house with a garment bag and a big tote when Jace pulled up.

"Running away, little girl?" he asked as I got in the car.

I checked him out: black pinstripe pants, cream-colored shirt open at the neck, dark suspenders, snazzy black and cream wingtips. Debonair. *Hot.* His jacket was folded between the seats, fedora on top.

"If I can run away with you, sure," I said with a grin, pleased that I wasn't the emotional mess I'd been the night before. Still, I felt giddy when I saw him, and I knew that wasn't good. The feeling went way beyond physical attraction.

"I hope I don't melt in this," he said, oblivious to my angst.

"Did you bring a change for after?"

"Absolutely. You?"

"Uh, yeah, this isn't for the photo shoot. All that's in the bags."

"Good God," he said, his eyes lingering on my legs and burning me all the way up to my belly, cleavage, lips and eyes. "This is your casual wear?"

"For a vintage car show, yeah."

"Maybe I will run away with you," he said under his breath as we rolled out.

I gave him directions to the historical museum, which adjoined a big lakefront park stuffed with flashy carnival rides. We parked as close as we could, then walked to the lakefront, where the cars were lined up — gleaming restored beauties from days gone by and the occasional rebellious, remodeled rat rod.

"Penelope!"

I looked around and saw Betty Lane, curvy and luscious

in a retro black bikini. Her wavy brown hair was pinned up on one side with a large, red hibiscus flower. We walked over, and I made the introductions.

"Thanks so much for doing this, Jace," she said, only mildly gushing.

"Happy to help, though you'd better hurry, before I sweat through these clothes."

"We'll do you next," she said, "but I want Penelope to do the swimsuit scene first. A bunch of us are going to do a shot with Wyatt Brooks over by that Mercury Monterey."

"What is that, 1955?" I asked, marveling at the bright blue-green paint, shiny chrome trim and gleaming wood panels on the wagon.

"Marvelous," Jace said as we moved closer. To his credit, he was looking at the car and not the cluster of my pinup friends hanging around in their swimsuits, sporting parasols. I spotted Cali several cars away, by a cherry-red 1956 Cadillac convertible, shooting a hunky firefighter with a kitten and another of the girls. She glanced up, and we exchanged a wave. Wyatt leaned against a car behind her, watching with amusement, his arm around a vintage longboard.

"Dressing room is there," Betty Lane said, pointing to a retro camper. "Come back in your swimsuit, and then we'll do your bit. What's your concept?"

"He might be a private eye. He might be a gangster. Either way, he's dangerous. I'm a femme fatale."

"You certainly are," Jace said.

"So are you. Dangerous, I mean." I raised an eyebrow at him. "You'll be OK while I change?"

"I have plenty to look at." He winked.

I rolled my eyes and took a step toward the trailer.

"Wait a minute." He cupped my elbow and pulled me

closer. "Thou art more lovely and more temperate," he whispered before slanting his lips across mine in a sweet, sultry kiss.

I sucked in a breath as he released me. Dizzy, I managed a nod and escaped to the trailer. If he was going to keep quoting Shakespeare at me, I had no chance at all.

I emerged in a navy and white retro bikini, with high-waisted bottoms and a halter top, trimmed in stripes and buttons and a couple of tiny bows. I still wore the wedge heels.

"Ahoy," Jace said appreciatively.

"Thanks." I smiled, but I felt shy all of a sudden. And I was never shy. This guy was seriously screwing with my balance.

"Let's go, ladies!" Betty Lane called from the Mercury. The pinups — ten, including me, in a rainbow of vintage-style swimsuits — gathered around the car. Wyatt moseyed over, too, holding the pretty wooden surfboard. It was trimmed with aqua that matched the car.

"OK, Wyatt," Cali said. "It's time."

Her boyfriend had a pained look on his face, but he set down the board, grasped his T-shirt by the hem and pulled it over his head. The appreciative murmurs among my friends almost made me laugh, especially when I saw Cali trying not to giggle. At least she wasn't overcome by jealousy, which was saying something when Wyatt's tan, muscled surfer body was a beacon to any red-blooded female.

He pushed back his dark, longish hair. The sun caught the unusual white streak in it and gave him a rakish look. He picked up the board again, leaned it against the bumper and stood in front of the car.

"Wyatt prefers to be behind the camera," Cali said. "Gather around him, girls. Don't be afraid to touch."

Wyatt scowled at her, his eyes promising revenge, but she just laughed. We all assumed perky positions, most standing, with a couple of women on one knee or sitting coquettishly. Cali took a bunch of shots, lining us up in one picture, and in another having us hold the surfboard above our heads. She even got us all more or less in the car at one point, though that lasted about a minute before we all tumbled out laughing and hot.

"Come here," Cali called to Wyatt, and she planted a big kiss on his mouth. He returned her smile — and put his shirt back on.

"Final costume changes," Betty Lane called out. "Pen and Jace, you're next."

I nodded and hastened to the trailer, noticing the other women's interest in my actor friend. Not boyfriend, I reminded myself. A few came up to talk to him, and he was polite and friendly, the way he'd been to everyone at the theater — at least up to the point when Holland threw herself at him.

I changed in record time, given the elaborate lingerie that went under the red dress, and emerged to find Jace waiting by the trailer door. He had on his jacket, tie and fedora now.

"Thank God," he said. "The sharks were circling. And don't you look delicious."

"Thanks, pretty boy."

Damn if he didn't pinch my ass.

"I think our decades are a little mixed up," Betty Lane said as we walked over to the 1950 Oldsmobile, an "88" four-door sedan in black. "But if you two are playing the '40s or the '50s, I'll buy it."

"I'm channeling Sam Spade," Jace said.

"I thought the suit said 'Humphrey Bogart,' " I admitted. "And you look crazy cool in it."

"Not as good as you look in that dress," he replied, a low fire banked in his dark eyes.

"OK, you two," Cali said, getting a flash stand in place. "Betty Lane, you have the prop?"

"I almost forgot," she said, rummaging in her bag and pulling out a gun.

"What?" Jace exclaimed.

"It's fake," she said, nonchalant. "Don't worry. I told the security staff we were doing this. I don't think they'll shoot you."

"Very comforting," he murmured as I chuckled.

I unbuttoned his jacket so he could stuff the pistol in his waistband. I loosened his tie, too. "Make sure they can see the suspenders. Very retro."

"Just lean up against the car, like that," Cali said as we fell into position. Jace put an arm around me. "Give me cocky."

I shot a sidelong glance at Jace, and he did look cocky. And sexy. Speaking of cocky, I cocked my hip, put a hand on it and pursed my lips.

"Damn, you two are cover material," Cali said as she fired off several shots. It was clear Jace had done his share of professional modeling. He moved often and responded deftly to direction. I did the same, making a mental note to go back and look at that spread he'd done for one of the men's magazines, where a shirt cost about the same as several months of my rent.

"Let's try a few in the back seat," Cali said.

"Shall we mop the sweat from our brow?" I asked.

"Absolutely not," she said. "I want you to do a little play-acting. Like you're just about to make out, and you're hot anyway."

"Uh, this is for the humane society, isn't it?" I asked. "Non-bohemian?"

"We'll keep it clean," Cali said. "Mostly. This is a pinup calendar. We have to titillate a little. And I know you have stockings on under that dress."

Jace raised his eyebrows.

"If the pics are too hot," she went on, "I'll send you the photos and none the wiser."

"All right." I sighed and crawled into the large back seat, Jace right behind me.

"Lie back, Penelope," Cali ordered. She'd clearly turned into Napoleon, so I went with it. "Against the corner, where the door meets the seat, so we see more of you. Jace, lean in like you're about to kiss her. Grab the hem of her dress."

Cali started snapping as Jace leaned over me.

Oh, my. I looked up at his shadowed face. His dark eyebrows were angled in concentration as he gazed at my lips, and something hard was pressing against my leg.

"Is that a gun in your pocket, or are you just happy to see me?"

"Both," he murmured, tossing the prop into the front seat and ignoring Cali's stream of instructions. He gave up his pose and kissed my chin, my neck. He looked down the length of my body and pulled the hem of my tight dress above my knee, then to mid-thigh, exposing the black lace edge of the stockings.

"Oh, yeah, that's it," Cali chattered. "Especially with you looking at her bod like that. Pen, just close your eyes and open your mouth. You're carried away."

That took no acting at all as Jace delicately ran a finger up my leg and swirled it on the bare skin above the stocking. With my eyes closed, there was only sensation and Cali's voice, now blurred in my consciousness as I gripped Jace's shoulder with one hand. He was tugging at my neckline, revealing at least the top of the bra, almost revealing much more. And then his lips were on mine, and I wrapped my arms around his neck, moaning into his mouth.

"OK, guys. OK, that's enough," I vaguely heard Cali say. And then she, or someone, shut the door, leaving us alone, and Jace's hand slipped between my legs.

"We can't do this here," I whispered as he tongued my ear and his finger stroked my thin, damp underpants.

"I'm not going to do anything," he whispered, kissing me again. "You're going to come."

"No, not here," I said again, though against my will, my body bucked against his hand.

"No one can see. Come for me, Penelope," he whispered. "I want to watch you fall apart. I want to make you come with just my fingers, my voice. God, you're so wet for me." He'd pulled the underwear down just enough to slip a finger inside me, seeking the spot that made my buzzer go. In a moment, he'd found it, and he stroked me until I mewled in desperate want. "That's my girl. Come for me. God, I want to put my cock inside you right now. I want to push it in your pussy. Your mouth. Every part of you that can take me."

That did it. He covered my cry with his mouth as I exploded against his hand and clutched his shoulders, and then I collapsed into his overwhelming kiss, my senses lusciously frazzled.

It took me a few minutes to cool down enough to straighten my clothes and his. I fervently hoped no one saw us, but at the same time, I just didn't care. I was boneless and oversexed and would give anything for Jace to fuck me properly.

He sat up and looked out the window, then pulled me up, too. The back door magically opened.

"You're lucky Cali kept everybody busy with photos in the back of that old Chevy pickup," Betty Lane said in a bored tone, "and that I was too busy on my phone to pay attention to what you were doing. And that Pinhead didn't see you violating his back seat."

"Hush, Betty Lane. Nothing was violated," I said.

Jace just looked amused.

"My advice?" she continued. "Get a room. And no hanky-panky in the trailer."

Jace guided me to the trailer, where I changed into the outfit I'd arrived in, and Jace put on loose khakis and a white linen shirt that did nothing to hide his magnificent physique. We only got distracted for a couple of minutes, and had our clothes half off again, when someone rattled the locked door. We hastened to get dressed and left.

"Want to walk around?" I asked him after we stowed our stuff in his car.

"I suppose, if we're not getting a room," he said in a droll tone. "And if I can walk."

"What's wrong with you?"

"I'm stiff for some reason."

I giggled. "You can walk it off and buy me some cotton candy."

"Mmm. Your hair is like cotton candy, pink and lemon." He lifted a few strands and kissed them.

"Jace," I murmured, but it was only part admonishment; it was also a noise of surrender, of desire and delight. He heard it and kissed my neck, too.

I hated losing control, and I was losing it, every inch of it, every time he kissed me, every time he touched me. Did he know that? Did he feel anything in return?

Damn it. I am not going to lose myself again. This heartbreak is even more guaranteed than the first one.

We wandered through the rest of the cars. Cali caught my eye and winked at me, and my face grew hot.

We spotted Thea, too. She was loitering behind a food truck, eating an ice cream cone, peeking around it to stare at a good-looking guy with unruly reddish-brown hair who was carrying around a video camera and interviewing people.

"Thea?" I called.

She jumped at the sound of my voice and whipped her head around. "Oh, hi, Penelope."

"Jace Edison," Jace said, reaching out to shake her hand.

"H-h-hi," she sputtered, dazzled.

"Who's that?" I asked her, pointing at the guy with the camera.

Her deep blue eyes lit up. "Oh, he's a video blogger. He's really building a following. I watch all of his videos."

"Why don't you go get interviewed?"

Thea looked terrified. "No way. He's too — there's just no way. Oh, I see Sloane and Alex. I'll catch you later."

Jace and I exchanged a glance at her obvious flight, waved at Sloane and Alex and meandered down the midway. We tried a game or three, losing everything except the ring toss, where Jace defied the laws of physics and actually hooked a bottle.

The carny, as sun-browned and wrinkled as a walnut, gap-toothed with a bald spot and a gray ponytail, ran a loud bell. "Big winner! Big winners get choice! Just one ring around the bottle!" After he was done shouting, he looked at Jace. "What'll it be, son?"

Jace turned to me. "You are the first person I've ever won a stuffed animal for. Your pick."

"Aw, it's so nice to be your cliché!" I teased, surveying the goofy giant toys. "Let's see. I love tigers, but I'm not sure if I want the stuffed one or the one that's a rug."

"Given that neither seems to be any more alive than the other, I think it probably won't affect their numbers in the wild," Jace said, then whispered in my ear, "but the rug might be fun."

"The white tiger rug!" I told the carny without hesitation. Yep. Still a one-track mind.

"One flat cat, coming up," he said, using a big hook to take down the plastic-wrapped bundle of faux fur from the rack along the back of the booth.

I talked Jace into the Ferris wheel, a sentimental favorite. The county fair had been a wonderful escape once a year when I could get away from my mother and go with my friends from school.

The view in Bohemia was a bit different from where I grew up. Here, from the top of the wheel, we could see over the lake and downtown Bohemia to the lagoon, and beyond that, the thin strip of land that was the barrier island and Bohemia Beach. Clouds were building out toward the west and I-95, on the sea breeze boundary generated by the moist summer day.

I was cozy, jammed between Jace and the bagged tiger rug. Despite the heat, I snuggled into him and breathed in his scent when he put an arm around my shoulders.

"Nice place you have here," he said, appreciating the view.

"I love it," I admitted.

"You never wanted to make your way in New York or maybe try Hollywood?"

"I'm not ruling it out, but I like small theaters. And ours is growing. And there's always Orlando. There are great theaters there, and even the theme parks need costumers." My subconscious had been working on job alternatives, apparently.

"I'd love to see what you'd do with a real Broadway show."

Wow. The truth was, I'd never even considered going the New York route. Costume design wasn't exactly like acting. You didn't just show up and blow somebody away in an audition and get to do *The Lion King.* You built up a book, a resume.

"Maybe your show will go to Broadway and someone will take a small interest in the original costumes," I said.

He laughed. "I doubt it — I mean, I doubt the play will go that far. It's far too esoteric for that."

"It's entertaining, and don't underestimate the power of having Jace Edison behind it."

"If it was by Joe Smith, I don't think it would get the time of day, here or anywhere," he mused as the wheel made another slow swoop to the bottom and started to climb again.

"False humility," I said, none too kindly. "I'm not going to go over your list of talents and accomplishments again. You make me feel like such a slacker."

"Are we that different?"

"Oh, Jace." I watched the world drop away from us again as we soared into the cloud-dotted blue sky. "Now you're talking nonsense."

"Probably."

The wheel started to jerk to brief halts to let people off and get more people on. An endless circle. People came into my life, rode the wheel and got right back off again. No, not people. Men. And I'd been on the wheel for longer than I'd ever expected with Jace, even if it had been only a month. I saw the world differently now, because I'd seen the view with him. Would the Chamberlain be enough for me now? Or would I be enough for it?

"I could use a swim," Jace said as we got off at the bottom, and I fell back into the moment. "Want to come to my place?"

"Can my tiger come?"

"I'm counting on it."

IN DAYLIGHT, Jace's pool didn't seem so private, so we both donned suits for our swim. It was pleasant to hear the salty ocean crashing onto shore while we relaxed in the cool, clean water of the pool. Decadent, really. Jace had made sandwiches, and we drank beer until the sun and the alcohol made us tipsy.

"I'm sure I got a burn today," I said as we climbed back up to the deck. I patted my cheeks. They felt warm and tender. "I used sunscreen, too."

"You have a healthy glow," Jace said, dropping his towel on the railing.

I did the same and followed him inside, admiring the definition of the muscles under his tanned skin. "I'm glad you didn't burn — sunburns make actors look like steamed lobsters under the stage lights, and we've had quite a few at the Chamberlain."

"Amateurs," Jace joked.

I didn't laugh. He was exactly right. "I suppose we are."

"Not you," he said, turning around and grabbing me by

the waist, his hands warm on my skin. "Besides, you'll look better with a burn."

"Am I really burned?" I touched my cheeks again and looked down at the curve of my breasts above the bikini. They had the slightest blush of pink.

"That's not the kind of burn I'm talking about." He kissed my cheek, his lips damp on the dry heat of my skin. Then he retrieved my carnival prize and held it up. "Rug burn, my lady?" He made the invitation with raised eyebrows.

I laughed. "Oh, I don't think I'm ready to do anything so unnatural to that tiger."

"He's fake, and it would be the most natural thing in the world."

"See, you already called it a 'he,' " I jested, though the idea of Jace having me on a rug, any rug, made my temperature run even hotter, especially given the alcohol fizzing in my veins. "We can't abuse the poor thing."

"I don't want to do anything to the *tiger*," he said, echoing my laugh. "I want to do terrible things to you."

I took a few steps closer, took off my bikini top and dropped it. "Oh, yeah? What kinds of things?"

"Penelope . . . " His voice was low and rough. "Do you want this to go slow or fast?"

I wriggled out of the bottoms and left them where they lay, taking another step closer. I looked him in the eye.

"Fast and hard," I said.

He dropped the silly tiger. In one step, he swept his arms under me and carried me to the much more plush white rug in the middle of the living room floor and practically dropped me on it. He yanked off his swim briefs and dropped down on top of me. I sank into the softness as he pressed against my body. He squeezed my breasts, and I cried out; he dipped a finger in my slit. Wet, of course. Around him, I seemed to be in a constant state of arousal.

"Beg for it," he whispered.

"I don't think I need to beg for it. Ahhh," I gasped as he slipped a second finger inside me. He worked magic with those fingers. "I think you want it so bad you'll give it to me anyway."

"You're right," he said. "I want it, and you'll take it." In a swift move, he shifted so his knees straddled my chest. Looking up, all I saw was a tower of lean muscle and a long, hard cock.

Now I did want to beg him, beg him to fuck my pussy; that's where I really wanted him right now, where I ached for him. But his erection, moist at the tip, hovered above me.

"Lick it," he said.

I did, slowly, taking the moisture off the tip, then swirling my tongue around the head. His eyes glowed with almost feral intensity.

"Yesss," he hissed, moving slightly against my lips.

I opened to him, taking his hot length into my mouth. He slid in slowly, mindful of his position of power, and I sucked. He groaned, pulling out, pushing in again, pulling all the way out.

"Now what do you have to say to me?" he asked, in that role I loved, commanding, driven by lust.

"Fuck me. Please, Jace."

"Fuck you where?"

"Right here between my legs. I need your cock, baby," I crooned.

"Yes, you fucking do," he said, shifting back down my body. He held his length in his hand and looked at me for a long moment, laid out for him on the floor, my arms thrown out to the sides, my breasts peaked and red for him. "And I need you, Penelope."

My heart skipped a beat.

He could have put on a condom, gone back to what he'd been before last night, before Demetrius and Helena's tryst backstage. Before that moment had whispered of love, however illusory.

He didn't. He notched his tip in my cleft and plunged.

I cried out in pleasure, and a little in pain, driven against the floor, the rug. His cock impaled me, delivered me of my senses, and I grasped his hips. opened my legs wider and lifted myself to meet his staccato thrusts. This was the hard and fast fuck I'd wanted, after that little tease of my mouth, and Jace delivered with primal proficiency. The orgasm ripped through me like a tornado, and I cried out as he kept pounding, pounding, until finally he surged inside of me with a gasp and a shudder that I answered with another. He collapsed against me, panting, and rolled me to the side. He pressed his mouth against mine, teasing with his tongue, his lips, surprisingly gentle after our fierce coupling. Then he just held me close, his breath warm against my neck.

Trembling, I clung to him, and that want expanded again inside of me, that want that went beyond the physical — the extraordinary physical — to the unattainable. The emotional.

If I couldn't tame it, this self-destructive yearning, then he couldn't know. I couldn't let him know. Because I didn't want lame apologies when he left, fake sentiment, bad feelings. I didn't want his goddamn pity.

For now, just having him would have to be enough.

A needle of pain went through me, anticipating the inevitable: losing him.

'Tis in my memory locked, I told myself. *And I shall keep the key of it.*

I STAYED at Jace's until Sunday morning, when he cooked me pancakes. There were few things that looked better than Jace in loose boxers and a thin white T-shirt cooking me breakfast, and the pancakes tasted good, too. But my creeping panic cut the sweetness of the moment. Cali had been right, though I didn't know it at the time: I was falling for him. And I needed to climb off that ledge as quickly as possible.

I asked him to drive me home after breakfast, and he politely agreed. When he wasn't ripping my clothes off, he was just that: polite. Noncommittal. As in never committing. He still had a broken heart, and let's face it, he was nothing if not weird about relationships. And I was no poster child in that department. Mad at myself for my own fragility, my damned emotional neediness, I thought a little distance between us might be wise. But it still hurt to say goodbye to him, even if it was just for the day. I was addicted to him; this was chemistry, emotional reaction to a physical connection. That's all it was. I needed to get off the junk and move on.

I napped away most of the afternoon as rain showers pattered on the windows — not the big summer storms, yet, but a rhythmic accompaniment to my restless dreams.

Monday, I took the scooter in to work, where I spent most of the day elbow-deep in fabric in the costume shop so we could be ready for fittings at rehearsal on Tuesday. Jace was busy, too, helping Dirk work with all of the designers to achieve the look they wanted. The pair of them came by in the afternoon, nodding their approval at the '50s-meets-fairies designs, though Dirk did ask if Oberon could "lose the silk hanky." I substituted an elaborate buttonhole flower, which suited the theme better, anyway, and he seemed satisfied.

Jace said little, but I could feel his gaze hot upon me as I worked with Dirk. On their way out, Jace subtly brushed against me, setting my body humming.

"That was so not fair," I texted him a few minutes later.

"No idea what you mean," he typed back. "BTW, I like how soft that dress is. Can't wait to take it off."

Just those few words gave me such a rush that I knew I couldn't count today as a sober one — that is, a day off the drug that was Jace. I wanted him still. I couldn't lie to myself. But could I keep myself from thinking about more than his body? From imagining what it would be like to wake up with him every weekend, to hear all his secrets and to share his bed every night? To sing with him in the car and swim with him on Bohemia Beach? He might be the best-looking guy I'd ever slept with, but now I was thinking about his protectiveness, his belief in me, his sense of humor, his deliciously strange ways of turning me on. What the hell was wrong with me? I was not a maudlin girl. Life had cured me of that. I should be obsessing about the pleasures he offered, not his goddamn personality.

I worked late on Monday, avoiding the temptation to be with Jace, and came in early Tuesday to help the costumers so we'd be ready for the actors. That evening, we had the cast come to us a few at a time for fittings so as to interfere as little as possible with the rehearsal.

Most of the appointments were uneventful. Wendy was delighted with the long, fitted jacket that went over her character's strapless dress. The dress would be all she'd be wearing by the time the play was over, as the actions in *Midsummer at Midnight* stripped away Helena's urban veneer and draped her in vines, flowers and the sensuality of the thin garment. In a similar way, Hermia would lose the sleekness of her modest dress as it became tattered and revealing by the play's end. We had to make her two dresses to achieve the effect. Hippolyta wasn't on stage as much, but she would don a wedding dress with a softer look by play's end.

Holland wasn't nearly as happy as the other female leads. As Titania, she was the emotional center of Jace's play, and I'd dressed her accordingly. Her dress had a 1950s cut to it, with a fitted, strapless sweetheart bodice under a sheer overlay; the circle skirt would puff out with a crinoline. But it was much more than that. I planned to layer sheer fabrics of different colors over the apple-green base fabric, and in between the layers would be realistic-looking silk flowers, making her both a neo-'50s modern woman and a lush fairy queen.

"The neckline isn't low enough," Holland informed Millie and me as we helped her into the dress. Across the room, the stitchers were wrapped up in dressing a couple of the game-designer characters.

"I think you look gorgeous," Millie said.

"I may look gorgeous, but the dress is — what is this? I'm supposed to be sexy. Titania is all sensuality. This is like June Cleaver on a camping trip."

Somehow, through the red haze of my barely contained fury, I sensed we had an audience. I glanced at the mirror in front of us and saw that Jace had come into the room and was watching with crossed arms.

"I showed you the drawing," I told Holland. "This is only the foundation of the dress. It's going to have these beautiful, creamy, feminine gauzy layers that evoke the enchantment of the forest and your powers as the queen of the fairies."

"You're going to stick a few flowers on it, right? Not enough," Holland said. "And you have some kind of fabric over these bust cups, don't you? So you're going to cover up what little cleavage is showing."

"The overlay will be made of tulle, and it's sleeveless. It's essentially transparent."

"I want more boob and more leg."

I took a deep breath and managed not to roll my eyes. "The hemline is non-negotiable. It fits with the theme and the rest of the costumes." I grabbed the fabric on either side of the bust and yanked upward. Holland gave a little gasp as her generous breasts jiggled. "Millie, write this down, will you? More support in the cups, and we'll trim the edge a bit so more skin shows."

"Fine," Holland choked out.

I grasped the fabric at her waist and gave her a good shake. "Seems a little tight here."

Holland batted my hands away. "It's all right. It needs to be tight. My waist is just right."

Millie was trying to hide a smile.

"OK!" I said brightly. "Everything else feel good?"

I moved a hand toward Holland again, and she flinched, backing a step away from me.

"Fine! It's fine. You make sure we have another fitting before we open. I don't want any surprises."

"Of course. You can go back in the changing room and take it off now. Leave it on the hanger, please."

Holland looked at Millie. "Zipper!" she barked.

Millie loosened it for her. Holland shot me an evil look — and then she dropped the dress right there, in the middle of the room. There was a whistle from the corner where the two guys were being fitted for their costumes, and I stepped back, not wanting to be in the same time zone as Holland's bikini-clad booty and shockingly bare breasts.

She turned slowly, making sure everyone had a good look, especially Jace. And then she smiled and sauntered to the dressing room to get back into her street clothes.

"Get that, would you?" I asked Millie, but she was a step ahead of me, already shaking out the crumpled dress.

"I think we've all seen enough boob from her," she muttered.

"You said it, sister. Can you grab Jace's costume?"

Millie walked away to hang up the dress and go through the rack of costumes in progress. I looked up to see Jace coming toward me, the corner of his mouth quirking.

"How's your day going?" he asked blandly, and I wanted to smack him and kiss him at the same time.

"Swell," I said, and he grinned at the look in my eye. "We have your trousers and jacket ready. You can change in the dressing room."

"Now?" he teased, knowing full well that Holland was still in there.

"Fuck, no," I murmured, and he laughed out loud. "Not that you'll see much you haven't seen already."

"I may need your personal assistance."

"Absolutely not." I leaned over and whispered in his ear. "But if you can't zip your pants up around that pretty boy penis, let me know."

Maintaining a deadpan expression, he whispered back, "Keep talking like that, and no zipper will contain me."

We stood there, faces almost touching, and looked into

each other's eyes. His breathing had picked up, and heat shot through my body.

"Found it!" Millie said, bringing over the suit. I swallowed and took a step back from Jace, and he subtly adjusted his jeans.

"Thank you," he said. "Dark and serious, like Demetrius at the start of the play. I like it."

"It's gabardine. Not as hot as wool. And as pockets are torn away, as you become more unbuttoned, and the jacket is removed to reveal more of the vest, you'll see more color. Then the vest will go, and the shirt will be unbuttoned. Plus you'll pick up bits of greenery as the play goes on."

"Will the prop master be involved?"

"Marty is too freaked out about Bottom's head, which should be done this week. I'll probably be the one to supervise the changes in costumes, at least at first, and there will be dressers."

"I can't wait," Millie interjected.

"This is why we love you," I told her. "She's awesome," I said to Jace.

"I bow to awesome," he said, literally bowing to her. Holland, who happened to be walking by on her way out of the room, scowled at Millie for stealing the attention she was so clearly trying to get from Jace.

He looked around to be sure she was gone. "I'll be right back," he said with a smile, and headed for the dressing room.

His fitting went smoothly, with just a few adjustments needed. I went into professional mode, trying to think of his body only in terms of how it would look in the suit. I almost succeeded.

When he re-emerged from the dressing room in his jeans and T-shirt, he stopped to ask me if I would see him later.

"I think we'll be working late again," I said, wanting badly to say yes. But I *would* be working late, and the way I felt around him was starting to scare me.

Jace held my gaze for a moment. His brow creased as if he was struggling with something, and that wrinkled-brow look always tore me apart. But all he said was, "OK, I'll see you tomorrow." He kissed me on the cheek, a sweet gesture that — the way he did it, with unhurried deliberation — felt like a red-hot brand on my skin.

Millie, who'd been waiting discreetly a few feet away, stepped up and watched him go.

"I'm sorry, but I couldn't help but hear," she said. "And I'd go to see him even if it was three in the morning."

"That's the problem," I said to her puzzled expression. "So would I."

THE NEXT NIGHT, I skipped rehearsal altogether, went home, put on soft cotton PJ shorts and a tank top and flopped in front of my little TV with a box of takeout sushi. I'd put in so many hours already this week that I needed a break.

Jace was coming in later each day, focusing more on rehearsals, and I tried not to think about him on stage, going through his paces as Demetrius, reciting that speech to Wendy. Not that I was jealous of Wendy — but I had to admit I was jealous of Helena. No one had ever declared love to me the way Demetrius did in the play. Reading through lines with Jace didn't count. Besides, Helena got to kiss him on stage.

My Fair Lady was playing on TCM, and I let myself get caught up in the wit and romanticism of it — certainly more romance than Shaw intended in *Pygmalion.* With such songs as "On the Street Where You Live," the musical couldn't help but make a girl's heart beat a little faster. Maybe Eliza's suitor Freddy was a fool, but that *song!* A great song could make up for a lot of foolishness.

So could great costumes. I imagined myself in Eliza's figure-hugging Ascot race dress, with ruffles, huge hat and all. Maybe I could work it up for Halloween, if I got invited to the right kind of party. While the other women wore less, I'd wear more.

My phone rang just as Eliza was scolding Freddy in "Show Me." She demanded he show her how he felt, not just talk about it.

I had the opposite problem. Too much show, not enough tell.

Because maybe there wasn't anything to tell.

The image that popped up on my phone was a shot of Jace in that TV drama he'd done, playing a womanizing grifter with a devilish smile. It was a great photo, but it didn't really seem like him, now that I knew him.

I debated letting the call go to voicemail and picked it up anyway.

"Hi, Jace."

"Hey, Penelope. Can I come over?"

"Is rehearsal over already?"

"It's 10:30. We ran late, but it's over. What are you doing?"

"Just watching a movie."

"What?"

"My Fair Lady."

"I played Freddy in that once, back in school."

"The pretty boy," I teased.

He groaned. "I'm going to get a complex. May I join you?"

"I don't know. I'm kind of tired."

"The moon is full, you know. Look out over the river and look up. It's like daylight out here."

Out here? I muted the TV, got off the couch and peered out the big picture window. The moon shone through the trees, casting crisp shadows. It really was beautiful. "Wow."

"I never waste a full moon."

"Do you turn into a werewolf or something?"

"I go for a walk or go somewhere I can get a good view of it. Sometimes just to the roof of my building. Maybe that's what drew me to *A Midsummer Night's Dream*. The moon is woven all through it."

"That's kind of sweet," I said.

"So I can come over?"

I laughed. "Was that stuff about the moon supposed to convince me? You can do better. Try quoting Shakespeare."

"Hmph. OK, I'll do better."

The call clicked off, and I looked at the screen just to be sure. The call was definitely over. He'd hung up on me?

I was about to unmute the TV when I thought I heard Freddy singing. But it wasn't Freddy on the screen, and it didn't sound right. And then I realized the sound was coming from outside.

It was "On the Street Where You Live," with its lyrics of lilacs and larks and that feeling of flying high when you're near the one you — well, love is never mentioned in the song, but at the very least, it was about infatuation. And the voice that sang it was absolutely marvelous.

I opened the door, and there was Jace, singing in the moonlight. I sucked in a breath and listened, caught up in his transcendent tenor, the elation on his face. I cut him off before he could repeat the chorus.

"OK, OK!" I said. "You're going to wake the neighbors! Come in!"

"Didn't you like it?" he asked as he brushed past me, and I got a whiff of him, forests and stars and manly heat from the balmy evening.

I turned to face him. Jace was flushed and merry after his song. His beautiful voice had gone right to my heart, but I didn't want to tell him so much.

"You're amazing," I said in a low voice. "You know that."

He let me close the door, and then he pushed me gently against it, put his hands in my hair and kissed me, engaging me with leisurely concentration, sucking on my lower lip, running his tongue along the seam of my mouth, coaxing me to open under his warm, masterful attentions. I moaned a little, and he paused in his kiss — but he didn't release me.

"Aren't you glad I came over?" he murmured.

"That's only my second serenade, so yeah, it was nice."

"Second!" He stepped back. "Who serenaded you before?"

"This guy who had a crush on me in the tenth grade. He came over to our trailer and sang 'Just a Gigolo' outside the door."

"Hardly romantic. Were you one of his stable of women?"

"He was a nerd. Nice enough, but he definitely didn't have a stable of women."

Jace laughed. "Did it get him anywhere?"

"I'm afraid my redneck neighbors scared him off with their car stereo. He never talked to me again."

"Your tale is Shakespearean in its tragic frustration of true love," he said.

"As if one serenade was any indication of true love," I said, then wished I hadn't.

A funny look crossed Jace's face, but he didn't respond. Instead, he walked over to the TV, where *My Fair Lady* was still muted. "Professor Higgins is getting his comeuppance, I see. I hope I get to play him someday."

"Don't rush it. You have several decades of hot leading men ahead of you before becoming the crusty linguist."

"I thought I was quite the cunning linguist already."

I rolled my eyes at the double entendre. "Don't get cocky."

"I've heard that's quite nice, too."

"Have you been drinking?" I asked.

"No, but I'd like to be."

I went to the fridge and pulled out a bottle of pinot grigio that was already open. "Will this work?"

"I'd love some."

"You're in awfully good spirits," I said as I poured two glasses and handed him one.

"We had a fantastic rehearsal, the moon is full, and you invited me over." He clinked his glass to mine. "Couch?"

I nodded and unmuted the TV so we could watch the end of the movie. He put an arm around me, and I nestled against him. This felt so nice, so natural. So loverly, to quote the musical.

"This is a good look for you," Jace said as the channel went into classic movie trailers to fill the gap between films.

"Oh, shut up," I said, muting the TV.

"I'm serious. You're not all dolled up. You're just pretty, wonderful you. Soft." He kissed my hair. "You're not screaming 'sex.' "

"I think you just insulted me on two levels. Whatever I'm wearing isn't sexy, and the rest of the time I'm a slut."

"No, no, no. You have to stop thinking 'slut' every time I say something like that. Unless we're playing." He grinned briefly. "I mean, you don't have your sexuality thrown up around you like a shield. You're beautiful, but you aren't — formidable."

"Now I'm formidable? You didn't seem to have any trouble breaking in."

He put his empty wine glass on the coffee table and pulled me closer. "I can't explain that. It was instinct, coming to you the way I did. Are you sorry?"

I looked into his eyes, his dark eyes, which tonight were so boyish. He was content and relaxed. No roles. Just Jace.

"No," I whispered. "I'm not sorry."

He took my glass and put it down next to his. "I'm happy I found you," he said. "I was nervous coming to Bohemia, not knowing anyone, not knowing how I'd be received."

Jace was nervous? The Babe of Broadway? But then I looked at him, thinking of all the pain he'd kept bottled up — the pain, and the twisted fear, and all that lust he'd unleashed on me.

I didn't want to try to build a wall between us anymore, even if I was just his summer fuck buddy. I slipped an arm around his neck and pulled him close and kissed him.

His response was absolute, a kiss that met and engulfed mine with sweet assurance, and then it was something more, edged with urgency, the passion that always seemed to ignite between us. He rubbed a hand across my breasts through the tank top, squeezing each in turn. Between my legs, heat blossomed, a fire that made me wet with wanting him. With no resistance from me, he pulled off my tank top. He licked one nipple, teasing it until it beaded, then feasted on the other, raspberries on mounds of cream.

Jace paused to slide off my soft shorts and smiled. "No underwear. Hmm." He touched my bud with one finger, making a delicate circling motion.

"I was relaxing," I croaked, leaning back on the couch.

"Do I appear to be complaining? I have a warm, naked woman next to me who happens to be the prettiest vision I've ever seen."

The prettiest? Certainly, the most aroused.

He paused in his caresses to take off his shirt and wriggle out of his jeans. I ached for him so badly that I touched myself, watching him, wanting him. Jace's eyes grew darker and his lips parted as he watched me fingering my clit. He seemed in no hurry to resume what he'd started, even though his erection was unmistakable.

"Spread your legs," he whispered. "That's it, Penelope. Touch yourself, sweetheart. Put a finger inside yourself. Show me how you masturbate."

I groaned at his words. I'd never done this for a man, not like this. I didn't count my little performance in his dressing room. Now, I had completely lost control, given it to him. I opened my legs farther and slipped a finger inside, and then two, probing in my creamy sex for the trigger that would release all this throbbing desire.

"Please, Jace."

"Go on, Penelope." He was touching himself, now, rubbing his hand up and down his hard cock, dark with arousal. With his other hand, he reached under me, to the seam of my buttocks, and stroked me there.

"God," I moaned. "Jace. *Jace.*"

He couldn't take it anymore, either. He grasped one of my legs, positioning it so it pointed almost straight up, and pushed my hand away. He guided his cock and coated the tip with my moisture as I begged again, *"Jace."*

"Yes, Penelope." He slid inside me, finally, *God,* so deep. Especially stretched as I was, with one leg in the air, the other bent with my foot on the floor. Jace had one knee on the couch, the other on the floor, and he plunged and held himself there until I whimpered. He did it again, and I could feel the first tickle of orgasm, the tendrils of ecstasy I strained to reach. He lifted and thrust a third time, and then he was pumping like the engine of a steam train, faster, harder. My whole body shifted with each penetration, and the muscles in my legs stretched with exquisite sensitivity. I'd never felt so connected with a lover as I did just then, so open, so exposed, so desperate. The steam built. The rhythm intensified. I clutched the couch, opening wider, wanting to give him everything. My body tensed with the terrible coiled power of need, a power that demanded release. Jace's expression was intense and possessive as he watched me. I reveled in it, sinking, spinning into a whirlpool of desire. He used his free hand to caress my breasts. But it wasn't until he pinched a nipple, hard, that I came with a long cry, my body convulsing around him. Still he kept grinding, teasing more and more waves of bliss from me until he finally detonated inside me, holding himself there with a guttural exhalation of pleasure.

With a long sigh, he slipped out of me and folded me up against him on the couch. I was sore and wet and trembling, exhausted, high. So high on him. I was dozing when he got up and shut out all the lights and the TV. He came back to the couch and spooned against me, hot and damp and strong against my back.

The last thing I saw before I fell asleep was the cool blue glow of moonlight.

"WHO'S NEXT?" Dirk asked the Chamberlain's marketing rep, a brisk brunette in a tight skirt, big jewelry and big heels.

She checked her clipboard. "Let's see. That was Channel 9 . . . looks like *The Bugle* is next. They're last on the schedule, so you can give them more than fifteen minutes if you want."

The Bugle meant the odious Joe Stier. Next to Dirk, Jace said nothing, just took a sip of his water.

Both were seated on the stage, with the set two-thirds built behind them. I was in the green room, watching the press interviews on the big monitor, during an afternoon break that had stretched well beyond two hours because of my fascination with the process. About ten news outlets had sent reporters and cameras to the media day — some print, some TV, some ambitious bloggers. Even a theater magazine from New York had sent someone, which I judged to be good news for Jace's play. Some had done interviews with the actors playing Titania and Oberon in the black box, but all had come to the main theater, one by one, to talk to Dirk and Jace.

Dirk had been subtly dominant throughout, exerting his authority as director, making it clear that he was the puppeteer behind *Midsummer at Midnight.*

Jace, despite his heavy input in the show, was modest about his play and his role in it. He'd deftly deflected questions about his personal life and emphasized the artistic goals of the production. When asked to pose for photos, he insisted that Dirk be included, and the marketing rep promised the press they'd get production shots soon. It was another reminder that we had to get the costumes done fast; we were going to stage a couple of scenes for Cali to shoot next week.

I sipped from my metal water bottle and shifted in the armchair, one of the eclectic pieces that provided seating in the green room. I'd been squirming a lot, stretching the muscles that had been used so wantonly last night. I really needed to get back to yoga, especially if I was going to keep playing with Jace. My exercise routine had gone to hell since production started.

Let's see, sex burns three or four calories a minute . . . close to low-impact yoga . . . I either need a lot more sex or a lot more yoga. And I knew which was more fun.

"And here's Joe Stier of *The Bohemia Bugle,*" the marketing rep said on the stage, leading in the columnist, who was in full swagger. "He's the arts columnist for the paper."

Dirk and Jace stood and shook his hand.

"Great to see you again!" Joe said to Jace, as if they were best friends.

"Mr. Stier." Jace nodded politely. I couldn't see the fine details of his face in the wide shot provided by the monitor, but he was such a good actor, I had no doubt Joe was unconscious of Jace's distaste.

"If it's OK, I'd like to film a couple of questions on video first. They like this stuff for the website," Joe said.

"Not a problem," Dirk answered.

The marketing maven left, and the men sat. Joe pulled out his smartphone. He aimed it at Jace first and started recording. "How do you like Bohemia?"

"This is a beautiful community, and I'm really enjoying Bohemia Beach. Everyone's been very supportive of the play. There's a lot of talent here."

Joe nodded and aimed the phone at Dirk. "What has been the biggest challenge in working with a hotshot from New York?"

Despite multiple implied insults in the question, Dirk took it in stride.

"Jace is one of us. We're all professionals, and he's been great to work with. The biggest challenge may be in that we have such an ambitious vision, it's taking a lot of work on the part of our design staff to make it happen, but I think you'll be impressed by the way the play looks and feels. And it's very entertaining."

"I understand you're appearing in the play after a last-minute replacement," Joe said, turning back to Jace. "Do you have any advice for your fellow actors?"

Jace shifted in his chair, taking a moment to respond. "My advice is to treasure their time in smaller productions like this one. I'm learning from them every day."

Damn, Jace and Dirk were diplomatic. Joe must have thought so, too, because his next question was designed to provoke.

"What's been the worst moment so far in getting ready for the opening?"

Neither Dirk nor Jace answered at first. Finally, Dirk said, "It was probably when I heard we'd sold out the first three weeks of performances. That puts a lot of pressure on the actors."

I laughed. Talk about turning a question on its head.

"And you?" Joe prodded Jace.

"Probably this interview," he joked, but there was an edge to his voice. Dirk laughed, and Joe belatedly joined in.

The columnist turned off his phone and put it in his pocket. "OK if I record the rest on audio?"

Jace and Dirk agreed, and Joe continued with a few more questions, most of them routine, about the themes in the play, the cast, and the schedule. Then he looked at his phone.

"I see our time is about up. Dirk, would you mind if I asked Jace a couple of questions about his New York career, just for background?"

Dirk, who was clearly weary of his hours on the hot seat, stood. "With pleasure. We'll look forward to seeing you opening night."

He and Joe shook hands, and Dirk went offstage.

"So, here we are," Joe said to Jace. There was something in his tone I didn't like. He clicked off his recorder and looked around, confirming the theater was empty. "I have a request."

"All right," Jace said neutrally.

A strange feeling tickled my spine, the kind that sometimes came when I played with my crystal ball. I pulled out my phone. I was alone in the green room, and Jace was alone with that creep on stage, and something didn't seem right about Joe's attitude. I hit record and filmed the monitor.

"I want to follow you around for the twenty-four hours leading up to opening night for a story I've pitched to a men's magazine," Joe said. "A very high-end men's magazine. I think you'll be pleased. They're very excited about it."

"Absolutely not," said Jace, not changing his tone at all.

Joe laughed.

"This would be great for you as well as me," Joe said. "I get to work at the next level, where I deserve to be, and the world finally gets an insight into Jace Edison, the man everyone thinks is a eunuch."

Jace stood. "I've heard enough."

"But we both know that's not true, don't we?" Joe still sat, smugly waiting for a reply.

Jace crossed his arms and didn't move, didn't speak.

"You're dating the costume designer, aren't you?" Joe asked. "Penelope Locke?"

My hand flew to my mouth. *What the fuck?*

"I have other contacts in the national media," Joe said. "Less exalted ones. And they'll pay a lot for gossip about the elusive Jace Edison and his piece of ass in Florida."

That motherfucker.

"Why aren't you working for them, then?" Jace replied, ice in his tone.

"I have a care for my reputation, but I do have a new wife with expensive tastes. It's either move up to the big magazines, or sell a little gossip. Either one works for me. And I did mention that the paper has me writing the first review of your debut as a playwright, didn't I?"

Jace took one step toward Joe, and even on the wide view of the monitor, I could tell he was furious.

"I don't give a shit about your review," Jace said, "but if you write about Penelope, I'll make your life miserable."

"So you care about her, right?"

"All you need to know is that she's a good person who doesn't need to be saddled with this kind of talk when I go back to New York. I won't let her be haunted by my ghost."

My heart crumpled like a paper lantern. He was defending me, yes. But he was also declaring how little I meant to him.

"Then your choice is clear," Joe said. "Let me follow you for a day, from dress rehearsal through the opening, and write about you. And I want personal stuff. I've done some digging already. I want to know about your family and the girl you dated in college and your early successes, your mysterious six-month hiatus, how you got the role here from the drunk guy, and how you're otherwise getting along with the cast."

Damn — everything from Lauren to poor drunken Paul.

Jace was silent for a moment. "But not Penelope?"

"I'll have to mention a romantic entanglement. I'll do the courtesy of withholding the name. I'll even be fair in my review. Word of honor."

"I'm reassured," Jace said with biting sarcasm. "I'll do it."

"Excellent." Joe stood and offered his hand. Jace didn't take it. Instead, he walked out of the theater.

A minute later, our marketing gal had reentered. "I saw Jace leave. You got everything you needed?"

"Everything," Joe said with a grin, giving her a gratuitous hug before he left.

I stopped my recording. I felt sick to my stomach. Jace was leaving at the end of the summer. Hell, I'd known that all along. But I couldn't let Jace reveal himself to that sleazeball, reveal his tragic history with Lauren, his struggles with stage fright — good God, it really could ruin him. And to do it on my account, out of some misplaced sense of chivalry? Ridiculous. I was a big girl. If I ended up in the gossip rags, I'd deal with it.

But I didn't want Joe Stier to win. Either way, that bastard couldn't win.

With shaking hands, I tapped my phone to retrieve my contacts and dialed Cali.

I DIDN'T SEEK out Jace that afternoon or evening. Instead, I focused on costumes, helping the shop complete the ones we'd need for the photo shoot. Notably, he didn't seek me out, either. Maybe he didn't know how to tell me what I already knew.

The truth was, I also wasn't sure what to say to him. I

couldn't wrap my mind around what had happened in his not-so-private chat with Joe Stier. Jace had protected me. He'd said he didn't want to be the ghost in my life after he left. He'd put a hell of a lot on the line.

But he was still leaving.

And I'd made a move that had its own dangers. If Cali could help me connect with the right person at *The Bugle,* we might be able to get Joe Stier out of the picture. According to Cali, female staffers at the newspaper had put up with his creepy advances for years. They liked to joke that Joe held compromising photos of the editor with a goat. It was the only way to explain his rise.

If Joe was invulnerable, who knew how vindictive he'd be? Maybe one review in a small newspaper didn't mean much, but it could set the tone for other coverage of Jace's play. It was important. And Jace would still have to go forward with a revealing interview.

Or I could plead with Jace to tell Joe to go to hell and let the gossips do as they may — and risk the bad review.

Either way, Jace was left exposed in a way he never would have been if he hadn't met me. And that made me feel like hell.

My mood didn't improve when I was awakened Friday morning by a phone call from my mother. Unfortunately, I answered before I was awake enough to process the caller ID.

"Hello?" I said just as my brain made the connection. I should keep the phone turned off in the mornings until I had my coffee.

"Penny? Penny, honey, I need you." She sounded especially piteous.

"Don't call me that," I managed, sitting up in the darkened room.

"Can you come see me tomorrow? There's something I need to tell you."

"So tell me." The air-conditioning unit was rattling something awful. I hoped it didn't die now. It was supposed to hit ninety today.

"It's important. I need to tell you in person."

I ran a hand through my hair and sighed. "I'm busy. I'm trying to get ready for a play."

"I'm sick," my mother said more emphatically.

"Sick?" I struggled to find some reason not to care, but that instinctual reservoir of daughterly devotion — a sense of obligation, if not love — compromised my judgment.

"Bad sick," she emphasized. "I need to talk to you about what happens next."

"What do you mean? Are you — how bad is it?"

"Bad. I need to talk to you."

My mother was going to die? Is that what she was saying? "I need details so we can get on the same page here. Have you been to the doctor?"

"I have to tell you *in person.*"

Fuck. She was manipulative, but it had to be important if she was saying it like that. Visions of a devastating cancer or years of dementia or a debilitating disease filled my head. She expected me to care for her, I supposed, though the very idea repelled me. I would find care for her, somehow, but I wasn't giving up my life for a woman who'd made mine a living hell.

All of that went through my head in a nanosecond, along with the question of whether I was a bad daughter — and how bad of a daughter could I be to a horrible mother?

"OK," I reluctantly agreed. "How about in the morning?"

"I have to work late tonight," she said. "Make it afternoon. Two o'clock should be all right."

"I'll see you then."

"Great. Thanks, Penny." She hung up, and I tried to clear the fuzz from my brain. Was I wrong, or did she have a note of triumph in her voice when she said goodbye?

There was a banging sound. I looked at the window that held the air conditioner. Fortunately, that didn't seem to be it. The other window showed the slanted light of early morning sneaking through the blinds.

I heard it again. *The door.*

I trudged out to the living room in my PJ shorts and tank top and opened it.

"Good morning, gorgeous." Jace wore the slightest of smiles and carried two cups of coffee in a tray.

"Smart-ass. I would close this door in your face, except that smells so fucking good I have to let you in."

"I figured I'd get in on my looks or the coffee." He entered, the embodiment of charm. Only he was flexing one hand as the other placed the tray on the counter, and he slipped it into the pocket of his jeans as if to tame it.

He was nervous.

I suddenly wanted to tell him everything, that I knew what Joe had asked, that I had an idea of how to get him out of it. But I was chicken. Jace would stop me, I was sure of that, not because of the risks to him, but because of the issues for me. Plus, I wasn't sure how he'd feel about me eavesdropping on the conversation, though he knew as well as anyone that someone could have seen the interview from the green room. With no actors around, he'd probably assumed that no one had.

"I have to brush my teeth and stuff," was all I said, and he nodded. No overture. No touch. I shook off the feeling that things had changed between us and took a hasty shower. I dashed back across the hall in my towel, but he wasn't in view. I made it a capri pants day, black with a boatneck red top, and went in search of him.

I could see through the living room window that he was sitting on the patio, and I took my coffee outside to join him. The day was already warm, not quite to the point of sweat-inducing, but another thirty minutes would take care of that.

"You OK?" I asked, sitting in the chair next to him. The light sifting through the trees along the glimmering lagoon dappled his face, making it hard to read. But it also lit up his eyes, and the mysterious darkness I was used to seeing there glowed with hints of gold.

"Of course," he said, presenting me with one of his beautiful smiles. "How are you?"

This was an opportunity to talk about what had happened yesterday. I didn't.

"Not thrilled. My mother wants me to come see her tomorrow afternoon."

"This is the mother of the year, right?"

I smiled grimly. "Right. I wouldn't go, but she says it's important. She says she's really sick and needs to talk to me."

His brow furrowed. God, that look killed me.

"That doesn't sound good," he said. "I'll go with you."

"What?"

"I'll go with you. You'll want a friend, going into that lion's den, especially if the news is as bad as she says."

"I — I don't know."

"Why not?" Jace asked, taking a sip of his coffee.

I huffed in frustration. "Because it's Skunk Lake, that's why."

He laughed. "I need to see this Skunk Lake."

"Believe me, it's nothing like your princely New Jersey suburbs."

"More interesting, I'm sure."

"That's the curse, isn't it? May you live in interesting times?"

"Come on, Pen. I'll drive. It'll be better with both of us."

My breath got all bungled up in my throat. A lot of things would be better with both of us. How could I start to say goodbye to him when he was getting so tangled up in my life?

"This would be a good time to just back away," I said. "You don't want to go, believe me."

Jace looked at me with utter seriousness, with a smoldering intensity. "I want to go."

And I gave in to that ember of kindness, of promise, knowing I was postponing the inevitable.

"OK," I said with a small, grateful smile.

We finished our coffees in silence, watching the light shift from gold to white, listening to a warbling mockingbird and the cries of ospreys hunting for their breakfast over the river.

He drove us to the Chamberlain. At my office door, we parted with a kiss. Did I taste melancholy on his lips today? Again, I had the feeling that the sands were shifting beneath us, and I cursed Joe Stier for hastening the demise of my midsummer dream.

My day brightened when I got word that a package had been delivered to reception. At the desk, the secretary handed me a lumpy object wrapped in a paint-spattered sheet that smelled faintly of art supplies.

"This didn't come from FedEx, I take it," I said.

"No," she said, "a young man all dressed up in black."

I smiled. *Damien.* So this was Bottom's head. I took the

elevator instead of the stairs, anxious to open it in the good light of the costume shop. Besides, I didn't want our cranky prop manager Marty to see it before I had a chance to work out any bugs.

Most of the staff was out to lunch, but Midge, the shop manager, was busy stitching tiny LED light strings into the fairies' sleeves. The girls would wear skater skirts, and the boys, long shorts, all in shades of green with gold accents. The costumes were designed for fluidity of motion as well as looks, since the teens playing the parts would be moving around on skates and boards.

Midge looked up when I entered. "What ya got?"

"It should be a donkey head," I said, going to the nearest empty worktable and gently unwrapping it. An envelope popped out first, containing a small remote control and a note:

> *Batteries not included. I'll bill you for the lights.*
> *Don't forget me in the program.*
> *Your ass, Damien*

HE'D SKETCHED an amusing donkey head next to his name, and I chuckled.

I finished unwrapping the parcel, revealing far more than what I'd given him. The metal frame was intricately enhanced with thin copper wire. Small gears, bits of computer parts and wires were woven into the design to create the impression of eyebrows and a mane. The virtual-reality glasses were well-defined, with one lens made of glass. Cleverly obscured amid the texture were LED lights.

It took me a minute to find the control box, hidden under the back part of the head, which would dip down to cover the actor's neck. It was nested in a soft pocket and buttoned in place. I removed it to take a closer look.

"Have any batteries?" I asked Midge. "Double A's?"

"Of course," she said, going to her desk, which contained all the gadgets that weren't found in her tool belt.

In a moment, I had the head lighting up in different patterns, depending on how I used the remote. There would be a learning curve for Doug, but I had a feeling Dirk would love playing with the comic possibilities of the lights dancing to the tune of Titania's enticements.

Later, in my office, I sent a note to marketing about crediting Damien in the program, and I sent an email to Marty requesting he stock up on AA batteries for all the light strings that would be used in the costumes.

"That's a lot of batteries," was his terse reply, which I ignored.

"Hey," came a voice from the open doorway. A voice as soothing as velvet, as incendiary as a bottle rocket.

He went right to my head, every time.

"Hey, Jace."

"When should I pick you up tomorrow?"

"About 12:30 should give us plenty of time, unless you want to get lunch ahead of time. Or breakfast," I said with a flirty grin.

"I wish I could," he said. "We're rehearsing tonight, and they've scheduled a fundraising breakfast tomorrow with me and several of your more well-heeled supporters. For some reason, they're willing to pay a hundred dollars a head to have breakfast with me."

I stood, and Jace stepped inside the office and closed the door.

"And just think," I said, "I got to have breakfast with you for *free*."

"I even *made* breakfast for you." He had stepped into my personal space, and the heat started to build in my body.

"And did extremely naughty things to me."

He ran his fingers through my blond and pink hair, his eyes searching my face. "Should I bill you?" he whispered.

"Just name your price," I whispered back, and our mouths met in a hungry kiss. Our hands drifted, sneaking under clothes, finding skin as we devoured each other. He pushed me back against my desk and inserted one knee between my legs. I whimpered.

He broke away with a gasp.

I was breathing hard, too. "Not a good time?"

He chuckled, trying to regain his composure. "Not a good time for this, you mean? Probably not. Although you are a very good time."

"That's my problem. I'm a good-time girl."

Jace slipped a hand behind my neck and pulled me in for one more hard kiss. "You're so much more."

"You have to stop being so nice to me," I said softly.

"Why is that?"

"I don't want to get used to it."

Jace regarded me for a moment with those opaque eyes of his, leaned toward me as if he were about to kiss me again, then shook his head. "I have to get to rehearsal. We're starting early so the cast doesn't have to spend their whole Friday night here."

"So you're getting out early?" I hated the pleading sound that snuck into my voice.

"There's some stuff I have to do. People I have to talk to at home. I just want to prepare them in case — in case they get any calls from the press about this show."

"Oh?" I stepped back. "Does that usually happen?"

He shrugged. He wasn't telling me. I wasn't telling him I knew. Both of us were acting. Somehow, the distance made it easier to let him go.

"Then I'll see you tomorrow," I said.

He reached up again and brushed my cheek, his actor's mask failing to hide his disquiet. And then he slipped out the door, and I sat at my desk and stared at nothing at all for a few minutes until I got up to go home.

I GREETED Jace with a kiss when I got into his car Saturday afternoon. Then I took a moment to admire him. He wore loose khaki shorts and a button-up short-sleeve shirt in light blue plaid, over a white T-shirt.

"That's probably the most summery thing I've seen you wear," I said.

"I'm surrendering to Florida. It's already eighty-five degrees. And you're probably the most casual I've seen you."

"I don't dress up for my mother." Though I'd still chosen my shorts, white scoop-neck T-shirt and heeled sandals carefully, knowing I'd be seeing Jace.

"You're gorgeous regardless," he said, and that little infusion of confidence made me smile.

"How was breakfast?"

"Truly awful," he said. "The people were nice enough, but

it was at some hotel, with a buffet of dried-out eggs and soggy bacon."

"Mimosas?"

"With terrible champagne."

"Snob," I joked as he drove us west through Bohemia. "At least it was a free breakfast."

"But they took a little piece of my soul," he said with faux drama, and I laughed. "Plus I didn't get to spend it with you."

"You'll get more than enough of me this afternoon, I promise," I said.

"Are we going to see a Skunk Ape?"

"Depends on who my mom is dating."

"Oh, snap," he said. "She's sick, remember."

"I know." I felt only a trace of guilt. "I just can't muster up all that much empathy for someone who has always made me miserable."

"It's hard for me to imagine. My mother has always been so supportive. If it weren't for her, I never would have become an actor."

"Did you talk to her last night?" I asked.

Jace glanced at me, his eyebrows raised, as if he'd forgotten he'd told me he was going to call home. "I did. She's fine. They're all fine. She and my dad might come down to see the play later in the run."

OK. So he wasn't going to go into details. I wondered if he'd warned them not to talk to Joe Stier, or when they did, to talk as little as possible.

"Do you miss your family?" I asked.

"I talk to them often enough. I call every few days."

"No wonder your mother loves you!"

"Penelope," he said as we got into the strip malls and red lights of west Bohemia, "mothers are *supposed* to love you."

"Oh, yeah. I forgot."

He wore a wry smile. "Should we turn on the Broadway channel?"

"Please!"

He switched on the satellite radio, and we listened, chatted about plays and even sang a little. We made our way beyond Bohemia, chasing the building clouds of the sea breeze, and took the isolated road that wound through the wetlands and would eventually lead to the land of the Mouse. The drive was so pleasant that I almost missed the turn, but as soon as Jace made it, the snakes in my stomach woke up.

These were even less traveled roads. We wound through a scrubby landscape of trees and occasional ranch houses until we got to the area around Skunk Lake.

"It's a left up here," I said as we approached the sign.

"Sunfish Estates?" Jace sounded skeptical.

"I think they marketed it as an angler's paradise. Perfect for my mother, who has never held a fisherman's pole in her life. At least, not literally."

"I don't need to have that image in my head right now," Jace said with a wince.

I chuckled. "Sorry. I'm pretending that you're not about to experience my horrible origins up close and in person."

He aimed a pout of pity at me. "Do I stay on this street?"

"Turn left on Catfish Way, then right on Chubsucker Drive."

He guffawed as he made the first turn, past a particularly shabby manufactured home. "Chubsucker?"

"It's a kind of fish. I know, I know."

"Are any of the streets named after skunks?" Jace asked.

"You'd think, but no." The trailers looked even worse than they had the last time, except for Mrs. Waller's. It had maintenance issues, too, but she planted flowers and kept the place clean. A sweet widow, she'd always opened her door to me and had cookies waiting when I needed to escape my mother for a couple of hours.

"Here it is," I said. "Black mailbox."

Jace slowed the Jaguar, which was way too nice for this neighborhood, and pulled into the gravel driveway. My mother's trailer, a shabby white with light-blue trim, was landscaped with a row of plastic sunflower pinwheels out front and a half-dead orange tree. The roof seemed to undulate slightly, as if a giant had been sitting on it. Flimsy white lattice covered the gap between the trailer and the ground. A small awning of unfinished corrugated metal extended over the door and out about eight feet, where it was supported by two slender posts of dubious sturdiness. On the haphazard concrete-paver patio beneath, a rusting charcoal grill shared space with two mismatched lawn chairs and a cooler.

At the back of the driveway was a freestanding carport, under which was a decaying old couch, a pile of flagstones waiting in vain for some future project, an assortment of plastic boxes, trash cans, tattered folding chairs, a broom, a shovel, and a reproduction of the *manneken pis* statue, though fortunately the peeing infant didn't appear to be connected to any plumbing. There was a motorcycle, too, which I found puzzling.

No car could actually fit under the carport, so my mother's old sedan was parked in the driveway. Jace parked partway on the weedy grass, and we got out. The air was stifling. No ocean breeze mitigated the heat, and the atmosphere was as dense as a wet sponge.

"Watch a lot of home and garden television, does she?" Jace quipped.

My laugh was tempered by my anticipation of the misery to follow. "I'm starting to think you shouldn't have come, but I was so grateful when you insisted. Now that we're here, I'm not so sure."

"The only way to do it is to do it," he said philosophically. He touched my shoulder, a comforting caress, and followed me to the door.

I went up the step and knocked.

"Just a minute!" came my mother's cigarette-gravel voice. And then the door opened, revealing her in all her faded glory. She'd maintained her blond hair with the help of chemistry, and her lipstick was too red for the situation. She seemed a little tired, maybe, but she looked pretty good, notwithstanding her heavy makeup. And for some reason, she was kind of dressed up, in a short denim skirt and a revealing red, silky blouse that made me glad I hadn't bothered.

"Well, come on in, Penelope," she said, eagerness in her tone. She didn't seem sick, but maybe her disease, whatever it was, was in the early stages. Her eyes lit up when she caught sight of Jace. "And who did you bring with you? Isn't he a stud muffin?"

"For God's sake, Mom," I said, but Jace's expression remained blank.

"Jace Edison." He held out his hand. "Nice to meet you, Mrs. Locke."

"Well, isn't that nice," my mother said, letting him clasp her limp-fish handshake. "He called me 'Missus.' You two come on in. Is he your boyfriend?"

"I'm working with him on the new play," I said. If she didn't recognize him, I wasn't going to get her all worked up about having a celebrity in her lair. "How are you feeling?"

"Great!" she said.

"I mean — how's your — are you going tell me what's wrong with you?"

"Oh, that. It was just a cold. I'm a lot better now."

"*What?*"

The sound of a toilet flushing was loud in the small, thin-walled mobile home, and I realized we weren't her only guests. With the classic sinking feeling I usually got when confronted with one of my mother's schemes, I looked toward the back expectantly. And almost choked when I saw the seedy blond Adonis in jeans, white T-shirt and black leather jacket who emerged from the back room.

"Penny!" he bellowed. "I wanted to be out here to greet you!" Before I could stop him, he'd dashed over and given me a big bear hug, lifting me in the process. He dropped me a few inches so I thumped to the floor, and suddenly I felt Jace at my back, his hand on my shoulder. I was reeling. *What the fuck?*

I guess Jace was, too. His polite tone had turned to ice. "And who's this?"

"What, didn't she tell you?" my mother cackled. "That's her husband!"

∾

"No, no, no. This can't be happening," I said.

Jace had taken a step back from me, and I turned to him with a pleading look. He looked confused and, to my surprise, angry.

"Don't listen to her," I said. "Dion's my ex-husband. He was my husband for about five minutes, a long time ago."

"For two months, you mean," Dion said cheerfully. He

pulled a beer out of the fridge and sat at the worn Formica table. "Damn, it's good to see you, girl. You look better than ever."

He still looked good, too, with his floppy blond hair and dazzling grin. Those looks had been a trap back then, when all I'd wanted was to get out of this trailer, and he'd seemed like the Greek god who could manage it. But now there were hints of dissipation, lines at his eyes, and rough skin that spoke of too much time in the sun. The once rock-hard stomach had softened. And, to my relief, none of the attraction remained, not one polyester thread of it.

"And I am here why? You're not really sick, are you?" I asked my mother.

"I told you, I got over it. I needed to get you in touch with Dion, here." She had taken a position behind his chair and put a hand on his shoulder.

Not again. I felt dizzy. "You had my phone number, not that I would have taken his call."

"Exactly," she responded. "Dion has a question for you."

"I don't care. I'm leaving."

"Wait," Jace said, his voice unusually cool. "Let's hear what Dion has to say. We came all this way, after all."

I shot him a look of disbelief. Why was he acting so weird all of a sudden?

"Is this your boyfriend?" Dion asked.

"As if," my mother interjected.

I scowled at her. "What do you want, Dion?"

He shrugged. "I'm going into the Army, and since your mom here said you weren't gainfully employed, I thought maybe you'd be interested in joining up with me."

"Joining the *Army?*" I asked dumbly.

"*You* wouldn't have to join the Army," he said with an

affable chuckle. "But I get better pay if I'm married. A lot of the guys do it. It could be just like old times."

"You have got to be kidding me. Aren't you too old to join the Army?" He was a few years older than I was, which had also been part of the problem.

"Oh, they take us old guys in the Army. They have so many wars and all."

My mother's red lipstick framed a devious smile, and my temper snapped.

"In what fantasy world did you cook this up?" I barked at her. "I'm 'not gainfully employed'? What the hell do you think I do over in Bohemia? I have a job. I have a fucking *career.*"

"Well, haven't you developed a cracklin' little temper!" Dion exclaimed in delight. "Don't be mad, hon. You'll get free healthcare. And fringe benefits, of course." He grinned again as his eyes slid up my body, and my stomach roiled.

"You don't have to act so highfalutin, Penny," said my mother, now massaging Dion's shoulders with both hands. "You always thought you were smarter than the rest of us. Now's your chance to have a normal life with Dion, here." She leaned over my ex, beaming, and her shirt gapped, showing cleavage and a scrap of a lacy black bra.

And then I got it. I was a pawn in her latest pathetic game.

But for me to win, I would also have to lose. It wasn't worth it.

"You win, Mom."

Out of the corner of my eye, I saw Jace's face turn to stone.

Confusion eroded my mother's triumphant expression. I savored the moment when she thought her plan was coming apart, and then I played my role, as she'd intended all along.

"I'm leaving. Dion? Suck it." I couldn't even enjoy

indulging in my fury, tinged as it was by that familiar sense of disappointment.

I spun and threw open the door of the trailer. It banged against the wall, and I walked out, hoping Jace would follow.

He did, not bothering to close the door behind him. He unlocked the car, and I got in and slammed that door, too. He slid into the driver's seat, cranked it up and backed out of the driveway. He turned the wrong way, but I didn't say anything. I was too mad to talk.

After a few minutes of Jace driving aimlessly and me seeing nothing but red, he spoke.

"So this is it?"

"What?" I asked, turning to him.

"Is this Skunk Lake?"

We were on the road that circled the lake, fringed by a few private docks, trees and public parking areas.

"That's it. Glamorous, isn't it?"

"So you're married?" he asked in a subdued tone.

"Was. *Was.* Divorced, ages ago. I was young. I was stupid. I was trapped in that goddamn latrine of a home."

"How old were you?"

"Eighteen."

"I thought you went to school for theater," Jace said.

"I did. But Dion was this speed bump I had to get past first. I'd just graduated high school, but I didn't believe in myself enough to think I could make it studying theater. Dion was this white knight on a motorcycle, or so I thought. I'd met him at a friend's pool party at the start of my senior year, and then I kept seeing him when I was working at the Dairy Spot."

"You're so much smarter than he is."

"Is it that obvious?" I laughed bitterly. "The thing is, I was living with my mother, and I thought I would have to live with her forever, which was akin to living in hell. I didn't think I could afford college. I'd been offered a couple of minor scholarships, but there was no way they would even come close to covering the tuition, and I guess I was scared. And Dion was gorgeous, even if he was an airhead. He had the hots for me, and I loved being appreciated."

"You could have had anyone."

"I didn't think so. I hated myself back then." I swallowed the lump in my throat. "Dion turned my head, because he acted like he was crazy about me. He was three years older than me, and I thought he was more mature than he was. I was infatuated. Plus me going out with him infuriated my mother."

"Why? She seemed taken with him just now."

"She was taken with him then, too. Once I came home and — " I gagged on the memory. "She was grinding up against him in the kitchen of our apartment. They had their clothes on, but he was drunk, and he didn't seem to mind. He was leaning back against the counter, and she was rubbing up and down. Her hands were on his — "

Jace responded to the catch in my voice. "You're jealous?"

"Of course not. Not now. Then I was jealous, jealous and furious. I went to a friend's house that night and obliterated myself with gin until I got sick. Until I realized that being angry was smarter than being jealous, because it gave me the fuel to do what I needed to do. Now — now I'm just pissed that I let her manipulate me again."

"But she wanted you to get together with him."

"I don't think so. She knew I would never agree to something as nuts as marrying him. Maybe he knew it, too. It was a ridiculous ploy, a way for her to justify getting together with him. I think this is her twisted way of fucking with me and maybe getting to sleep with Dion, finally. Assuming she never has. I don't know, now."

Jace made a noise — of anger or disgust, I wasn't sure.

"She's always had this sick competition thing with me," I said. "She hates getting older. And she knew how much power Dion had over me then, so maybe she thought it would be fun to stir the pot. Get to me while she got to him."

"I see." Jace's voice was cold and furious at the same time.

"I don't think you *do* see. I'd wanted him in the worst way, when I was in high school, but I was young and scared and a virgin. All the extra attention from my mother's 'dates' had made me really gun-shy around men. Dion softened me up with kisses. I suppose I was deranged by teen hormones. I thought it could only get better, more fool me. Dion started talking about marriage like it was some kind of fairy-tale option and not just a way for him to fuck me. He even said he could help me pay for school. Maybe that's what convinced me. I saw a way out of my life. We got married at the courthouse a week after I graduated."

"And was he all you dreamed?" Jace's sarcasm was painful.

I shook my head. "If you mean, was the sex good, I had no way to compare at the time. The idea was more exciting than the execution. It wasn't interesting, and he lasted about as long as a firecracker. Once we consummated the craving, all the gas went out of it. Plus we lived in an apartment he shared with a slob of a roommate for two months. Dion never did anything except tinker with his bike and the occasional odd job while I worked *two* jobs to pay the rent. Seeing him standing there, letting my mother rub up against him — " I shuddered. "That was the last straw. Finally, I saw the light and got the hell out."

"When did you go to college?"

"Right away. I decided I'd make it on my own, even if it killed me. I found part-time jobs and worked in the costume department at school. I still have loans to pay off, but they're not too heavy. I learned to believe in myself."

Jace nodded but said nothing as he drove on the road that curved around the lake. The sun played hide-and-seek behind the towering clouds.

"The Army. What a joke," I muttered. "Dion's never followed a rule in his life."

"And I thought you didn't have any secrets," Jace said.

"Why should you care?" I disliked the shrewish tone that crept into my voice, but I barreled ahead anyway. "You're full of secrets, and you're going to take them all with you when you go back to New York."

It took him a moment to respond. "I don't want to leave you with anything that would cause you pain."

"That's a fucking diplomatic answer."

"I'm sorry. I don't know what I'm saying. I just thought I knew you better, that's all. I'm a little shell-shocked."

Though he sounded calm, his face was flushed, and his mouth was compressed.

All my anger fizzled, replaced with regret. "Are you upset? Don't be upset, Jace. I didn't think it was important. I never tell anybody about Dion. It's embarrassing. And since I've only just gotten to know you, and you're leaving . . . " *Shit.* I was making a hash of this. "Either way, as a friend, I would have told you eventually. Probably. It's just something I've put behind me, and I prefer to leave it back here at Skunk Lake."

"I do understand that," he said, then continued darkly,

"and since you don't have stage fright or any other crippling neuroses, you haven't had much of a reason to talk about it."

Not that I didn't have problems. But my chain-dating didn't seem all that dysfunctional compared with his issues. I was overcome with remorse for snapping at him as I recalled all he'd told me about losing Lauren, losing his way.

"Jace, pull over. Just anywhere."

God, his face was grim. He found a little picnic area shrouded by trees and parked in the shade. He left the car on but the radio off; I thanked the fates for both the silence and the air conditioning as I turned to him. I wished I could hug him, but the center console was in the way.

"I'm so sorry I didn't tell you," I said. "It just didn't seem like the right time. I — I don't know what this is between us. But you've trusted me, and I should have trusted you with this. I'm sorry."

He nodded, looking at the dash. Not looking at me.

Tears filled my eyes.

"Damn it," I hissed, brushing them away.

He looked up, and his face softened. "Oh, Pen, don't cry. He's not worth crying over."

"I'm not crying over him! I'm crying over — I'm crying because I've made you upset, and that's something I never want to do. I've been closer to you than I've been to any guy since then. Actually, since ever. *Ever*. Do you understand that? Do you know that? Please don't hate me."

"I don't hate you. God, I don't hate you." Jace popped open his car door, came around to mine and pulled me out. He enfolded me in his arms, and I sobbed into his chest like the little fool I was.

Thunder rumbled, and still I held him, wishing he was mine, wishing he'd always been mine, that he'd never had his heart broken, that he didn't have another life in a place far, far away. I lifted my face to his, and he kissed me. I vibrated with longing as I opened to him, and he tightened his hold on me. The first raindrops fell on our faces and mixed with my tears. I clutched him closer as the warm rain embraced us. I needed to show him I wanted all of him, all of his fears and his kindness and his heart, even if he was going to throw mine away. Soon. So soon.

A flash and a nearly simultaneous crack of thunder made us jump apart. Without a word, we got into the car, a little wet, but somehow better. At least I felt better. And maybe Jace did, too. As he pulled onto the road, and the shower became a cloudburst, he reached across the center console to grab my hand. He drove like that until we reached the next intersection, and then he put both hands on the wheel.

"How the hell do we get to Bohemia Beach?"

My smile was rueful. I crossed my arms against the chill created by my damp clothes and the air conditioning and got him going in the right direction.

WE DIDN'T TALK about Dion or my mother for the rest of the day. We didn't talk about much. But we made love as if we might never have sex again in the big bed at Jace's place as thunderstorms rolled overhead, until our bodies were slick with sweat. And then we took a candlelit bath together in the giant tub.

I straddled him and slid down over his cock, making waves in the soapy water, rocking against him, my breasts and hair dripping. I stared into his eyes and saw the storms echoed there. There was so much we weren't saying, but our bodies did the speaking for us, until we clutched each other and came with wild cries.

He dropped me back at home on Sunday afternoon. Wearing his *Rent* T-shirt, I could feel the Jace hangover setting in. I was headlong into this bender, fuck the consequences, and the more Jace I had in my veins, the more the withdrawal was going to be a bitch. But like a good little addict, I found reasons not to care. I wanted him, as much of him as I could get, before he left me. I tried not to worry on what terms we'd part, if we could remain friends, though I had to admit that one of the novelties of being with Jace was that he was also my friend. Even if we never slept together again, I would miss his friendship. It was worth keeping, if columnist Joe Stier's threats didn't get in the way.

They were at the top of my mind when Cali came to rehearsal on Tuesday to shoot a few of the characters in costume — Titania (still carping about the décolletage of her more-or-less finished dress) and Oberon; Demetrius (Jace, devastating in black) and Helena (lovely Wendy); Lysander and Hermia. Cali particularly loved shooting Doug as Nick Bottom with his donkey head, lounging with Titania in her bower, especially when she heard her brother had executed the final head design.

Alan manipulated the lighting on stage for the shots, which incorporated only a little of the scenery — Karen's crew was running behind, and Dirk, I could tell, was trying not to blow a gasket. Still, our director posed the characters in dramatic and funny moments for about forty minutes of shooting, and then he shooed Cali off so he could get rehearsal under way. I asked Millie and Theresa to make sure the costumes were stored properly and caught up with Cali at the exit.

"Do you have a minute to talk?" I asked her.

"I was hoping you'd find me. I have an update."

I led her to my office, not wanting to run into actors in the green room.

"Nice art," she said with a twinkle, nodding at the *Alice in Wonderland* poster that featured her photography.

"I love it," I said as we both grabbed a chair. I took a deep breath. "Is there any hope?"

"I have a meeting set up with the managing editor."

"Does he have the power to do anything?"

"*She* is Nell Banker, and she's second in command of the newsroom, so I hope so. She's been hearing stories about Joe for a while. There just hasn't been enough to act. Women have been afraid to go to human resources, because Joe is the editor's golden child. Since I spoke to her about you, she's asked a few of them to file the reports they've been holding back, and she's agreed to meet with you tomorrow."

"Tomorrow!"

"Is that all right?"

"Yes, more than all right. Does she understand what I'm bringing?"

"She knows it's a recording. She doesn't know the content, only that you describe it as blackmail. I'm curious myself."

"It's still on my phone," I said, digging it out of my bag.

"Then you should make a copy of it and put it on something that's easier to see. Let's see your tablet there."

A couple of minutes later, Cali had the video synched to the tablet and was calling it up.

She watched the conversation between Jace and Joe; it was the first time I'd seen it since that day, and my stomach hurt all over again to hear it.

"That rat fuck," Cali said.

"I know."

"But Jace — he really cares about you." She turned to me, her blue eyes wide and bright. "Oh, Pen."

"He's chivalrous, is all. He's leaving soon."

She smiled and shook her head. "I thought the same thing about Wyatt. How do you feel about Jace?"

I didn't respond, but my eyes filled with tears.

"Oh, shit, you have it bad. Don't let him go. And tell him about this."

"Not till I have an answer."

"Tell him as soon as you can, then. Tell him everything. Tell him how you feel."

"I don't even know how I feel," I said.

"Don't you?" Cali gave my arm a squeeze, then stood with her photographer's baggage. "The meeting's at 10."

"Is it at the paper? Won't Joe see me?"

"It's in the publisher's conference room, which is at the front of the building. He's unlikely to see you, if he's even there. But I'll go with you. If we run into him, and he asks, I'll say we're talking about photos for the entertainment section. Which we are, of course. Did you know they're going to put *Midsummer* on the cover?" Cali grinned.

"You're the best," I said, showing her to the door.

"Listen. This will work out. But you have something bigger to think about. I know what it's like to be scared to lose the thing you want most. Don't be afraid. I almost waited too long. I waited for him to make up his mind."

"And it all worked out. You're lucky."

"Sometimes luck needs a kick in the ass." She hugged me. "See you tomorrow."

Cali was already in the spacious, three-story lobby of *The Bohemia Bugle* when I arrived. She had a small camera bag with her — I rarely saw her without one — and her long, blond hair was pinned up in a twist.

She stood to meet me. "It's so weird coming back in here. I haven't been in the building since I was laid off."

"But they're still using your photos."

"Yeah, because they're getting them free from the Chamberlain," she joked. "The change has been good for me. Everyone's still civil. And I think you'll like Nell."

A secretary showed us into the conference room and offered us bottles of water, which we both took. It was another really hot day, and it looked as if more storms were in the offing. It was finally the rainy season. The big windows on one side of the room showed a retention pond rippling in the breeze under a sky thick with clouds. Palms, hibiscus and bougainvillea swayed amid a mass of dark green foliage.

Nell arrived, her look sleek, classy and smart. She shook both of our hands, and Cali did the introductions.

"Why don't you both sit down," Nell said. We took comfy roller chairs at the long, glossy table, and she looked at me. "I understand you have something to show me?"

"Yes. It's a conversation your reporter had with Jace Edison, the playwright and an actor in our production."

I pulled out my tablet, and Nell fished into the wires nestled in the middle of the table to plug it in.

"Might as well see it in HD," she said. "Penelope, would you find the video on your iPad and hit play?"

I found it just as the big TV at one end of the room came on. My screen was mirrored on it. I started the video.

It was almost like watching it that first time in the green room, though my hand-held phone video of the monitor wasn't perfectly steady. I could see the cold anger in Jace's expression as Joe laid out his plan for fame. I hoped I was doing the right thing.

I watched Nell for a reaction as it ended. She unplugged the iPad and gave it back to me without comment, and then she looked directly into my eyes.

"You are seeing this actor?"

"I have been, yes."

"And you don't care if your name ends up in the tabloids? Because that very well may happen if we remove Joe Stier."

Yes. She was actually talking about removing Joe Stier.

"I don't mind. I mean, I don't love it, but I don't think Jace should have to open up his life just to feed the ambitions of your reporter."

"Who apparently isn't writing his big story for us, anyway," said Nell, her tone acerbic. "Would you mind if I showed this video to the editor?"

I glanced at Cali, but she gave me no hints, then back at Nell. "Isn't Joe the teacher's pet?"

Nell laughed. "He has been, but not so much lately. Even outside of his treatment of women in the newsroom, his stories have been suffering. It appears his extracurricular activities have affected his work to the point that even my boss is unhappy."

"OK," I said. "Whatever it takes. But I really don't want the world to see this video."

"I promise they won't. In fact, if you have five minutes, I'll take your tablet to the editor and let him watch it right now. I told him earlier today that we had to talk about Joe. HR has been getting reports of some concern."

This time, Cali nodded, and I handed over my device. When Nell left, I turned to her. "What do you think?"

"Nell is smart. She's been wanting to get rid of Joe for a

long time. If I'm right, she's already built a very good case. This could help sway the editor."

It was more like fifteen minutes, but when Nell returned, her eyes were bright. "We'll need a few days to work out the details," she said, handing me my iPad.

"What details?" I asked.

"I'll let you know when there's word. We have to get human resources involved. Legal likes to cover their butts in situations like this. If possible, we can do this without ever mentioning your video."

"I'd prefer that," I said. "The last thing I want is this ending up in court, as a public record. I never actually considered that until now. I really don't want that."

"Don't worry," Nell said. "Besides, we can't show what we don't have. If there comes a time when he sues us — and trust me, we will not leave any openings for him to do so — I don't think your video would help, anyway. This is an internal matter, and we don't want the details released, either."

There was the hard-nosed businesswoman who didn't want her company known for sexual harassment. And that was good for me.

"Thanks for looking at this," I said.

"Yeah, thank you," Cali added.

"My pleasure, ladies. You may have given me just what I needed. I'll be in touch."

On the wide steps outside, Cali put a hand on my arm and halted me. She nodded toward the parking lot. There, several rows away, was Joe Stier. I held my breath. Almost as if he sensed us looking at him, he turned his head and saw us. To my surprise, he grinned, nodded and gave us one of his classic leers. He went right up to the back door and went in.

"He doesn't know we know," I said.

Cali scowled. "Slimeball."

"Do you think it will work?"

"I think the women are about to get their turn. But you should be prepared for consequences, either way."

It wasn't the happy statement I'd hoped for, but still, I felt better as I drove my old VW bug back to downtown and the theater. If Joe got fired, the worst thing that would happen would be tabloid gossip. It wasn't great, but it wasn't like forcing Jace to reveal everything. His heart and his career would be safe when he went back to New York.

And my love life? It couldn't be any shittier than it was before he came to town.

Except that now, I would have an idea of what I was missing.

TIME SEEMED to speed up as all of us fully embraced the fact that the play would open in just over a week. There was no longer any thought of fresh inspirations or details for costumes. Tech week was imminent, and that meant that all the costumes would have to be perfected in just a few days.

And there were so many of them. We had the principals' costumes finished for the photo shoot, mostly, but there were still details that had to be added, especially since the city characters' outfits would become more loose, ragged and revealing by the end of the play. For Helena and Hermia, we also had to make the slinky undergarments that would be glimpsed as their dishabille increased.

I sat in rehearsals Wednesday and Thursday night, making detailed charts for each character to mark every scene where their costumes evolved. I also noted every costume that needed batteries for the delicate strings of lights — specifically, the fairies, the game designers and Nick Bottom, with his magical donkey head.

Meanwhile, in the costume shop, the outfits for the game designers and the teen fairies were hemmed and tailored and finished and hung on neat racks that would be rolled onto the elevator and taken backstage Sunday morning. That would be an all-day marathon — a full run-through with lighting and sound cues, costume changes and revolving scenery that would help Dirk and the designers identify glitches and solve any problems.

I called Cali once, Thursday afternoon, and she said she hadn't heard anything definitive about Joe Stier. But one of her old colleagues who was plugged into the rumor mill said Joe was in trouble because one woman on staff had come forward with a raft of unwanted raunchy texts he'd sent.

"Hang in there," Cali told me.

Throughout, I barely saw Jace, except for a discreet kiss or a cup of coffee here and there, though he was much on my mind. He had to rehearse as an actor, and he was at Dirk's side the rest of the time, acting as his assistant. He smoothed conflicts with the lagging construction crew and offered last-minute advice on production questions relevant to the play's themes. In short, when I ran into him Thursday night on the way out the door, he was exhausted, and I was the same. And neither of us were talking about the forces conspiring against us. Still, we promised each other that we'd get together Saturday, if not sooner, before the hell of tech week commenced.

Tension was high on stage Friday. Dirk had scheduled a rehearsal for early Friday evening, but an afternoon lightning strike had taken out the theater's air conditioning. The actors showed up to find a steamy temperature of eighty-seven degrees in the performance space and were correspondingly grumpy. The crew had set up a couple of large fans to keep the air moving on stage, but their roar just made it hard for the actors to hear one another.

Holland was the first to shed clothing. I looked up from my note-taking to see her flinging her shirt into the empty audience seats, leaving us all to admire her (fortunately opaque) black bra and the bounty it barely contained.

When Dirk didn't object — his lust for his leading lady was no secret — most of the guys quickly followed, baring their torsos, laughing and grinning. But not Jace. He took off his button-up shirt but retained the sleeveless undershirt underneath. For someone who could be so impulsive offstage, he was completely in control when he was working, and he shot me a wry look as the other guys flashed their chests. Still, I found myself distracted by the play of muscles in his arms and back as he moved, and I filled in the gaps with my memories of his chest — and everything else. And felt even hotter.

Equally modest were Wendy and the woman playing Hermia, who did little more than shed outer layers and unbutton blouses to tasteful depths. I was quietly thankful that the teen fairies weren't around, given the dubious dress code. My own retro sundress was thin and light, and there was no way I was stripping to my unmentionables for the pleasure of the cast. I'd save that for the next pinup shoot.

Apparently, our artistic director had more qualms than Dirk. A half-hour before rehearsal was to end, Anne Friar bustled into the theater and practically dragged Dirk into a corner for a private conference. I couldn't get much of it, except that she was almost angry enough to spit at our sweating director, and I heard the word "inappropriate" at least three times.

"OK, kids, get dressed and get out of here," Dirk said with a glower when Anne stalked out again. "I'll see Alan and Bill tomorrow for the lighting and sound run-through. We'll see the rest of you Sunday at 10 a.m., fully clothed, please, for the official start of tech week. And we all know how much fun that will be."

There were groans and laughs as the actors gathered their garments and belongings. Jace wandered over to me. I realized it was the first time he'd publicly approached me in days, and I knew his distance had to be because of Joe.

"Want to go outside and cool off?" he asked with a small smile.

"You're not too tired?"

"Dirk's giving me a whole day off tomorrow. I feel like a new man. Especially if I get to see you. You don't have to be here tomorrow, do you?"

"No, thank God. We got the last major costume work done today, though I expect we'll have our needle and thread out for Sunday."

"Can you sew scenery? It will be a miracle if the stage crew is done with the trees by then."

"Karen will get it done." I sounded more confident than I felt.

Humor danced in Jace's eyes. "We'll see. I'll paint if I have to. Where should we go?"

"Someplace with air conditioning."

"Then my place."

"Mine is almost working," I joked, but I was glad to acquiesce. He followed my car home first, where I packed a quick bag before settling into his.

"I feel like Cinderella when I ride in this car," I said, enjoying its cool comfort and glide, nothing like my rattle-trap. "Did you drive it all the way from home to Bohemia Beach?"

"Yeah, and I loved it. I usually keep it at my parents' house. It's such a pain to have a car in the city. I was excited that I'd get to drive it all summer."

"I can see why."

"Why are we talking about my car?" He was taking the Jag over the arch of the causeway now, soaring into the warm night.

The question surprised me. "I don't know. Because it's nice? Because I wonder what it's like to have nice things?"

"It's just a thing. Other things are more important."

"True."

"I got a strange phone call this afternoon."

"You did?" A little frisson of worry passed through me.

"It was a reporter at *The Bugle*. She wanted to do a quick phone interview with me because the guy who did the original interview just quit and hadn't written his story about the play."

I couldn't help it. A grin took over my face.

Jace saw it. "You knew, didn't you?"

"I didn't know he'd be fired. I mean, I hoped he would, but I didn't know."

"He was fired? Why did you know, Penelope? How much do you know?"

Shit. We were on A1A now, driving into the quiet stretch where Jace lived. I let him pull into his driveway before I spoke.

"I should have told you," I said. "I was watching the interviews on media day."

"From the green room?" He turned off the car and looked at me.

I nodded. "I was curious. There was no reason not to watch. I like to watch you work."

He nodded as if he were thinking it over. "Let's go inside."

"Are you angry?" I asked when we got to the living room.

"I'm more worried than angry." He flopped onto a couch and stared at me. "I'm wondering if I should be thanking the stars for a miracle or freaking out about what comes next. And it would have been nice to hear it from you. I knew when that reporter told me that Stier was gone that it couldn't have been a random coincidence."

I gingerly sat next to him. "I just wanted to help, Jace."

"Tell me."

So I told him about recording the conversation and the meeting at *The Bugle* and Joe's history there.

"So *The Bugle* has this video?" he asked, his brow furrowed.

"No. The top editors watched it and gave it back. They could have copied it, I guess, but I trust the woman who met with me and Cali. She said they would never have to acknowledge it, even. It just tipped them over the edge. It let her convince the editor to do what they needed to do anyway. Joe had been harassing women there for a long, long time."

"Do you understand that he's probably going to go to the tabloids with whatever he has?"

"I'm sorry, Jace. I know that will suck for you, but it seemed like it would be even worse if you had to let him into your life like that. You didn't *want* to do the interview, did you?" I asked, horrified that I might have completely misread the situation.

"Hell, no." He sighed deeply, put an arm around my

shoulders and pulled me closer to him. "And I appreciate what you tried to do, though I wish you'd told me about it. I was so relieved when I heard he was gone, that he couldn't touch the opening of the play, that I wouldn't have to talk to him ever again. But then I realized that he can do whatever he wants if he's not protecting his job at the paper. He can go to the tabloids with whatever crazy story he cooks up. This could really screw up your life for a while, Pen. I didn't want to see that happen."

I tried to smile. "There's no reason for you to protect me. And hey, there are worse things than being connected with Jace Edison."

"This could dog you for a long time," he said quietly. "Whenever some journalist does a Google search on you, when they're about to write about your fantastic work for whatever production comes next, they're going to find out that you were . . . "

"I know. Your 'piece of ass in Florida.' "

Jace made a sound of disgust. "That bastard. I wish you hadn't heard that."

"I can't sue them over the truth." But damn, it hurt.

He touched my cheek and gently kissed me. "I hope you know you're much more than that to me."

I struggled to sound unaffected. "It is what it is, Jace. I'm just sorry that you'll have to go back to New York and face that gaggle of gossipmongers in the entertainment press. Now every story will pair you with whatever voracious female happens to cross your path. You won't be the asexual untouchable anymore."

His voice was low and distant, as if he was caught up in some dark thought. "It was getting old, anyway."

It took me a full minute to give up on my wisp of a wish

that maybe — just maybe — he wouldn't be leaving me behind when he left. Not entirely. Some crazy part of me had thought maybe we could still see each other, even if it was long-distance.

Maybe Cali was right. Maybe I should jump in and tell him how much I wanted that, wanted more.

But the way he sat there, hands clasped, distant and wrapped up in his world, that world so far away, dissolved my last hope. I took a deep breath and prepared to ride out the last tremors of the earthquake that he'd created in my life.

"Got any beer?" I asked.

He blinked as if coming out of a dream. His half-smile, part melancholy, part merry, almost broke my heart. "There's a six-pack of one of those Bohemia Brewing Company beers. They're pretty good. Grab me one?"

I nodded, smiled my little-used actor's smile and got up to get them. I came back with the cold bottles and settled against him as he flipped on the TV and went to TCM. I realized the movie was one of my favorites, *How To Steal a Million,* with Audrey Hepburn (apparently the star of the month) and a deliciously slinky Peter O'Toole as the art expert she talks into stealing a forged statue from a museum before its fakery is discovered. She thinks he's a burglar. Her father is a forger. There's deception upon deception, but somehow, love wins.

The absurdity of it abruptly annoyed me. But before I could get angry at the ridiculous idea of love conquering all, Jace turned off the TV and kissed my neck. I wanted to resist. I tried. But his busy lips said more than his silence, and I wanted to believe his body as he kissed my shoulder and slipped down the strap of my sundress. He licked the skin there, and then lower, tasting the curve of my breast before pulling the dress down to lick my nipple.

I gasped. Nothing had faded between us, not when we touched. If anything, his mouth stoked an even higher flame in me. I had never realized that an emotional attachment — I refused to call it more — could feed the conflagration of our bodies. I'd never known that feeling with Dion, back in my five-minute, lust-spurred marriage, and it was a shock to experience it with Jace.

He slipped off the other strap and pushed my dress down to my waist, revealing both breasts, and whatever restraint I had was burned away. We were stripping each other, kissing, touching, as urgent as ever.

Moments later, naked and beautiful, he stood before me, grasped my legs and pushed me against the back of the couch. He positioned my ankles on his shoulders, leaving me entirely exposed to his turbulent gaze. Supporting me with one hand, he touched me with the other, sliding a finger through my warm, wet heat, slipping it inside me. I loved it when he possessed me like this, and I lost myself to the hazy, intoxicating sensation of his invasive finger, the feeling of being on display for him.

He, too, seemed lost in a daze of desire. He moved both hands to my rear. Undulating against me, he stroked my folds with the head of his hot, hard erection.

"Penelope," he whispered, my name a caress. The sweet sound undid me, as did his midnight eyes and the heady feeling of giving myself up to his ravishment, bent as I was to his penetration. I moaned at the velvet of his voice, the steel of his sex sliding into my honey, and I clenched around him. I was bound to the moment. Come what may, Jace was inside me, dear Jace, and I braced myself against the hard pleasure of his deep, angled fucking.

I would take what I could. I would treasure this moment,

however brief, however high. I would listen to what his body was saying and let myself fall.

"I THOUGHT you said you could roller skate?" Dirk bellowed at a 16-year-old fairy in a skater skirt, who was sprawled on the stage where she'd just crashed.

"I can. I mean, I can ice skate, so I thought it would be the same thing." She burst into tears.

It wasn't the first day of tech week without someone bursting into tears. I'd spent much of the endless run-through backstage. Most of the costume tweaks had been done or noted, so I'd gone into the theater to get some air (in the now-working air conditioning) and watch the actors. We'd been here for eight hours, and nerves were frayed worse than fake silk.

Adorable Harry as Puck was idling on his unicycle offstage, peddling back and forth to stay in place. He nodded to the fallen girl. "She'll be hell on wheels in two days," said the affable college student. "I'll teach her myself."

"Make it work, or we'll have one less fairy," Dirk said, and the girl gulped another sob. "For now, take those skates off before you maim someone, and let's go through this scene from the top. Doug! Holland!"

Fairies scattered so they could reenter, two with skateboards but most on in-line skates, except for the girl who'd fallen. Now she wore fluffy pink socks.

Doug as Nick Bottom, who was struggling a bit with his donkey head, turned and whacked Holland in the face with his elongated wire nose.

"Would you please watch where you're putting that thing?" she barked, pushing him away.

"That's not what you said a couple of weeks ago," Doug muttered, to the laughter of everyone in earshot. That included Hermia, Lysander, Demetrius and Helena — the actors were all lying about the stage on park benches for their enchanted doze. Wendy looked so cozy lying against Jace, I had to suppress an ugly surge of jealousy, even though he and I had spent the day before in happy, idle hours at the beach and in his bed.

Despite Holland's scowl, she looked gorgeous in her dress, even if she did keep pulling down on the neckline so more of her breasts would show. She took her position just backstage with Doug, and they entered, as Titania and Bottom, trailed by fairies.

"Music! Lights on the bed!" Dirk hollered up at the booth.

The light scheme changed a couple of times as Dirk sighed in a dramatic manner. Finally, the actors were in position, the lights were correct, the musical cue had played, and Titania and Bottom, chattering, nestled into her bower — now much more ornate than when Jace and I had visited it.

The repartee Jace had written between the fairy queen and the game designer about game play and technology rolled trippingly off their tongues. The fairies/skater kids were eager to do Nick's will, to find him batteries for his virtual-reality glasses, which is what he thought the donkey head was. The kids agreed, willing to do anything to get a copy of his newest game. It was wildly silly. The fairies parted, wheeling toward the back of the stage, and a skateboarder who'd been hot-dogging all day did an impressive kickflip, spinning the board under him as he jumped.

Only he landed too late and plowed right into one of the two-dimensional wooden trees.

"Look out!" the stage manager yelled offstage as the tree crashed on top of the kid and three other trees fell around him, domino-style, in a deafening clatter. Fairies jumped out of the way, and Dirk ran into the cloud of dust and pile of wood.

He and two stage hands got the tree off the teen, who sat up, stunned and dotted with splotches of wet paint. "It's cool," he said with a grin.

"It is not cool, and no more tricks," Dirk commanded, but I could tell he was shaken. "Is everyone OK?"

There was a chorus of yeses from the kids, and then Karen, the scenic designer, strode into the mess as the crew erected the fallen trees.

"Shit!" she said. "We're going to have to paint them all again!"

"And clean up the stage," Dirk said, pointing to the smudges of paint on the floor. "And then touch up the floor and reinforce those trees, *after* we're gone. Somebody get a mop so we can finish this goddamn rehearsal!"

A beleaguered member of the crew appeared with a mop and bucket a couple of minutes later and worked on the spots. The actors playing the sleeping couples stood and stretched.

"Nobody goes nowhere," Dirk growled, his pale face flushed under his red beard. "Get your heads in the game, people. This is not the time to add bells and whistles to your performance. Let's get through this without getting killed, all right?"

Chastened, tired actors stood or sat patiently, just wanting it to be over. Holland, lounging on the flowers and colorful cloths of the round bed, said "Hmph!" and yanked at her neckline again.

A distinct ripping sound cut through the silence.

"Fuck," I said out loud as the split overlay of tulle flopped over her now exposed breast. "Millie!" I shouted.

Millie appeared ten seconds later, running from back-stage, where she'd been wrangling costumes. We converged on an unrepentant Holland, who'd done nothing to cover up her tit.

Not even Dirk was aroused. "We're not doing *Oh! Calcutta!* Get that dress off — NOT HERE!" he shouted as Holland started yanking at the gown, "and put on some real clothes! You have two minutes!"

"Stop doing that," I snapped at Holland, who was still trying to squirm out of the dress as we led her backstage. "You're just going to make it worse. We're going to have to redo the bodice and maybe some of the overlays."

"If the neckline had been lower, this wouldn't have been an issue," she retorted as we got her to the green room and an adjacent dressing room. "Can you give me some privacy?"

"Now you want privacy?" I laughed as Millie unzipped the dress and Holland stepped out of it. "You can have it. I just want to get the dress back so we can salvage the wreck."

I probably would have slammed the door of the dressing room if Millie hadn't been right behind me.

"We can fix it," she assured me as we left the green room.

"But it's going to take most of tomorrow," I said. "I know. Shit happens."

"I'll put it in the costume shop."

"Thanks for your help. I wish everyone was as non-dramatic as you."

Millie grinned and shrugged. "They're actors. That's why we love them."

Indeed. I went back into the theater proper to see order more or less restored. Wendy was off chatting with the hunky Oberon, who was waiting in the wings, and Jace sat on the park bench, wearing a bemused look. He looked up as I walked by, and his face broke into a slow smile that chased all my clouds away.

They're actors. That's why we love them.

I smiled back, drinking in his gaze for another moment as Holland huffed back onto the stage in shorts and a clingy T-shirt.

"Hang on to that lovestruck expression, Edison," Dirk said wryly to Jace as he walked past. "You'll need it in the next scene. Places, everyone! Let's pick up after the fairies' exit."

I knew I'd turned red. Lovestruck? Hardly. But there was something so warm and intimate in Jace's eyes that I felt a rush of heat from head to toe. He winked and resumed his position on the bench. Wendy curled up next to him, Helena to his Demetrius, and I slipped out of the theater. I couldn't watch that speech again, not now.

Not when I so badly wanted him to say it to me.

Despite Sunday's horrible run-through, I sent email invitations to my friends to the dress rehearsal on Thursday. It was always better for the cast to have an audience, and the actors all invited a few people to buoy them and give them the reactions they needed to do their jobs. Pretty much all of my buddies said they'd be there Friday for opening night, too.

I hoped desperately that the play would come together by

then, and my fears were eased as Monday and Tuesday's run-throughs — with a few of the more technical costumes — went more smoothly. Wednesday gave everyone a start when our Oberon didn't show up for rehearsal. Many frantic phone calls and two hours later, as a quaking understudy read the part, he walked in the door with sheepish apologies about car trouble in the middle of nowhere and a dead cell phone.

The second act went well, the paint was almost dry on the trees, the lights and music were working and there were only minor issues with the props. Even the hapless roller girl could get around the stage on skates now. I was a little nervous, even though we'd worked with the most difficult costumes every day. Doug had mastered the remote for Bottom's donkey head so that the lights would blink crazily or settle into colors, depending on the mood of his character. I'd mended Holland's dress and lowered the neckline to a point where even she would think it was daring. Her dresser also had plans to use tape to head off a wardrobe malfunction.

"Be here no later than 6 tomorrow for makeup and costumes," Dirk said to the cast on stage at the end of the evening. We designers listened from the audience. "Fairies — I like the way you're using your wheels, but don't roll in front of Titania when she's doing her lines. I don't like that."

"Neither do I," Holland said to chuckles.

"Holland, you're lovely," Dirk continued, "but I want you to let yourself get a little ugly when you're arguing with Oberon about the clockwork baby. He's criticizing you for wanting a real baby; make it personal." She nodded. "The couples all look great up there. Don't be afraid to lay it on thick, Wendy. You're funny and vocal, and everyone should know that. Jace — if we could just have a few rewrites ... "

The cast exploded in laughter, knowing that Jace, to

Dirk's horror, had tried to sneak in one or two new lines this week. Jace grinned, but his face sobered as Dirk continued.

"There will be a fair crowd for the dress rehearsal. It's invite-only, but a lot of people have been clamoring for tickets given that this is a hot new play." He didn't need to add, *starring a hot actor.* "Treat this like the real thing. Get psyched. Turn on. We've had our problems, but I want you all to know that you are tremendous together. People are going to laugh, and they're going to be moved. We'll meet again tomorrow in the green room and do this thing. All right?"

The cast clapped and cheered, and Dirk waved at them to go. The crowd broke up, overflowing with a joyous, tired energy, and I stood and stretched. Tomorrow would be my toughest day, but I felt good about where we stood. I smiled at Jace as he walked over to me, but he didn't smile back.

"What is it?"

He shook his head, as if to say, *Not here.*

"Want to go to my office?"

"How about a walk?" he said.

"If you don't mind sweating a little."

We stowed our stuff in our respective vehicles and started our stroll through downtown Bohemia. It was off-season and midweek, but still there were patrons flowing in and out of the bars and restaurants. The air was warm, but not oppressive, and Jace took my hand.

"Let's go visit Ponce de Leon," he said as we neared the square. We moved into the quiet park and headed for the fountain, where the bubbling water obscured the sounds of downtown. He sat on the edge and pulled me down next to him. "I don't know if I can do this."

For a minute, I wasn't sure what *this* was, and then I realized he had to be talking about the play.

"Haven't you worked through it?" I asked. "Are you still afraid?"

"As rehearsals have gone on, it's gotten better, but now that the dress is tomorrow, with a real audience — "

"Jace, listen to me." I shifted to face him and took both of his hands. "What's the worst thing that could happen?"

His brow furrowed, and I longed to kiss that spot in the middle of his forehead. "What do you mean?"

"What's the worst that could happen? You might freeze on stage. You might have to run off and throw up."

"Is this supposed to be a pep talk?" he asked with a half-smile.

"In a way. What I'm trying to tell you is that your fear has built up a monster far bigger than anything you'll encounter on stage."

"Any of those things would be bad for my career."

"You once told me you thought you were a fraud for your string of successes right out of the box. When you got a couple of dings in one review of *Piece of Work,* all your confidence crumbled. Maybe that's because you haven't failed enough."

He shook his head.

"Failure makes you stronger," I said. "Maybe it would be good for you to fail. Maybe you should look forward to it. The thing that makes a great actor, or even a great costume designer, isn't always succeeding. It's learning how to fail gracefully. It's about taking the big risk. Like this play is a big risk for you, but a great one."

Jace pondered my words. "I suppose a failure at the Chamberlain wouldn't end my career."

"Of course it wouldn't," I said. "Wait a minute — what do mean, 'at the Chamberlain'?"

"I mean — "

"You mean we're a hick community theater working on becoming a regional theater and that no one's ever heard of us anyway," I said flatly.

"That's not what I mean. The Chamberlain is a great little theater."

"A great 'little' theater. Where you're slumming for the summer. I get it."

"What the hell just happened to this conversation?" he asked. "That's not what I was saying. I was saying that I'm still scared to go on stage."

But I was on a roll, no longer the voice of reason. I gushed with bad feeling. I'd found another motive for him to leave me.

"I'm just a mediocre little artist in a tropical backwater, far from the bright lights of the big city," I said, almost to myself. "Not Broadway enough for you." I stood and started walking out of the park.

"Penelope? Are you drunk or something?" Jace walked after me. "I'm in no state to argue with crazy."

"This crazy girl is going home," I shouted over my shoulder. Back on the sidewalk, I doubled my pace, heading back to the Chamberlain and my car.

"Penelope!" he called again, but this time, he didn't try to catch me.

Tears flowed down my face. *What the fuck?* I'd jumped down Jace's throat, and for what? The truth was, I was looking for any explanation that justified why we couldn't be together, because geography wasn't satisfactory enough. Neither was the crap I'd thrown at him back in the park, and I knew it. And the poor guy had wanted to talk about his own problems. His stage fright. Jesus, I was an insensitive bitch. And why the hell was I crying? If it was over Jace, well, I hadn't cried over a guy since Dion, and that was more out of regret for my stupidity than it was over actually breaking up with him. Because breaking up with him had been my idea.

Maybe I was trying to make breaking up with Jace my idea, too. But that wasn't what I wanted at all.

I got to my car, got in and cranked it up, filled with remorse. Before I drove home, I texted him: "I'm sorry. I'll talk to you tomorrow. You'll be great."

"Let's talk now," he messaged back.

"Tomorrow. Please. Goodnight."

I ROLLED into the theater about 2 p.m. so I'd have enough time to go over each costume but not so much time that I would drive myself nuts worrying about the dress rehearsal. I was always nervous for the dress; this is when the costumes absolutely had to work. Millie, Theresa and I had been doing virtual run-throughs all week. We'd also memorized the charts I'd made with all the changes, but there was always an opportunity for disaster.

I anxiously awaited Jace's arrival. I had to clear the air with him, or at least clear my heart. I couldn't blame hormones. I couldn't blame indignation. I could blame only myself for last night.

The actors started arriving around 5:30, eager to get ready for the big night. The dressing rooms were full, and the makeup crew was helping those who couldn't help them-selves. I was dressed for work, in black capris and a white blouse, and I did my best to touch base with everyone about their costumes. Midge walked around with her tool belt, prepared to make emergency stitches.

"Millie," I said as I fluffed Hippolyta's skirt, "can you go get the fresh batteries from Marty for the light-up costumes?"

"No problem," she said, heading off to find the prop manager.

When she came back ten minutes later, as I was sorting through the teen fairy costumes, she had a ghastly look on her face.

"What is it?" I asked.

"He didn't get any batteries."

"He didn't get any batteries?"

"That's what he said."

"Can you please show me where he's lurking?" I said, and she nodded in response to my icy tone.

"Marty!" I called when I found him. He perched, toadlike, on a stool, counting out paper coffee cups in the little room where he organized the props for each production. "Where are our batteries?"

"I didn't order batteries." He turned to me with a smug look on his face. "You didn't pay me for any batteries."

"You know very well they were supposed to come out of your budget and we needed a *lot* of them when performances started. And guess what? *Performances are starting!*" I screamed as Millie scurried in the other direction.

He blanched. "There's no need to take that tone."

"There is absolutely a need to take that tone!" I shouted. "Don't give me your passive-aggressive shit." I glanced at the clock on the wall. "You have one hour to come to me with at least five dozen AA batteries, or we're going to put you on stage with a flashlight."

"OK, OK! I'll send my assistant."

"Thanks." I threw him a chilly smile and spun on my heel to leave.

In the hallway, I almost tripped over Dirk.

"Very nice," he murmured. "Maybe you should consider directing someday."

I laughed and headed back to the dressing rooms.

I attended to the women first, then Oberon. When Marty sent his assistant over with the batteries, I had Theresa put fresh cells in every power pack in every costume with lights, including Bottom's head. She and Millie dealt with the fairies and the game designers.

I took a spin through the lobby about twenty minutes before show time and found a group of my friends drinking wine and chattering.

"Is my head still awesome?" asked Damien, looking elegantly punk in black clothes and black eyeliner.

"Your head is still awesome, if empty," I said, to Cali's giggle. Her brother elbowed her. "Thanks for coming, you guys."

"I hate to miss opening night, but I have a gig. I'm glad I could make it tonight," Ez said. "I dragged Gary along."

"She never has to drag me along," Gary said, smiling and impish under his mop of curly hair.

Thea and Sloane made appropriate expressions of enthusiasm, and I gave them all hugs before heading backstage again.

Fifteen minutes to go, and I still hadn't seen Jace. At the least, I had to make sure his costume was perfect. I found Midge and quietly asked whether she knew where he was.

"He grabbed the smallest dressing room and asked if he could have some time to himself. Caused a few remarks about him being the big star, but we have plenty of room.

He's been locked up in there for a while." Midge sounded worried. "You go check on him, honey."

I found the dressing room, where someone had taped a star on the door. It was cut out of a magazine ad, one of the fashion spreads Jace had appeared in. *Everybody's a comic.*

I knocked, and there was no answer. "Jace, it's me," I called softly. A moment later, he opened the door.

He looked marvelous and awful at the same time. I slipped inside and closed the door behind me.

"Are you OK?" I asked quietly, mindful of the thin walls. Though there was so much noise around us, no one could hear us, anyway.

"I have no idea," he said, his face mournful.

"Because you look fucking fantastic. Is the costume working out all right for you?"

He nodded and spun for me, and there was no doubt. He was elegant in the dark suit and narrow tie, a dashing, difficult Demetrius. His face was subtly made up for the stage. Physically, he was perfect.

I stepped closer, trying to get a read on his dark eyes. "How do you feel?" I asked.

"Like it's the first play I ever did in first grade," he said.

The image of him as a first-grader made me smile. "What was that?"

"We did an elementary thing called *King Arthur's Court.*"

"Hmm," I said. "Adultery. Strong stuff for first-graders."

"We kind of skipped that part."

"And you played King Arthur?"

"Lancelot."

"The pretty boy," I said. "Of course."

That earned me a small smile.

"Jace, I'm so sorry I flipped out last night. I should have

been thinking about you. You know you're going to be great, don't you? This play is marvelous, and so are you."

He stepped closer and slipped his arms around me, and I returned his embrace.

"I hated that you ran away from me," he said.

"I was a jerk. Also, as you pointed out, possibly crazy."

"What was that about? I was worried about you."

Just then, we heard Dirk call out in the adjacent green room. "Actors!"

Jace released me, his face still grim.

"You'll like this," I said. "Come on."

I opened the dressing room door. Jace took a deep breath and walked out to the green room.

The actors were gathered in the middle.

"Hugs!" Dirk said.

Dirk and the members of the cast slipped their arms around one another's waists, making room for Jace. Some hung onto others' shoulders on the outside, listening.

"Energy, energy, energy!" Dirk said, and the actors repeated it.

"Pace, pace, pace!" The newcomers caught on this time.

Dirk gathered them even closer, and the positive energy filled the room as he bounced a little and they joined in.

"We have a pretty good crowd out there tonight," he said after a minute. "I know you're going to go out there and make great art, and make people think, and make them happy. Listen to each other. And have fun. What's our word of the day? How about Bottom?"

The actors laughed.

"Say it three times," Dirk said. "Bottom, Bottom, Bottom!" they chimed in, with a "Whoo!" at the end, and they released one another with smiles on their faces.

"I'm going out to introduce us," the director said. "Here we go, kids."

"Places!" the stage manager called.

Jace stood still as the world moved around him. And he wasn't smiling. I grabbed him by the arm and guided him toward the backstage area where he'd be entering in the first scene. I could hear Dirk addressing the audience, telling them a little about *Midsummer at Midnight.*

"You look so serious," I said. "Are you in character? Should I go away?"

In response, Jace grabbed my hand, but he didn't say anything. He was looking off into the shadows, the jumble of scenery, as if dazed. There was applause as Dirk left the stage.

I touched Jace's face so he would look at me.

"They're going to love you," I whispered. "I love you, Jace."

I kissed him, hot and fast and true. His eyes widened. His mouth dropped open. And then it was his cue, and with one long, last look at me, he entered *Midsummer at Midnight,* stage left.

The first of his lines rolled out of him, resonant and flawless.

All the air left my lungs in a whoosh. I had to get back to the others, oversee the costumes and the changes. But I'd just jumped off a cliff, and I wanted to decide how it felt.

It felt kind of like flying.

∾

I SPENT intermission helping Millie and Theresa make necessary tweaks in the evolving costumes. I deliberately let Millie deal with Jace's suit. I didn't think it would be a great idea to distract him in the middle of the play, not given the bomb I'd dropped on him. Plus I was just a little scared about how he'd react. Maybe I felt as if I were flying, but hitting the ground was going to hurt.

As the second act reached its climax, with Demetrius's speech to Helena, I took a moment to watch it on the monitor. Jace was on fire, and Wendy was both funny and poignant as the defiant Helena who's finally convinced of his love.

I heard a sigh next to me. It was Midge.

"Makes your heart go pitter-pat, doesn't it?" she said.

"You have no idea," I murmured as the play spun into the final farce with the game designers, who pitched their comical virtual-reality game of love to Mr. Duke, to the amusement of the other characters. It was shorter than Shakespeare's play-within-a-play, thank God. And then the couples repeated their vows of love, with the blessing of Oberon — and finally, with Puck's epilogue, the transformed baby cried in Titania's arms.

We all waited for a breathless moment, and then it came, applause and shouts of approval from the audience. Granted, we knew a lot of the people in the audience, but for a dress rehearsal, they'd been gratifyingly responsive, laughing in the right places and even in some places where the comedy hadn't been all that obvious. No doubt the actors would bring out those moments even more.

They made their curtain call, and the leads got an especially big round of applause, which made me happy for Jace. The actors started tumbling back into the green room, flushed with adulation. I waited with a kind of frazzled excitement, fear, resignation, elation, all mixed up. It didn't matter what happened, I told myself. At least I'd spoken my heart.

There was a flurry of actors changing out of their costumes and grabbing snacks from the craft table and hugging each other, and then, in the middle of them, standing still and staring intently at me, was Jace, now in just the open white shirt, undershirt and trousers of his costume. A broad smile lit up his face, like a spotlight on stage. We rushed to close the few steps between us and hugged, hard.

"You were wonderful," I said. "I told you you'd be wonderful."

"It felt good. It actually felt good. I'm so relieved." He grasped my shoulders and looked into my eyes. "Penelope . . . "

"You don't have to say anything, Jace," I whispered.

"But I do." He pulled me away, taking me into the dressing room he'd used earlier, and shut the door. Now he looked serious. "Did you — did you say that back there just to get me on stage? To help me?"

My eyes widened. "I — no. I mean, I wanted to help you, but what I told you — Jace, I meant it. I mean it. Look, you don't have to feel any obligation. It's just something I needed to say. I had to tell you. Please don't worry about letting me down easy. I'm a big girl — "

"Penelope, wouldst thou listen?" he interrupted. He took a step closer to me and ran his hands up my arms, squeezing them lightly. "I thought you didn't want me. You kept talking about your life after I was gone, that it was a foregone conclusion. I was so sure you didn't want me in your life that I just assumed we had no future."

"You what?" I knew I had lapsed into dumb hillbilly mode, because I could hear it in my accent.

He smiled. *"You will be my constant, always, the northern*

star that guides me home, the sun that every morning lights me to my happiest days. You're the dream I want to keep."

I started trembling. "Are you quoting famous playwright Jace Edison? Or are you lapsing into another one of your roles?"

"I'm quoting myself." He ran a finger along my cheek. His dark eyes were warm and mesmerizing. "I'm in love with you, Penelope Locke. I can't believe you couldn't see that."

"I never know what you're thinking," I said, not believing what I was hearing, afraid of the euphoria blossoming inside me. "You're such a good actor."

"Well, I'm not acting now." And he swooped in and clasped my neck and my waist and kissed me with sweet, aching yearning, with a thrillingly confident sense of possession. With love.

Yes, it was love, because I felt it, too. I opened to him with a small sound of surrender that had him slipping his arms around me and holding me fast against his hard body.

I wanted to yell at him to hang up his shirt and pants when he started taking them off, but hell. I could iron them tomorrow. He unfastened my blouse so fast, two buttons popped off, and I kicked off my shoes and helped him take off my pants, too.

"Lock the door," I whispered. He did, then picked me up and lay me down on the dressing room's funky chaise lounge. There was no preamble. He was inside me in a moment, and I wrapped my legs around him and met his thrusts with an urgent need to consummate this new, splendid bond between us. He crushed my cry of ecstasy with a kiss and pumped hard inside me; I clenched around him in a wave of joy and held him tightly as he came.

"Penelope," Jace said softly, gently withdrawing and

curling up next to me, holding me against his chest. "The way we are together — I've never known anything like this."

"Never?" I asked, thinking of Lauren.

"I've known a kind of passionate fascination," he said, "something that I thought was love. It was a kind of love, but it was untested and enshrined in a memory that I could never allow myself to doubt. It wasn't like what I have with you. I think I knew when I first kissed you backstage."

"You mean when I kissed you."

"And I kissed you back. It was the first time in years that I'd felt anything like that. And then when you told my fortune at the party, it was like you reached into my soul and unlocked it."

"That was strange," I admitted. "Like lightning going through me."

"You had me," Jace said. "I didn't know how much, how thoroughly. I just knew I had to have you. And then it grew, this feeling grew, and you were right there with me. You gave me courage. You listened. You've seen parts of me no one has ever seen, and you didn't run."

"I couldn't keep away. God knows I tried."

He laughed, a sound I loved, would always love.

"Lucky me," he said.

" 'Me?' Angelo? My lord?"

"I'm those things. And more. And me. Just me."

"Never 'just' you." I lifted my face to his and kissed him. "You're everything to me. My Jace."

THERE'S ALWAYS a certain amount of electricity on opening night. The paying public and VIPs appear in all their finery, and the performers reach a new level of giddy nervousness knowing they're there. Some say a bad dress rehearsal means a good opening night, but I knew better. A good dress rehearsal could mean a great opening night, and this play had come together in the magical way that only some plays do.

Jace and I hadn't gone out with the cast and crew for drinks after the dress, as we had some celebrating to do on our own, but we were caught up in the same happy mood as everyone else as we all prepped for the show. A bunch of my friends were in the audience, including Cali and Wyatt, Sloane and Alex, and Thea. Dirk was in a good mood.

I was starting to feel invincible until Jace came to me about twenty minutes before curtain, wearing a grave expression. He was already in costume and ready to go, as was pretty much everyone. He pulled me into an unoccupied corner of the busy green room, where we sat on a love seat.

"What is it?" I asked him.

"There's a story in the *National Eye* about us. It's very short," he said.

I took a deep breath. "What does it say?"

"It says that Jace Edison has found love with a beautiful costume designer in Florida."

I narrowed my eyes at him. "That doesn't sound very sleazy."

"It's not, because I planted the story myself." Jace smiled. "It seemed like the easiest way to take the gas out of anything Joe Stier was planning. In fact, they apparently got a call from him and blew him off because they already had the story," he said with satisfaction.

"But — how?"

"I know a guy who used to be a big deal with them. He's a

reporter on a paper on Florida's west coast now, but he has connections. It didn't take much. They were pretty happy to get the story."

"Is — is there a photo?"

"Only of me," he said. "One of the theater's publicity photos."

That made me smile. "Great. Now Cali's a tabloid photographer, and she doesn't even know it."

Jace laughed. "Well, if we ever have her shoot an engagement photo, we can send them that, too."

My mouth dropped open.

"I mean," he said, "if we decide that's right for us."

"You know how much I loved being married," I said darkly, but inside, my heart was doing a happy dance.

He grinned. "I know."

"Does this mean you would have a clockwork baby with me?"

Jace leaned close and whispered in my ear. "Someday, I'll have a real baby with you."

I pulled back and looked into his eyes. These were such domestic dreams for two theater vagabonds. But for him, the idea of a baby had to be a huge deal, given his history.

I leaned in and kissed him, and I felt the emotion in his response. My heart twisted as he slid a hand into my hair and opened his mouth on mine.

I sighed when he released me. "All this will be after a few years of stunning theatrical successes, of course."

"Of course," Jace said. "I'm talking to a theater in Orlando that does really good work. I can spend part of the year there, and it will give me a chance to do some of the more serious roles I've been wanting to do, along with more writing. And I can work in New York, too. I have movie offers. I have options.

And you can do whatever you want, as long as you're with me as much as possible."

"I love the Chamberlain and Bohemia Beach, but the atmosphere's been weird lately. Since they're talking about hiring somebody with a gold-plated resume for future shows, maybe it's time for me to look into new challenges."

"You can do anything you want. *Anything.* And I've grown attached to Bohemia Beach, too. I'm going to buy a place here that we can always come back to."

"And we'll make it work?" The possibilities were almost overwhelming. Magnificent, wonderful and overwhelming.

Jace's luscious lips curved into a smile, and his dark eyes danced. "We'll make it sing."

AFTERWORD

Thanks for reading! Sign up for my newsletter to get fun original content, giveaways, news and cocktail recipes, and I'll send you a free story. I also have a Facebook group where readers can hang out and chat about books and life — please join us in Lucy's Lounge.

MORE ONLINE:
LucyLakestone.com
Facebook.com/LucyLakestone
Twitter.com/LucyLakestone
Bookbub.com/authors/lucy-lakestone
Pinterest.com/lucylakestone/
Amazon
Goodreads
YouTube

ACKNOWLEDGMENTS

I have a lot of people to thank for their insights and support as I wrote *Bohemia Heat*. While I covered arts topics as a journalist and have dabbled in the arts myself, many of the backstage mysteries of the theater required research. As the writer of this novel, of course, I take responsibility for any errors, fictional liberties and, essential for a story about the theater, dramatic license. I made a lot of stuff up!

Thank you to costume designer Aimee M. Johnson for her insights into how costumes are produced for a professional show. I imagine my fictional Chamberlain Theater as being well-heeled enough to produce all-original costumes, though smaller theaters often don't have that option.

Thanks also to Christina LaFortune for answering questions and connecting me with Melbourne Civic Theatre and Artistic Director Peg Girard. The cast and crew allowed me to sit backstage and observe during a dress rehearsal. Theater maven Pam Harbaugh also gave me valuable insights into how theaters work. A hat tip goes to Orlando Shakespeare Theater, as well, for the open house that gave me more insight into lighting, sound and backstage construction. The performance space at OST inspired my fictional one.

In case you are wondering about the identity of the former tabloid reporter whom Jace mentions in the final chapter, it's Alden Knox, the hero of my Barefoot Bay novel *Desire on Deadline.* Thanks to Roxanne St. Claire for inviting me to be a part of the launch of the expansion of her fictional world and for her encouragement and advice.

Thanks, as always, to the members of Spacecoast Authors of Romance for their kindness and inspiration and to all of my writing friends, especially Karen Ann Dell. I learn so much from all of you, all the time.

I'm very grateful to editor and friend Holly Martin for her judicious eye and encouragement. More thanks go to Mr. Lakestone for his support of my writing obsession. And lastly, thank *you* for reading!

ABOUT THE AUTHOR

Lucy Lakestone is an award-winning author who lives on Florida's east central coast, among the towns that serve as an inspiration for the hot romances of her Bohemia Beach Series, including *Bohemia Beach, Bohemia Light, Bohemia Blues* (winner of the Golden Quill), *Bohemia Heat, Bohemia Nights* and *Bohemia Bells*. She's been a journalist, photographer, editor and video producer but prefers living in her imagination, where the moon is full and the cocktails are divine. She is also the author of a novel of romantic suspense, *Desire on Deadline*.

BOHEMIA NIGHTS

The fifth BOHEMIA BEACH *novel*

◦✐◦

a hot Scot, a deliciously indecent proposal

Thea McKay likes her quiet, private life well enough.
She creates pop-up paper art that no one ever sees,
hangs out with her friends and admires men from afar.
But then, at a play premiere, she meets gregarious video
blogger Duncan Flyte. An incorrigible charmer with
dubious motives, he's handsome, hilarious and overwhelming. When he says he won't stop showcasing her
to his legions of fans unless she agrees to spend seven
nights with him, her world turns upside-down. The of-
fer is both outrageous and tempting. Those seven
nights don't have to be passionate, but what if Thea
wants them to be? Can she raise the stakes with this
adorable Scottish import — especially when Duncan's
cheerful campaign to woo her may be just one more
spectacular lie that will break her heart?

LEARN MORE AT
LucyLakestone.com